SPELLBOUND

By

Sylvia Kincaid

Fantasy Romance

New Concepts

Georgia

Spellbound is an original publication of NCP. This work has never before appeared in book form. This work is a novel. Any similarity to actual persons or events is purely coincidental.

New Concepts Publishing, Inc.
5202 Humphreys Rd.
Lake Park, GA 31636

ISBN 1-58608-794-0

NCP books are available at special quantity discounts for bulk purchases for sales promotions, premiums, fund raising, or educational use. For details, write, email, or phone New Concepts Publishing, Inc., 5202 Humphreys Rd., Lake Park, GA 31636; Ph. 229-257-0367, Fax 229-219-1097; orders@newconceptspublishing.com.

First NCP Trade Paperback Printing: July 2006

THE WARLOCK

Chapter One

An alarm was sounded as soon as the lookout spotted the flutter of a battle flag at the distant end of the wide fields that surrounded the principle fortification of Aradan. Even as the first soldiers crested the rise, the gates of Aradan Castle were swiftly closed and locked down tight with the great timber braces that took ten men to fit them in place. All along the walls, the men at arms checked their weapons and then waited in rigid tension, staring hard into the distance, watching as the small dots on the distant horizon slowly began to resolve themselves into men garbed in gleaming armor and battle horses decked out in the trappings of war. In the keep below the walls men at arms who had been loitering in the keep, cleaning weaponry and armor, practicing their craft, or whiling away their free time gambling their meager pay, froze at the sound of the warning horn and the sudden activity on the walls for a handful of minutes. Abruptly, they sprang into action themselves, racing to the armory to don leather armor and gather swords and long bows and quivers full of arrows. King Gerard had never been a popular king and they knew he had many more enemies than friends or allies among his neighbors.

Still, relief flooded the hearts of many as they took up their battle positions along the walls and stared out toward the threat approaching their keep. The army that marched forward with such discipline and precision--if it deserved such an exalted name--was a small one. They made up nearly thrice that number and had the added advantage of position.

Puzzlement began to take the place of their uneasiness as the army advanced purposefully, still displaying battle readiness, still flying the colors of war. None recognized the crest on the tabard of the man who led the army, but he wore the gold and purple of a king.

Their confusion intensified as the army halted at a signal from their leader before they'd covered much more than half the distance between the castle and the rise where they had first appeared. Expecting a messenger to break away and ride forward with their demands, a murmur of surprise rippled through the waiting troops as the leader himself left his army and came forward. Without any sign of wariness or hesitation, he spurred his great black horse with his spurs and closed the distance, bringing his restive mount to a halt only when he when he reached the outer rim of the moat, when he was so close that many of those on the wall above him could see his face clearly.

A dark cape, lined in scarlet, fluttered in the wind that coursed around him, outlining the proportions of a man of surprising stature and build. Long hair, darker still than the cape and gleaming with bluish highlights flowed with the cape almost taunting them with the fact that he was so bold he saw no need for a helmet, or even to bind the mass to prevent an opponent from grabbing a fistful for leverage to lop his head from his shoulders.

Beyond that, the purple and gold tabard of royalty he flaunted was worn over nothing more substantial than a quilted vest. A wicked looking sword hung by his side that was clearly a weapon and not merely there for ornamentation, but, in his sword hand he held the staff of a conjurer, a dabbler in the black arts, which would make it impossible for him to draw the sword with any speed if he found it necessary.

He was either a fool or a madman to come so close. A good marksman could have pierced his heart from twice the distance. As close as he had come, it would take no great shot to slay him where he stood.

Oddly enough, that thought comforted none. There was grim determination on the man's face, but no sign of fear, and intelligence gleamed in his strangely piercing eyes. He was an enigma that made them uneasy in an indefinable way for such obvious fearlessness indicated he had reason to believe there was nothing to fear.

To rout their uneasiness, some of the men voiced taunts and jeers, but he remained maddeningly cool and undaunted, taunting them by his very presence and attitude.

Silencing them, the captain of the guard, Bryon, placed a foot on the low edge of the wall and leaned over just as brazenly to call down to the intruder, drawing chuckles of admiration from his men. "What business brings you to Aradan leading an--army?"

the captain demanded sharply, emphasizing his contempt for the threat the army represented by his hesitation in honoring them with that distinction.

The stranger studied him for a full minute before he spoke. "My business is with the man who calls himself King of Aradan. I will discuss it with him and none other."

A murmur of both surprise and outrage rippled through the men at arms at the brazen demand. Their captain lifted an arm to silence them, however, and they desisted almost at once, waiting to see what their captain would have to say to this arrogant lunatic.

"Commoners do not summon kings," the captain spat contemptuously.

The man's eyes narrowed. "Nor question their commands," he responded coldly.

The captain was taken aback for several moments. "Off with you before I have you shot as a spy, lack-wit."

The man said nothing, merely waited.

"Suit yourself. Kill him," the captain commanded, nodding to the nearest archer and turning back to watch the slaughter with amusement.

An arrow was loosed. It shot true, so fast it was little more than a blur as the missile spanned the short distance. Three feet from the mounted rider, the arrow shattered, dropping to the ground. Several of the men who'd witness it gasped and crossed themselves. The captain frowned angrily, nodded to the two archers on either side of him. Two bolts were notched. Two bolts launched and both shattered a full arm's length from the target.

The stranger smiled grimly.

Unnerved and furious now, the captain commanded his archers to fire. A hundred arrows flew from the walls, peppering the ground around the rider, bouncing off something none could see, shattering--but not a single arrow touched him.

"What trickery is this?" the captain demanded, disbelieving, trying without absolute success to hide the fear that had begun to worm its way around his confidence.

The captain's words were cut off abruptly and the men around him whirled to look at him, certain a stray arrow from the waiting army had caught their commander. Instead they saw him clawing at his throat, as if invisible hands had closed around it in a vise hold.

"Bring me the man who calls himself king of Aradan!" commanded a voice so powerful that seasoned warriors trembled and new recruits went weak in the knees.

* * * *

"You are a willful child, Rhiannon, but you must accept that I know what is best for you," King Gerard said coolly, "Or I will be forced to send you to bide a while in the tower until you come to your senses."

The knot in Rhiannon's stomach wound a little tighter, setting off a wave of nausea. She did not lift her head to look up at the man seated on the throne on the dais above her. She didn't need to see the chill blue of his gaze to know that he was in deadly earnest.

Her body had already begun to cramp from her position of subservience on the floor, and her knees to ache from the cold stone, but she resisted the urge to shift and give away her discomfort and uneasiness. Her mind was chaotic, however, her fear so overpowering that the wisdom of weighing each of her words very carefully eluded her. "If I am a child, Uncle, then surely I am not ready to wed?"

She knew the moment the words were out that that tact was a grave misstep and risked a quick glance upward to gauge the magnitude of it.

Gerard's eyes narrowed. "I have spoiled you. Do not test my patience, my dear, or you will see that I am a king first and devoted uncle second. You have always known that you must marry to form an alliance for the kingdom, not for your own pleasure."

Swallowing with an effort Rhiannon bowed her head once more but a surge of anger had displaced much of her fear of her uncle. By rights, she should have been queen as her father's only heir, but she had been a small child when he was killed and his brother, Gerard, had taken the throne--originally with the announced intention of preserving it for his niece and protecting her until she reached an age where she was fit to rule, but all had known long before she reached that age that she would never see it if Gerard were not crowned in her stead.

It was outrageous to be usurped and then used by the very villain who'd done so to further his own ends. Had she assumed the throne as was her right, she would have been no happier that her union would be used to form some alliance, but she would have at least had reason to want to. Then, it would have been for the good of the realm. Then it would have been her choice and she might at least have had a little more latitude in deciding who she would ally herself with.

If she had not known better, she would have thought her uncle had gone out of his way to find the most repellent suitor possible for her. For King Linea of Midea was not only a foul toad, he was sixty if he was a day--and a randy old pervert besides! She had met him only once, but that was more than sufficient.

Her uncle's choice hadn't been based on malice, of course, though he was certainly not above it. His choice had been based solely on greed. She had no doubt that her uncle expected King Linea to be so obliging as to croak as soon as he'd planted his nasty seed in her and leave his kingdom, with its considerable wealth, within his grasp.

She gritted her teeth, determined if she could not evade the fate her uncle had in mind for her then she would see him in hell before he got his hands on yet another kingdom at her expense.

As uplifting as that thought was, the one that followed it made her shudder, for she could not erase the vision of King Linea from her mind and it was revolting to think of what would be expected of her. "I am willing enough to do my duty, *Uncle--to the realm and my people*--but I confess I cannot see how wedding that--King Linea is to benefit anyone above any of the others who sought to wed me."

Gerard smiled thinly. "Alas, that my brother begat no son before his untimely death, for the weight of this office is a heavy one--but, princess or not, you are little more than a child--a female at that, and you cannot be expected to understand the complicated world of politics."

That comment made her so angry she felt even more ill, for if she was ignorant of politics it was precisely because Gerard had no intention of enlightening her for fear his beleaguered subjects might decide to overthrow him in favor of the old king's heir.

Dangerous thoughts, those, and likely to bring her a swift end if her uncle even suspected she harbored them.

Which she didn't, actually. She resented the theft of her birthright. She resented being used. She pitied those who suffered because of her uncle's cruelty and greed, but harbored no real desire to rule herself. She had often wished she had been born of some other household altogether so that she might be spared the tedium and intrigue of the courts, so that she could be spared being used as a pawn in a game she was not even allowed to play.

"But I do understand the need for a strong alliance, Uncle. What I do not understand is why it must be King Linea. Midea is a tiny kingdom. Surely it would be far more useful if I were to be allied with one of the larger kingdoms--perhaps to buy peace with one of your enemies? He is--a toad and ancient besides!"

Gerard smiled a little more easily, but she could see anger simmering just below the surface and wondered a little uneasily if he realized that she was far more likely to encourage his enemies than to discourage them. "In which case, you should not have to suffer his presence long and, the gods willing, will find yourself a wealthy widow ere you are much older."

Disgust filled Rhiannon that her uncle would so brazenly outline his plans, for she didn't doubt for a moment that he fully intended to help her new husband along the path to his grave if he proved more hardy than expected. She forced a tremulous smile, though it was becoming harder and harder to play the role of weak minded female. "I had not considered that, Uncle."

She'd not considered it before he spoke it aloud because she'd been too naive to believe her uncle was truly as cold and calculating as he appeared to be. Even now she could hardly credit it. He had seemed kind enough to her as child. She had never felt comfortable in his presence, primarily because his displays of affection had always seemed 'wrong' to her, just a little too excessive, a little too familiar, and yet he had indulged her a great deal, just as he claimed.

She could hardly remember her own father, and her mother not at all since her mother had died when she born, but her uncle had always said he stood in her father's place and when she had been a child she had tried to think of him as a father.

It made her uneasy that she was not entirely certain of her uncle's motives in the alliance he proposed--insisted upon. King Linea's motives seemed straightforward enough. He *was* old enough to be her grandfather, but she didn't doubt that he believed himself capable of begetting the son he required as heir--though he'd been married twice already and had failed to produce a child that lived beyond babyhood. Moreover, although she also looked upon her uncle as old, he was still considered by most to be in his prime, and would be a strong ally for the tiny kingdom of Midea, which lay across the sea that formed Aradan's northern border.

Midea was less than half the size of Aradan in lands, but thrice as rich. Perhaps that was motive enough?

And yet her uncle had refused the offer made by King Saliem's emissaries and his was a far wealthier kingdom.

Then again, King Saliem was a more powerful king altogether, not even as old as her uncle, and perhaps her uncle had realized the chance of actually getting his hands on King Saliem's wealth was very remote?

She might have put it down to the fact that she'd scarcely attained womanhood when the offer had been made except that now she knew better. Her tender age would not have weighed with her uncle if there had been benefit to himself in it.

She saw when she emerged from her abstraction that her uncle was studying her appraisingly and wondered if it would be wise to capitulate now--or at least appear to--or if folding so quickly would make him more suspicious instead of less so. Before she'd quite made up her mind which was the safest course, a breathless messenger stumbled to a halt before the guards at the entrance to the receiving chamber, distracting both her and her uncle.

"What is it?" King Gerard demanded testily.

The messenger gulped, but hurried forward and fell to his knees. "Sire--There is-- I believe it must be a powerful sorcerer at the gates, though he has claimed no such thing--but we fired upon him for his brazen demands and our arrows simply bounced off, causing him no harm at all."

King Gerard frowned. "A wizard?"

The messenger glanced up at his king. "He has demanded to speak with you."

Gerard reddened with fury. "Demanded?" he roared, on his feet instantly. "*He* demanded? The cur summoned *me*?"

The messenger turned white as death. No doubt he saw the possibility looming before him for Gerard had been known to strike down more than one messenger who'd delivered unwelcome news. "Captain Bryon ordered him shot for his impertinence, Sire! I saw myself. The arrows shattered and fell to the ground all around him. He commands the dark forces! Captain Bryon was seen to have been seized by the throat, as if by invisible hands that lifted him clear off the wall!"

Gerard glared at the messenger for several moments. Finally, his anger seemed to dissipate and a thoughtful expression crossed his features. He stared at the hapless messenger for some moments, scratching his beard and finally got to his feet decisively. "Captain Bryon was right to refuse entrance and to send for me. I will see this conjurer myself. If he is as skilled as you say, I may have use of him."

When the king departed the chamber, Rhiannon at last rose gratefully to her feet. Her uncle had not ordered her to remain where she was and await his return, however, and after a moment, curiosity drove her to see if she could get a look at the madman herself.

He must be mad! Conjurer or not, no one in their right mind would offer their services to Gerard, who was known to be dangerously fickle--and certainly not demand the king's presence so that he might petition for a place in the household.

But perhaps that particular part of the message had been garbled?

Gerard, she saw, was already climbing the stairs to the wall when she reached the keep. She waited until he had reached the top and strode purposely toward the stair, ignoring the curious looks of the guards and proceeding as if she was expected to be just where she was.

She gave her uncle a wide berth when she reached the wall, however, moving somewhat further along the battlements and taking up a position at last where she could peer over the crenulations.

She was startled when she saw how close the man had come, for he stood just beyond the moat, well within range of the archers who'd lined up along the walls.

He did not look mad. There was no wildness about the intense gaze he had trained upon her uncle as he, too, moved close enough to the battlements to look down at the man who'd summoned him.

A sense of uneasiness moved through her. She wasn't certain of the source at first, but finally realized that it was pity. Poor fool! They would crush him, or worse!

After eyeing the stranger speculatively for some moments, Gerard finally spoke. "I am King Gerard. I was told that you are a dabbler in the black arts. As it happens, I may have some use for you."

The stranger's lips curled derisively. "But I have no desire to serve you," he said almost apologetically.

Gerard's lips tightened. "Then why have you come?" he demanded.

"To kill you."

A wave of goose flesh lifted along Rhiannon's nape at the simple comment, chasing the shock of his words. Mutely, she simply stared at the man for several moments before it occurred to her to wonder what her uncle's reaction to the challenge would be.

He looked as stunned as she. After a moment, he managed a cold chuckle. "Kill him."

The archer he'd commanded simply gaped at him for a handful of seconds.

"Now!" Gerard roared.

Almost, the archer seemed to shrug. Turning, he notched an arrow, took aim and fired. Rhiannon gasped, her hand flying to her throat as the bolt flashed through the air--and then shattered and fell to earth before it had come closer than an arm's length to the man.

Gerard stared at the stranger in disbelief. "Who are you?" he roared.

The man smiled. "I am the warlock, Daigon, son of the murdered King Rhainor and I have come to claim what it rightfully mine, the Castle Aradan and all the lands that lie between it and the sea of Midae."

Chapter Two

Gerard turned so deathly pale and then fiery red with fury that Rhiannon wondered for several moments if he wouldn't simply drop dead from his rage. He stuttered with it when he spoke again, spitting flecks of spittle in every direction like a mad dog. "Alone?" he raged, waving a hand in the direction of the small army that waited at some distance from the castle. "With no more than a handful men? You think you can challenge me so brazenly and I will simply hand over what is mine?"

"I think you will yield up what is mine," the warlock Daigon responded coldly. Lifting the staff he held in one hand high, he recited an incantation. Mist rose from the fields at his back. As the wind rifled it into swirls, shredding it, Rhiannon saw the dim outline of riders. Slowly the mist cleared and where once there had been no more than a small army, a great army stood.

As if at some command that only they could hear, the army began to advance slowly across the field, gaining speed as they closed the distance, the hooves of the steeds they rode pounding out a rhythm against the ground like the distant rumble of thunder. And as they grew nearer and nearer horror began to shiver along Rhiannon's spine. The hair at her nape prickled.

Around her she heard gasps of fear, curses, muttered prayers--but she was only dimly aware of the growing horror of those surrounding her. She could not seem to tear her gaze from the riders as the dark shapes took form and she saw the pale gleam of bones, rotting flesh, eyeless sockets. Dirt clung to their tattered chausses and here and there pale bones gleamed through great tears that bore the look of sword cuts. Dirt clung to their tunics and capes that whipped frenziedly about them. Skeletal hands gripped duly gleaming swords and bony arms held them aloft. Their faces bore lipless grins and clods of rotting flesh. Rhiannon imagined she could almost see the insects crawling over the decaying flesh.

She could almost imagine she could hear eerie battle cries issuing forth from fleshless throats.

"Who *are* you?" King Gerard roared again, though this time his voice was laced with the high notes of terror.

Drawn by her uncle's cry, Rhiannon glanced at him before focusing her attention on the warlock once more.

"I have told you. I am Daigon--whose father and mother were murdered by your brother, Nordain while they slept."

Rage, fed by her terror, erupted inside Rhiannon. "Liar!" she screamed. "Liar! My father murdered no one! He was a good man, a man of honor! He would never have committed such a cowardly act!"

For the first time, the warlock, Daigon, turned to look directly at her and Rhiannon felt a jagged shock run through her. Her breath caught in her throat, threatening to strangle her. His piercing eyes seemed to delve inside of her, to know her in a way that no one ever had.

"It is the truth. Either you are lying to yourself. Or you were lied to. My family was murdered by assassins sent by your father."

Rhiannon's knees went weak when at last he released her from his stare and pinned her uncle with that unnerving gaze once more. "I have reconsidered. You may keep your life if you will leave peacefully, now--I will take the child of my father's murderer in exchange for their lives."

Rhiannon's mind went perfectly blank with terror at that. Almost as if she was looking down upon someone else, she saw herself seize an arrow and wrest the bow from the lax fingers of the archer standing nearest her. Notching it, she drew the string back, sighted along the shaft of the arrow and let it fly. As if the commotion had drawn his attention, the warlock turned to fix her with an enigmatic stare as she launched her arrow at his heart. He lifted his hand, as if he would catch the deadly shaft. It swerved, to Rhiannon's horror, piercing his palm.

She blinked in disbelief, fear douching her in a cold wash.

"You have your answer!" King Gerard screamed gleefully. "To arms, men!" he roared at the men along the walls.

Rhiannon had not been able to tear her gaze from the warlock. She watched as he studied the arrow in his hand almost with a look of surprise. Finally, he broke the shaft and pulled the broken piece from his hand. A slow grin curled his lips as he lifted his hand and as she watched the blood ceased to flow and the hole slowly sealed itself until his hand was whole and unblemished.

The deep rumble of his voice rolled over her and all who stood upon the wall. "Behold my army! Those you and your brother have unjustly slain!"

Rhiannon gasped, for even as he spoke the army that had been racing toward them only moments before appeared at his back, swarmed around him and urged their mounts to leap the moat.

"The princess Rhiannon is mine!"

The command whipped Rhiannon's head in the direction of the speaker as if some invisible ribbon had jerked her around. She saw that the warlock was staring directly at her. With an effort, she dragged her gaze from him to gauge the progress of the army of the dead. The mounted knights had vanished. Foot soldiers were swarming up the walls like spiders.

Around her, terror created absolute chaos. Men slammed into each other as half tried to flee and half raced to fire upon the advancing hoard. "Fight, damn you!" Captain Bryon roared, failing about him with the flat of his sword as he tried to rally his men. "Or I will cut you down myself!"

The men seemed deaf to his commands, mindless in their terror. There was no order and even many of those who had instinctively turned to fight, whirled to flee as the dead began to crawl over the crenulations.

The scrape of metal against stone caught her attention and Rhiannon glanced quickly toward the sound as a grinning skeleton scrambled over the wall almost on top of her. She leapt back from the nightmare creature even as one bony hand shot out to grasp her wrist. One of the men at arms fell upon it, hacking at the bones with his sword. "Run, princess! Save yourself!"

Freed from her stupor at last by a surge of adrenaline, Rhiannon fled, ducking and weaving her way through the surging mass of men and walking dead, searching for her uncle among them. When she spied him at last, she saw that he was surrounded by the palace guard and racing down the stairs toward the keep. Below, in the keep itself, she saw the mounted knights of Daigon's army, who had passed through the massive stone walls of the castle as if they were no more substantial than mist.

They were all going to die!

* * * *

Rhiannon was gasping so hard with fright, with horror, with the exertion of struggling over the mass of bodies and around the writhing tangle of battling warriors, that she felt for several moments after she'd managed to close the massive door behind her that she would be sick. When she mastered the urge, she realized the great hall was as silent as the tomb. A hysterical sob escaped her.

How appropriate! For it would almost certainly be their tomb!

A chill crept over her and she shivered, hugging her arms to herself as she stared uncomprehendingly around at the deserted hall. Her uncle was nowhere in sight, but she had seen him enter the main castle with his men.

Faintly, she heard sounds in the distance. Frowning, for it sounded more like the rattle of pots than battle, she debated whether to explore the origins or go the other way. Finally, certain that the metallic rattle and the low murmur of voices did not indicate a deadly engagement, she pushed away from the door and crossed the great hall, pausing now and again to try to discern the direction of the faint noises. When she reached the stair that wound upward toward the sleeping chambers, she realized the sounds were not drifting downward from above, but upward from below.

Frowning, she looked around. At the rear of the corridor, a door stood slightly ajar, as if it had been flung closed but not caught. It led to the guard rooms in the dungeon, she knew. She had never been down there. Few who passed through that door were ever seen again.

Ignoring the creeping of her flesh, she moved as quickly and quietly as possible toward the door and listened.

She'd been right! She could hear the sounds more distinctly. She might have turned away even so, but as she hesitated, she heard her uncle's voice, low but unmistakable. "Leave that!" he hissed. "We must move quickly!"

More curious now than afraid, Rhiannon pushed the door open a little wider and peered down the stairs into the bowels of the earth. A single torch had been set into a sconce at the foot of the steep stone stairway, casting a globe of light over the damp stones of the walls, the hard packed earthen floor and the lower quarter of the stairs.

"Hsst! What was that?"

Rhiannon paused, her heart hammering in her chest.

"The wind!" her uncle snarled. "Hurry!"

Apparently they decided to take her uncle's word for it, for she heard the clanking begin again, as if metal objects were being banged together. Moving as quickly as she dared down the stairs, Rhiannon paused again at the foot and glanced up and down the darkened corridor. Dimly, at one distant end, she saw the glow of a torch from beneath a door. She had only traversed half the distance when the door abruptly opened, spilling light and men into the corridor in front of her. Everyone, Rhiannon included, froze for a handful of heartbeats, staring, and Rhiannon realized with belated fear that she would likely have been skewered on one of the guard's swords if she had managed to get nearer before they erupted from her uncle's treasury--for she saw that that was where they were.

"What are you doing?"

Gerard's eyes narrowed. "What are you doing here?"

"I came to find you!" Rhiannon said almost accusingly. "They are dying up there! The warlock's army is cutting them down like ... helpless children. Our men cannot hope to defend the keep from such creatures! What are we to do?"

"Flee and live to fight another day!" Gerard snarled.

Rhiannon felt her jaw go slack. "You would leave them? Abandon those who fight to protect you to die without their leader?"

Gerard strode toward her, grasped her shoulders and shook her until her head rocked on her shoulders and threatened to snap. "Fool! Do you think it will help them if I die with them?"

Rhiannon caught her uncle's forearms, struggling to push him away. "Coward!" she screamed at him.

He released her then, but slapped her so hard her head snapped sideways on her neck and the side of her head collided with the stone wall. Stunned, she slid to the muddy floor. "Fool! It's me he wants! If I leave there will be no reason to slay them!" he growled furiously.

With an effort, Rhiannon shook off the dizziness that swarmed around her and looked up at her uncle speechlessly, wondering if he actually believed what he was saying. She could not credit it. He was obliged to know the warlock would take the castle apart stone by stone until he found his prey. "Yield," she managed to say, though her tongue and lips felt numb and swollen. "He offered you your life."

"For you!" Gerard snarled. "Which is why, although it pains me, you must stay."

Dully, Rhiannon watched as Gerard and his guard, carrying as much of the treasury as they could manage, passed her where she sat crumpled on the floor and raced toward the other end of the corridor. Confusion filled her when they passed the stair.

Dimly, she recalled that there had always been persistent rumors of hidden corridors within the castle, corridors which linked every part of any importance. When the men paused near the opposite end of the corridor, fumbled with something in the wall for several moments and then promptly vanished, she knew that the rumors were not tales at all, but truth.

Struggling to her feet, Rhiannon stumbled after them, one hand braced against the wall to steady herself against the waves of dizziness that made the walls and floor and ceiling seem to undulate before her. She found nothing when she reached the point where they had disappeared but a wall.

After staring at it in stupefaction for several moments, she began to run her hands over the stones, searching for a hidden latch, a depression in the stone. When she found nothing, she stepped back to look at the puzzle in the dimness. Her eyes had adjusted to the deep gloom of the dungeon, but she could see no lever--nothing that might be used to move the stones. Frowning, she closed her eyes, summoning the image from her memory.

Her uncle had reached for the sconce on the wall!

Moving toward it, she stretched as far as she could, coming up on her tiptoes. Finally, she managed to grasp the sconce. She pulled. Nothing happened. Frustrated, she was on the point of releasing it when she thought to try to twist it. Almost immediately, the whispering scrape of stone against stone tickled at her ears. A chilling breeze, like the breath of the dead, wafted across her. When she released the sconce, the door immediately began to close. Without time to consider whether she actually wished to follow or not, Rhiannon leapt inside.

Almost instantly, she found herself in a blackness so deep it felt solid. Terror swarmed up through her like stinging insects. Hysteria bubbled in her throat. She'd entombed herself! Blind with panic, she felt around for the wall. Marginally relieved when she found it, she ran her hands over the wet stones, searching for the lever that would open the door once more.

She found nothing. Despite the chill, she was sweating with fear.

A fresh, painful blast of terror burst in her heart when a distant sound echoed eerily through the gloom. Clasping a hand over the pain in her chest, Rhiannon whirled to face the horrible creature she knew must be stalking her.

The sound came again. This time, despite her fear, she recognized it.

Horses!

Her uncle had horses waiting!

Fighting sobs of fright, Rhiannon ran her hands over the stones again until she found the corner she was seeking. Turning, she stumbled blindly through the darkness, one hand on the wall to guide her. It seemed she walked blindly for hours, fearing any moment that she would take a step and find nothing beneath her feet but air, although she knew it could not possibly have been more than a few minutes. Abruptly the wall ended.

Too frightened to move in any direction for several moments, Rhiannon strained to pierce the darkness as she turned in a slow circle. In the distance, she saw a faint glow of light. As faint as it was, it sliced through the gloom, illuminating the water that ran down the walls in rivulets and transforming the water into sparkling jewels. Fisting her hand around her long, heavy skirt, she lifted it and began to hurry toward the light. It grew brighter and brighter as she ran and she realized finally that she was in a long, curving tunnel. It was climbing. She didn't notice the pull against her muscles at first. She thought it was the pounding of her heart and her running that caused her breathlessness. As her body labored harder and harder, however, and she found herself holding a stitch in her side, she realized the air was growing warmer, as well, and salt was carried upon it.

They heard her this time before she reached them. As she stumbled to a halt at the mouth of the tunnel, she discovered she was facing six drawn swords.

"What are you doing here?" her uncle demanded furiously.

"Don't leave us!" Rhiannon begged him. "Your people need you!"

An expression marred his features as if he smelled something that stank. He spat at her feet. "Do you think I mean to die for commoners? Slaves?"

Rhiannon stared at him, realizing that she didn't really know him at all. He had always been cruel, but she would never have believed he was a complete coward. The thought abruptly recalled another and an unpleasant sensation washed through her. "You really are running! I would never have believed that you were such a coward! Is it true--what he said? Tell me!"

For several moments, she thought he would strike her down. Apparently deciding against it, he turned away from her and hurried toward the horse that awaited him. His men rushed to follow, swiftly securing the last of the bundles they carried in the packs behind their saddles.

"What he said about my father? Tell me the truth! Did my father send assassins to slay his parents while they slept?"

Ignoring her, he steadied his horse and launched himself into the saddle. Without stopping to consider the possible consequences of her actions, Rhiannon grabbed his leg. He tried to shake her loose. Failing that, he swung at her. This time she expected it, however, and dodged the blow, clinging determinedly though she knew her weight was hardly enough to prevent him from fleeing.

"Yes!" he roared furiously, his patience at an end. "My brother sent assassins to kill his king and queen! But he was not *your* father! Only the gods know with whom your whore of a mother slept, but it was not her husband's child she bore-- And it was not the warlock's parents Nordain slew!"

Rhiannon was so stunned, her fingers went lax, allowing him at last to shake free of her. She shook her head, trying to make sense of what he'd said, too stunned to assimilate his words and comprehend the enormity of what he'd flung at her. "I don't understand," she murmured, taking a step back as he swung at her again with his fist.

"King Rhainor's heir died with him and his queen--still cradled in his mother's womb!"

Numbly, Rhiannon watched as the man she'd always believed to be her uncle dug his spurs into his horse's side and led his men charging toward the mouth of the cavern. The horses' hooves, clattering against the stones in the enclosed space, pounded out a rhythm of sound that was nearly deafening. She covered her ears with her hands, staring after them long after they had vanished from sight.

Finally, she lowered her arms, blinked, looked around the cavern. She was alone. As shock gave way to pain, a sob tore its way through her chest and throat, erupting loud in the silence. She covered her mouth with her hands, trying to think what she should do.

She was a bastard.

Nothing that she had ever believed to be true about herself was.

Should she return and try to save those she could from slaughter? Or was it already too late? Would sacrificing herself actually help anyone at all?

A true royal would know their place--but she wasn't, was she?

And yet, would there really be any escape for her? Her uncle had taken all of the horses. She could walk, run and hide, but how far would she get, on foot, without food or water?

She was so afraid! It was so tempting to at least try to escape that she felt ill.

Her chances of actually succeeding were slim, though, and she knew it. If she was going to die anyway, wouldn't it be better to die with some honor? Some dignity?

But then, how much honor and dignity could a bastard actually lay claim to?

A strange uneasiness began to creep over her as she stood indecisively in the cavern, a coldness. The hair on the nape of her neck began to prickle. Slowly, she turned, searching the dim cavern around her for the threat she knew was there.

She saw nothing at first but a thin layer of mist that seemed to hover perhaps four feet from the floor of the cavern. The mist began to assume form, shape, definition, became a pair of disembodied eyes--*his* eyes. The warlock had found her!

Chapter Three

Daigon watched as his *mort du armée* swarmed the castle walls and engaged the defenders at the top, wreaking further havoc among his already demoralized enemy. With his vision, he penetrated the castle walls and looked upon the mounted knights who had stormed the keep and saw that they, too, were progressing well in breaking down the castle's defense.

Risking good men he could ill afford to loose had been no part of his plan.

Satisfaction filled him that his strategy appeared to be working so well. With stealth, cunning, and magic, he and his army had taken every fortification south of Castle Aradan, the jewel of Aradan's crown. It was time to finish it.

A sense of elation filled him at that realization. He had spent much of his life dreaming of this moment, striving toward the time when he could avenge the deaths of his parents and take back what had been stolen from them and from him.

It would not be the victory he had dreamed of when he was a young boy, yearning for the comfort, security, and love of parents he had never known. The man who had murdered his parents as they lay sleeping peacefully in their bed had fled beyond his reach--for even the powers he had attained would not allow him to reach beyond the grave.

Briefly, the old anger surged forward again, but he tamped it. Hatred was good if it fired the soul but useless if it so befouled one's heart that one could find no pleasure in life. Time had helped to mellow that youthful rage and allow reason, not anger, to rule him.

It would be enough to take back what had been taken, to usurp those who had profited from the death of his parents, even if they had not been directly responsible.

He frowned as that thought conjured an image of the girl, wondering what demon of mischief had prompted his demand to have her. Somewhere in his mind he must have realized that Nordain would have propagated his seed, and yet he had not counted on her presence. He had not considered the complications that could arise with the discovery of a female heir.

He would have felt no compunction about banishing a male of Nordain's line, or killing him if he saw it was necessary to maintain peace. What was he to do with the girl?

He should have simply told Gerard to take her--he supposed he still could if Gerard had not managed to escape. But there was always the possibility that Gerard had fled, leaving her behind as he had demanded--or was dead. If either possibility was the case, he would have to decide what to do with her.

He felt confident that he had adequately convinced the people of Aradan that he was not someone they could flout with impunity, but even so he had no desire to rule his people solely through fear--and the girl could create complications in that respect. As unlikely as it seemed, given her sire, it wasn't beyond the realms of possibility that the people looked upon her with fondness--in which case they could become difficult if they felt she was being ill treated.

Shelving the problem for the moment, he returned his attention to the assault and decided it was time to summon his men for the *coup de grace*. They still waited beyond the range of the archers as instructed, chafing at their inaction he saw with some amusement when he had used a simple spell to allow his spirit to cross the field and appear before them. Assuring them that there was still plenty of bloodletting to assuage their appetite, he gave his captain, Martunae, the order to advance his troops and returned to his body.

Lifting his staff, he began to murmur the incantation that would open the castle to him. Inside the keep, the stout oak that had been used to brace the gate groaned. After a few moments, the wood began to heave, as if it were a live thing dragging in lungfuls of air. Abruptly it shattered into flying splinters that peppered the men struggling nearest it, killing a half a dozen and wounding twice that many.

Moments later, the drawbridge fell outward, landing with a deafening concussion on the bracing on the outer edge of the moat and the gates began to swing inward.

Thrusting his staff into its holder, Daigon drew his sword. Victory sang in his blood as he spurred his horse toward the drawbridge. Without sparing a glance behind him to see how close his men were, or even if they had obeyed his command, he kicked his horse into motion and charged across the drawbridge.

Seeing his intent, Captain Martunae dug his heels into his horse's sides, urging for more speed, struggling to close the distance between them before Daigon could enter the keep alone. The hooves of his horse struck the heavy planking at the end of the drawbridge just as Daigon disappeared through the yawning mouth of Castle Aradan's gates. Behind him, his men spurred their horses and clattered onto the bridge, as well.

He saw when he reached the keep that his alarm had not been unwarranted. Daigon, his lips curled into a grim smile, had already dismounted. Even as Captain Martunae watched, two soldiers, screaming a challenge, fell upon him.

"To arms!" he bellowed. "To your king!"

Dust kicked up by the hooves of their horses swirled around them as Daigon's men brought their stampeding horses to a skidding halt. Swinging their swords to the right and left, they cut a path through the heaving mass of battling men until they had surrounded their king. Dismounting, they slapped their horse's rumps to send them charging into the melee and began to systematically hack at the already beleaguered castle defense.

The sun had reached its zenith before the men defending Aradan began to show signs of yielding. As much as Daigon admired the ferocity with which they had defended the castle and their king, Daigon's patience had reached an end. He was hot from his armor, his exertions, and the growing heat of the day; tired; and covered with gore, both his own and the blood of those he'd slain.

Abruptly, he summoned the dark forces, repelling a wide circle around himself that sent men flying in every direction. "ENOUGH!" he roared in a voice that reverberated off of every wall as if the gods had spoken.

It had the desired effect. Everyone in the keep froze, his army of dead included. "Yield now, and you will be given quarter! Put me to the trouble of taking this keep apart stone by stone and there will be no quarter given!"

The defenders threw down their swords.

Daigon's eyes narrowed as he studied them, one by one, but he saw the fight had gone out of them. Ordering Captain Martunae to round them up and collect their weapons, he waited until the captain and his men had that well in hand and banished his *mort du armée*. Everyone, including his own men, seemed almost to sag with relief when the gruesome warriors vanished.

When all who could still stand had been contained in one corner of the keep, he approached them. "I am Daigon, son of King Rhainor and Queen Saraphine. And I am hereditary ruler of all of

Aradan. Give me your allegiance and I will give you both your lives and your livelihood."

The men looked at each other, no doubt wondering what the alternative was.

Captain Bryon nerved himself to speak. "King Rhainor *was* the rightful king, but it has always been said that his heir died with him."

Daigon studied him for several moments. "And you have only my word for it that I am who I claim to be?"

Captain Bryon shifted uncomfortably. "Yes."

Daigon smiled thinly. "For now, that will have to be enough."

Captain Bryon's lips tightened, but he nodded. Ignoring his injuries, he knelt with some difficulty. "I give you my fealty, Daigon, son of King Rhainor, who has won these lands by right of might."

A grim smile curled Daigon's lips, but he found that he didn't particularly care that they still had reservations that he was the son of Rhainor. Right of might was enough. He nodded. Taking their cue from their captain, the others knelt and swore fealty to their new king, as well.

When Daigon had accepted his due, he summoned his captains, addressing Captain Martunae first. "As men of honor, we will accept the fealty of these men--for now. If you see any sign of treachery, however, the traitor is to be dealt with swiftly."

Captain Martunae nodded.

He turned to Captain Bryon. "You will divide your men who are the least injured into two parties, one to take care of the dead, the other to help the injured. Summon your healer to attend them." Daigon produced a pouch. "He is to clean the wounds thoroughly--with clean water. Then sprinkle this into the wounds and seal them with a firebrand--no exceptions. If he fails to do exactly as I've instructed and even one man becomes ill with infection, I will have his head on a pike--be sure that he knows this."

Captain Bryon nodded sharply and appeared to relax fractionally as he took the pouch. Daigon produced another and held it out to Captain Martunae, who took it without a word, as if he was familiar with what was expected of him.

"When you have relayed my orders, Captain Bryon, you will find me in the throne room."

* * * *

Contrary to what he'd expected, Captain Bryon found when he reported that the warlock, Daigon was not seated upon the throne of Aradan, but standing at one long window, staring out, no doubt, at the lands that he had so recently won. Since the man did not immediately acknowledge his presence, he looked around the room uneasily and finally knelt anyway. Instead of bowing his head, however, he took the time to study his new overlord.

He had the bearing of a king. Tired as he no doubt was, there was no slump of weariness to his broad shoulders, and the man was tall, taller than most men. He had been young when King Rhainor ruled Aradan, and he could not entirely trust his memories of such an early age, but it seemed to him that the warlock bore a striking resemblance to the old king--which might mean nothing at all. He could as easily be the whelp of some commoner. King Rhainor had not had the reputation of sprinkling bastards about the countryside, but that didn't mean he had had none.

"As it happens, he didn't," Daigon said, turning to look at Captain Bryon finally.

Bryon felt his jaw sag and his heart flutter uncomfortably. "Sire?"

"No bastards. My father had no bastards," Daigon responded patiently.

Captain Bryon blinked rapidly several times. "You read minds?"

Daigon smiled thinly, but he laid no claim that he could--nor admitted that he could not, and Captain Bryon was left with the uncomfortable feeling that he could. Either that or he was extraordinarily perceptive.

"Where is the princess, Rhiannon?"

Captain Bryon felt a brief surge of satisfaction. So the warlock did not know and see all? "Beyond your reach I should think," he responded.

Daigon stared at the man, feeling an uncomfortable, and unaccountable twinge of dread. "She is dead?" he demanded sharply.

Captain Bryon realized at once that he had no desire to rouse Daigon to fury. "Nay--at least, not to my knowledge. I expect she escaped with her uncle through the tunnels beneath the castle."

Daigon's eyes narrowed. Wryly, he admitted it was contrary of him to be so displeased with the news when he had not been looking forward to dealing with the problem. He decided, however, that his displeasure stemmed from the fact that he had only just taken the keep and already his commands had been ignored. Concentrating, he separated his spirit and searched for her using the link that she had so generously given him with the arrow she placed through his palm. He found her in a cavern that opened to the sea.

"She is in the caverns below. Send someone to fetch her to my private chambers."

Captain Bryon saluted, but looked uneasy. "Your private chambers?"

"The king's apartments," Daigon clarified, although he knew very well that the captain's hesitancy had had nothing to do with confusion over which chamber to take her to.

When Captain Bryon still looked uncomfortable, Daigon lifted his brows. "There is some part of the order that confuses you?"

Captain Bryon stared at him unhappily for several moments and finally shook his head. "No, Sire. I will see to it."

Daigon studied the man's stiff shoulders as he strode quickly from the room. When Captain Bryon had disappeared, he turned and looked toward the rear of the room. "You can come out now."

He waited. Minutes passed. Finally, an elderly man got to his feet shakily.

Daigon looked the man over appraisingly. "Who are you?"

Nervously, the man darted from behind the benches where he'd been hiding and dropped to his knees on the floor in the aisle. "The King's steward--Sire."

Daigon cocked his head curiously. "And what name are you known by, steward?"

Startled, the old man darted a quick glance at him before ducking his head once more. "Meekin, Sire," he said shakily.

"Good!" Daigon said decisively. "You are just the man I need to see, Meekin. As you have no doubt noticed, I am soiled from my--travels."

The man glanced at the blood spatters that coated Daigon's clothing, his cloak and his boots and swallowed a little sickly. "You've need of a bath, Sire?"

Daigon smiled. "A man of perception. Yes. I will give you the task of rounding up the servants and coaxing them out of hiding--my men will need to be fed and the castle and keep will need to be set to rights. Send someone to fetch my personal effects and have a bath prepared so that I can wash the muck off."

* * * *

When Rhiannon first began to swim upwards toward consciousness, the sound that greeted her confused her. The rhythmic clatter grew louder, however, and she finally realized that it was not someone throwing pebbles, but rather the scrape of feet against stone. Still far too groggy to feel any alarm, she merely groaned and sat up.

Her head was pounding and she lifted a hand to examine it, pausing in shock when she saw her wrists were manacled together by a chain. After several stunned moments, she completed the action she'd begun, discovering a goose egg of interesting proportions on her head but no blood. Had she fallen, she wondered, still more than a little confused? Had her uncle trampled her with his horse in his haste to flee?

Abruptly, she remembered the eyes and shivered. Too late, that memory connected in her mind with the manacles that had appeared upon her wrists and the sounds of men approaching. Even as she struggled to her feet, soldiers appeared in the mouth of the tunnel. She stared at them, recognizing Captain Bryon almost at once. There was something about his demeanor, however, that prevented the flood of relief she should have felt.

"Princess Rhiannon! Are you injured?"

She must look like hell if that was his first thought, Rhiannon thought wryly. She shook her head, but a wave of dizziness followed. "I--uh--I must have fallen."

"Can you walk?"

This time, she didn't dare move her head. "Yes."

His face hardened. "King Daigon has sent us to fetch you to his chambers."

"King!" Rhiannon said, so outraged by that that it was several moments before she assimilated the remainder of his speech. "His chambers?" she asked a little faintly. "You're certain he didn't say throne room? Receiving chambers?"

He reddened. "The king's chambers."

"Well! I won't go!" she snapped. "How dare he command my presence in private chambers!"

Captain Bryon looked dismayed. "My king has ordered it. I dare not disobey, princess."

Rhiannon studied him belligerently for several moments, but she knew she was no match for Captain Bryon and the three soldiers who had accompanied him. Moreover, she had no desire to get the men killed, or worse, by demanding that they disobey a direct order. Her lips tightened. "Fine!"

Gathering her skirts, she stalked past them toward the tunnel. After a few moments, one of the men passed her carrying a torch high and led the way. Her anger sustained her until she reached the dungeons once more. Her rigid spine and angry march had only made her head hurt worse, however, and pain and fear had gained the upper hand long before she climbed the stairs from the dungeon. It took an effort to rekindle her righteous wrath, but the sight of the guards stationed outside the king's chambers helped a good deal.

He'd wasted no time in making himself at home, she thought indignantly. Well! If he thought for one moment that he could order her around, he had another think coming! She would let him know right off that she wasn't about to kowtow to him just because he had learned a few magical tricks to frighten the ignorant with!

How dare he order her to be brought to his private chambers anyway! As if she were nothing but a – a harlot!

It went a long way toward boosting her flagging anger that, instead of announcing her, the guards at the door simply stepped aside, pushed the door open and thrust her inside.

She'd already drawn breath to give him a taste of the sharp side of her tongue when the door closed sharply behind her. She froze, her mouth still agape as the warlock, Daigon, who wasn't wearing a stitch of clothing, turned at the commotion at the door. She felt her mouth working, but she couldn't seem to summon a single word, or thought, or even to remember to exhale.

Chapter Four

Surprise flickered across his features followed by a twinge of color that indicated discomfort, but both were gone so swiftly that Rhiannon could never afterwards be certain that she'd seen it at all. A sardonic smile curled his lips. Without haste, he climbed into the steaming tub of water as if he hadn't been interrupted at all and, once settled, examined her from head to foot in a thorough, leisurely manner that finally penetrated her stupor.

Embarrassment should have been her first reaction as soon as some of the shock had worn off. It wasn't. She couldn't precisely pinpoint *what* her reaction was, but the tingling warmth that spread through her seemed to defy identification as discomfiture or even revulsion. On the contrary, she seemed overly warm and overly conscious of her own body in a way she couldn't remember ever being.

She could not recall that she'd ever seen a man completely naked before--half naked, to be sure--the upper half, not the lower regions--but even at that she thought she might *still* have been stunned for, contrary to her first impression of him as a man of magic, there was nothing soft on him--not on his entire body that she could see. Nor was he quite as slender as his height made him appear. His arms, his back, and his chest were covered in the heavy, bulging, well defined muscles of a swordsman and not even veiled from view by heavy, dark hair, for his body was surprisingly bereft of that, save for a sprinkling of dark hair in the center of his chest, a thin trail that arrowed downward.

And the dark thatch from which his unnervingly huge man-root sprouted.

"The timing is not what I'd hoped for," he said wryly, breaking the silence at last. "I shall have to remember next time that the guards can be counted upon for their swiftness--and the servants for their slowness."

Rhiannon blinked, several times, rapidly. She was still too much in shock to grasp the whole of his comments, however, and simply seized upon the first. "You intended this!" she said accusingly.

He tilted his head questioningly.

It only fired her anger higher that he had so cunningly planned her seduction and now was trying to make himself appear innocent of evil thoughts. "I suppose you expected me to simply fall at your feet in a swoon because of your magnificent--uh--uh--form and make it easier for you to ravish me!"

His lips twitched and finally curled up at one corner in an unmistakable smile. Laughter gleamed in his eyes, which she realized abruptly were not dark as she had thought but a deep sapphire blue. "I hadn't considered it actually. Do you anticipate that there is danger of it?"

Rhiannon frowned, confused. "What?"

"The swoon. I must tell you," he added thoughtfully, "that I'm not at all certain that I can oblige at the moment--with the ravishment. Perhaps after I've rested a bit?"

Rhiannon gasped in outrage. "Oblige?" she repeated indignantly. "Oblige!"

Shrugging, he looked her over once more. "I like to think I'm an agreeable sort, but you're not precisely to my taste. If you had a little more meat on your bones...." He shook his head. "But then there is the yellow hair...."

It was several moments before Rhiannon realized she was gaping at him like a fish that had just been pulled from the water. She was having a similar problem in breathing if it came to that. "You--you--bastard!" she snarled. "As if I've *any* desire to suit your fancy!"

His dark brows rose. "No? Then you should not have offered. I'm excruciatingly disappointed."

Rhiannon stared at him as if his wits had gone a-begging. "Offered?" she said faintly. "I did no such thing!"

"Then I was mistaken?"

Rhiannon blinked at him, realizing abruptly that he was thoroughly enjoying himself teasing her. "Yes--and since I can see I'm disturbing your bath, I will await your pleasure in the receiving chambers," she said haughtily and, gathering her skirts, stalked to the door.

"I thought we'd established that you had no interest in my pleasure?"

Rhiannon gritted her teeth, but discovered she was unable to make the grand exit that she'd intended. The door latch wouldn't budge. She tossed a glare at him over her shoulder. "The door is bolted!"

"Is it?"

"Why is it bolted if you had no intention of...no plans to...if you didn't mean to--uh--do anything?" Rhiannon asked with forced bravado as her sense of righteous indignation abandoned her and uneasiness began to creep in in its place.

"I did send for you," he pointed out pensively, focusing on his bath.

Mesmerized by his glistening skin as he slid the soapy cloth over his chest and arms, Rhiannon found she had difficulty pulling her gaze away. "For what purpose?" she managed to ask finally.

"Not the one that so obviously plagues your mind," he responded wryly.

Rhiannon felt color flood her cheeks until she had to resist the urge to fan herself.

"My back," he said, holding the soapy cloth out and sitting forward in the tub.

"What?" Rhiannon asked blankly.

"Scrub my back, if you please."

Rhiannon licked her lips. She didn't want to get that close to him, particularly when she'd been raging at him like a fishwife.

Especially with him naked.

She had a sinking feeling, however, that it was a test of some sort, that he wanted to know just how defiant she was. Would she dare defy a direct order? And if so, what else would she do?

Or maybe he'd only demanded it to humble her?

He was king now, conqueror. It didn't matter if she *did* think of him of some common upstart. He held the power of life and death.

Feeling a little ill that her shock and fear had so far gotten the upper hand with her that she'd actually had the audacity--and stupidity--to challenge him, Rhiannon's blush vanished and most of her natural color with it. Numbly, she curtsied low--as she should have done the moment she entered the room--and moved to the tub.

Her hand trembled in spite of all she could do as she took the cloth. It was almost a relief to sink down on her knees at the foot of the tub. A few minutes more and they would have given out and dropped her ignominiously on the floor.

Breaking a sweat, she scrubbed his back in hard, jerky movements. He winced, sucking in a sharp gasp as she rubbed the cloth over a reddened patch of skin near his ribs and she dropped the cloth from suddenly nerveless fingers. "Pardon," she said quickly. "I didn't realize you were injured."

He twisted his head to look back over his shoulder, then lifted his arm to get a better look. "It's nothing that won't heal quickly. Finish."

Rhiannon felt her face redden. "I--uh--I dropped the cloth."

He looked back at her again and amusement lit his eyes. "Retrieve it."

Rhiannon's jaw dropped, but she was far too wary now to give vent to her sharp tongue. Closing her eyes, she slid her arm into the tub and felt around. A jolt went through her when she encountered something that was definitely flesh, not metal.

"A little to the left."

She moved her hand.

"Your left."

She felt around in the other direction.

"Lower."

She felt a little lower, trying to ignore the flesh her hand was rubbing against.

His shoulders started shaking. "I believe this is what you're looking for."

Rhiannon gaped at the cloth in his hand and abruptly snatched her arm out of the water. She was tempted to slap him in the face with the soggy cloth when he placed it in her hand again. Instead, she contented herself with scrubbing his back so thoroughly that every inch of flesh was reddened when she'd finished.

He said nothing more, not even when she scrubbed the massive bruised area.

Dropping the cloth, she pushed herself to her feet, locking her limp knees. "If that is all, my lord?"

"Not quite," he murmured, grasping her wrist before she could retreat very far.

Rhiannon's heart began to hammer unpleasantly fast as it occurred to her to wonder if the request had been no more than a trap to get her close enough to catch without difficulty. "I don't flatter myself that your uncle left you because I had ordered him to. Why did he abandon you?"

Rhiannon merely stared at him as those terrible moments in the caverns came flooding back. It was on the tip of her tongue to tell him it was because Gerard wasn't her uncle at all, but wariness had finally usurped the shock and fear that had suppressed it before and she held her tongue, considering her answer. She didn't care if it would make Gerard sound like the coward he was if she told the truth--that he was so desperate to escape that he would take nothing that might slow him down beyond his coin. But her status as a princess might be the only security she had--little as it was. The warlock might well take liberties, but he would not torture her--she didn't think, or imprison her in the dudgeon, or cast her out to make her way the best she could, or kill her outright. He might have conquered the kingdom, but he would know that it could not win the people's favor if he treated her with malice.

And, as princess, she at least had value as a hostage, a pawn.

If she admitted that she was no such thing, then what use would he have for her?

She didn't doubt that what Gerard had told her was true. She supposed she had always felt, in the back of her mind, that some things simply didn't fit--the coloring the warlock had spoken of, for instance, for both of her parents had been dark--and even Gerard was dark.

"He could not take me," she said finally. "There were not enough horses."

It sounded lame even to her, but it was the best that she could do when she had not had a chance even to formulate a more convincing lie.

The look he gave her made it clear he didn't buy it for a moment. She lifted her chin. "He will come back for me," she said, failing to infuse even a thread of conviction in the statement.

The warlock's dark brows rose. Something gleamed in his eyes, but this time she doubted it was amusement. "Do you think he would be so rash?" he asked with interest. "I have the castle--and his men."

Rhiannon realized later that the desire to wipe the smug look from his face was one she would have been wiser to resist. "Since he cleaned out the treasury and took it with him I should think he can raise another army without much difficulty!"

The warlock stared at her for almost a full minute while his anger climbed to a slow boil. "What!" he roared abruptly, climbing out of the tub.

Rhiannon's eyes widened. She retreated several steps before she realized he still had a grip on her wrist.

Without waiting for a response, Daigon stalked to the door of his chambers, dragging her behind him, and snatched the door open, bellowing down the hallway for Captain Bryon. The guards nearly fell over themselves in their rush to find the captain.

When he'd slammed the door again, he turned to glare at Rhiannon. "Is there no end to the treachery the house of Huaven is capable of?"

Rhiannon gaped at him, wondering suddenly if it wouldn't have been far better to have admitted right off that her uncle had disclaimed any familial connection. It was only after he'd released her and stalked away to snatch up a robe and shrug it onto his shoulders that it suddenly occurred to her that he was accusing her of deliberately distracting him to allow her uncle time to get away.

Relief flooded her when he turned away and began to pace the room. She glanced at the door a few times--wondering if she could slip away, but decided he was furious enough as it was. It would be stupid to risk angering him more and would gain her nothing since she couldn't possibly reach any place of safety before he came after her, or sent the guards.

When she glanced toward the warlock again to see if he had noticed her contemplation of escape, she found that he had ceased to pace and was staring directly at her. Before she could even gasp in surprise, she felt herself impelled backwards until she was plastered against the wall like a fly captured by a spider web. He had not touched her. He was not near enough. It was more as if the wall had sucked her against it, but in the blink of an eye he was standing toe to toe with her.

In an almost leisurely manner, he scooped her breasts from her bodice and teased her nipples with his fingers until they stood erect and pouting. "You were to distract me, yes?"

Rhiannon merely gaped at him blankly, still too stunned by her predicament to think when the realization sank in that she truly was stuck, that she could not so much as twitch.

When she said nothing, he dipped his head, traced a teasing circle around one erect nipple and then sucked the strangely sensitive bud into his mouth. Her paralysis did nothing to protect her from sensation. The heat and suction of his mouth sent escalating currents of fire along her blood stream and nerve endings, making her entire body clench. The feel of his mouth on her and the sensations it created was like nothing she had ever felt before, or ever imagined her body capable of. Her breath caught in her chest. Her heart seemed to jerk to a halt and then commenced to pounding in double time, as if scurrying to make up the lost beats. Dizziness swept through her. The muscles low in her belly clenched tightly. Warmth spread through her nether regions, making her woman's place seem as swollen and achingly sensitive as the nipples he was teasing with his mouth and tongue and fingers.

Just when she thought she couldn't bear it any more, and had begun to think she would die if he stopped, he released her nipple and lifted his head, rolling both between his fingers as he fixed her with a penetrating stare. "Is that the task he left you?"

It took a tremendous effort to lift her eyelids and look up at him. Rhiannon licked lips dried by the rush of air between them as she struggled to drag air into her laboring lungs. "Task?" she asked in confusion.

He studied her for several moments and lowered his mouth to her other nipple.

A harder jolt than before went through Rhiannon as he captured it, rolling it about in his mouth as if it was a ripe berry, sucking it. The faintness increased to a swirling blackness and Rhiannon abruptly realized she was teetering on the brink of some exquisite plain. If she fell, she would never be the same again.

"He only said he could not take me, that you would come after him," she gasped, struggling against the moan of pleasure that was threatening.

He stopped, lifting his head to study her again. Abruptly, she found herself freed. She had to lock her knees to keep from sliding down the wall. Confusion filled her when she lifted her lids at last and saw that the warlock was pacing as before, halfway across the room from her.

When she looked down at herself, she saw her bodice as it had been before, as if it had not been touched.

Frowning, she wrapped her arms around herself, struggling against the pounding fire in her blood, trying to figure out what, or even if, anything had happened.

Something had happened. Her body had quickened, as if a fever had suddenly come upon her. Her nipples still throbbed almost painfully. An echoing throb filled her loins with heat and moisture, as if her body wept for something it had been denied.

Cool air wafted across her heated flesh, sending a shiver through her, but cooling the fever in her blood, as well. Rhiannon wrapped her arms around herself, staring suspiciously at the warlock now, though she found she could not bring herself to demand to know if he'd bespelled her since that would entail what might be an awkward explanation of what she'd experienced.

It was a relief when she heard the march of footsteps along the corridor outside that heralded an arrival.

Captain Bryon was white faced when he presented himself, and breathing heavily, as if he'd run most of the way.

The warlock rounded on him, fire in his eyes. If possible, that fury leached even more color from the man's face. "Is there some particular reason you failed to notify me that Gerard had cleaned out the treasury before his departure?"

Captain Bryon's mouth fell open in shocked surprise that no one could doubt was genuine. "Sire! I swear on my mother's grave I had no knowledge of it!"

The warlock's gaze slid to Rhiannon, where she stood uneasily near the door, wondering if she might escape while the warlock's attention was trained on the captain.

"The princess said nothing of it to you?"

Captain Bryon whirled to look at her as if he'd never seen her before. His face was red when he turned to look at the warlock again. "She only--that is, she seemed disoriented when we found her, and she--uh--was not pleased at the summons. She told me nothing about the Kin--nothing about her uncle."

After studying the shaken man for so long that he looked as if he would crumple to the floor, Daigon whirled away and stalked to the staff that leaned against the wall near the bed. Wrapping his fingers around the gnarled staff, he moved to the center of the room and lifted it. Almost at once, the crystal that topped the staff began to cloud with swirling mist.

Rhiannon gasped, covering her mouth with her hand as a strange light appeared at his feet. Slowly, the dancing light seemed to solidify, take form. To her amazement, she saw her uncle, surrounded by his men at arms, settled near a campfire.

"Do you know this place?" Daigon demanded, pointing.

Captain Bryon, who'd been staring at the image in stupefaction, blinked. Frowning, he began to actually study what he could see of the woods around the party. "I think so, Sire. They have left the coast and taken a trail northward--toward Tsenvia." He looked up at the warlock. "He will not go there. King Howard is a bitter enemy."

"Go to Captain Martunae and tell him that I said you were to take six of his most able men and go after Gerard. Relieve him of *my* gold and bring it back. Is that understood?"

Captain Bryon had reddened when Daigon had pointed out that he was not to ride with his own men, a silent accusation of lack of trust, but he merely nodded. "And--Gerard and his men?"

Daigon considered it for a moment. "Leave him. Without the gold to hire an army he is no threat to me."

Briefly, Bryon looked surprised, but he did not question the order. Turning on his heel, he left as swiftly as he had come.

When he had left, the image Daigon had conjured died and he returned the staff to its place beside his bed. Shifting uneasily, Rhiannon remained silent, unwilling to draw his wrath once more now that it seemed to have abated somewhat. When he continued to ignore her, however, pacing the room for a time and finally moving to the window to stare out of it at the settling sun, she began to think he had forgotten about her. After glancing at the door several times, she took a cautious step in that direction.

Her heart leapt in her throat as Daigon turned, pinning her with a hard look. She swallowed with an effort. The man must have the ears of a predator to hear such a furtive movement.

Her eyes widened as he strode toward her, but to her relief, he only went to the bell pull to summon a servant. A servant appeared at once. "Remove the water and bring more."

The elderly man looked surprised but merely bowed deeply and disappeared again. A brigade of servants appeared next, carefully removing the water from the tub bucket by bucket. The last had scarcely exited with the final pail when a new procession arrived, filling the tub once more.

Rhiannon watched with scant interest. Emotionally, she was exhausted. She'd endured a great many shocks throughout the day and the trek through the secret passages had wearied her physically as well as emotionally. By her count, the warlock had kept her standing for nigh an hour on top of that. She was too proud to beg to be released, and fairly certain anyway that he would not allow it, but it was becoming more and more difficult to hide the fact that she was beginning to feel like she might drop where she stood.

"Now," Daigon said when the servants had left at last. "Your turn."

Chapter Five

Rhiannon was certain she could not have heard him correctly. "Sire?"

He gestured toward the tub of steaming water.

Rhiannon looked down at herself, realizing for the first time that she didn't just feel terrible, she looked awful. The once lovely dusky rose colored gown she wore was torn in several places--tears she hadn't even noticed in her fear and distress as she'd fought her way through the battle to the castle. Mud liberally smeared it, as well, from her adventures in the secret tunnels.

Embarrassment climbed into her cheeks as she recalled the accusations she'd flung at the warlock. He was obviously far too fastidious to find any female who looked as she now did the least appealing--and considering some of the insulting things she'd said to him, possessed a good deal of restraint for not pointing out her undesirability.

Regardless of her condition, she was not keen on the idea of stripping for him.

She glanced around the room a little helplessly, as if inspiration would come to her--or a rescuer magically appear.

The sense of helplessness gave way to anger after a moment. Setting her jaw, she met his gaze unflinchingly and held out her manacled wrists. Surprise and dismay filled her when the metal bands immediately disappeared, leaving her with no excuse to ignore the order. After that brief moment of confusion, however, she set her jaw and began to disrobe. He watched with keen interest, his eyes narrowed, almost slumberous.

Rhiannon found that her heart was beating unpleasantly fast as she dropped her gown from her shoulders and stepped out of it. Leaving it where it landed, she reached behind her waist and struggled with the lacing of her corset until at last she'd loosened it. When she lifted her gaze to Daigon again, his skin was slightly flushed and his breathing noticeably irregular--like her own. She dropped the corset, hesitated a moment and then pushed her under gown from her shoulders and allowed it to fall to the floor.

Heaving a deep, sustaining breath as she stepped out of it, she looked up at Daigon again. His gaze was fastened to her breasts, she saw, and a blush rose from her breasts all the way to her hairline. Gritting her teeth, she reached for the tie of her pantalets.

The movement drew his gaze. He studied her fingers for several moments, almost seeming to hold his breath. Abruptly, his gaze met hers for several thudding heartbeats and then he turned and strode across the room and into his dressing room.

Shaking--she wasn't certain if it was just from relief, or a combination of relief and something else--Rhiannon discarded her pantalets and climbed quickly into the tub. The heated water soothed her, making the tension curling inside her and in every muscle of her body begin to uncoil almost at once. Pulling her knees up, she wrapped her arms around her legs and propped her forehead on her knees. She didn't look up when the door to Daigon's dressing room opened again and she heard him cross his bed chamber and halt near the tub where she sat. For several moments he said nothing, but she could feel his gaze. Finally, he moved toward the door.

"I will send your ladies to attend you," he said, then opened the door and departed.

When he had gone, Rhiannon lifted her head to stare at the door, trying to sort through her tumultuous emotions. She felt unlike herself, which was hardly surprising since she had discovered she was not the person she had believed herself to be when she had woken that morning. In the space of one day, everything she had ever known had crumbled to dust around her along with far too much that she'd believed were truths.

She was confused by Daigon's behavior. She had seen absolute ruthlessness in him when he had come to conquer, but he had been patient, even amused, when she had lost her mind and berated him as if she had every right to do so and an expectation of impunity. She could not even say that his teasing had been malicious, though she'd been so upset at the time that every teasing remark had only made her more furious--possibly because she was scared to death and confused by everything that had happened.

She had been terrified the moment she heard that she was to be escorted to his chambers that he had rape on his mind, insulted when he'd coolly informed her that she wasn't to his taste and both frightened and elated when she'd seen that he was not as immune to her as she'd claimed.

Was she his prisoner? Destined to become his mistress? Or was he toying with her because it amused him to do so?

What, if anything, could she do about any of it?

She thought the old guards might still have some sense of loyalty to her, but could she ask them to forfeit their lives when she had no reason, at the moment, to think hers would be forfeit without their help?

She didn't think she could ask that of them. Even if they were willing to risk their lives to protect her, she had never felt that such a thing was her 'due' and she certainly did not feel that way now--knowing she did not even have the right of 'birth.'

Was it true? Or simply something her uncle had said in the heat of the moment to push her away?

She rather thought it the opposite, that he'd been so frantic to leave he'd hardly been aware of what he was saying and, perhaps, had given her a truth that he might never have otherwise.

But why had he kept it to himself? If he knew, why hadn't he denounced her the moment her father died?

It was a power issue, she decided. She had some grasp of politics, but perhaps not a thorough enough understanding to figure that part of it out. Pride must have entered into it. Her father had acknowledged her as his heir--because there had been no other children that lived beyond infancy. Maybe he hadn't wanted to make her father, and by virtue of family connection, himself, look like the cuckold he obviously was? Or maybe he figured an announcement that she was a bastard *after* her father's death would not be believed? And he could not have used her as a pawn in his power game if it had become widely known that she was not even related to him by blood.

Briefly, she wondered who her real father had been. Her mother's true love? Had she given herself to the man she loved because she knew that she had no choice in her marriage?

Rhiannon found that she liked to think that might have been the case--that her mother, finding herself in much the same situation as she would be in now if Daigon had not completely overturned her world, took the happiness she could by sharing her love with the man she cared for while she had the opportunity to do so.

That did not help her now.

Daigon might or might not find her physically appealing, but he despised the family that had taken everything from him--and she didn't doubt that he at least believed that to be true whether it was or not.

She supposed it might make no difference to him in a way that would be of benefit to her. He might hate her and still take her to his bed--might actually relish the idea of despoiling the daughter of the man who'd had his parents slain as a way of getting his revenge beyond the grave.

If any part of that was true, though, it still would not help her if she managed to convince him she was not of King Nordain's seed. He would have no use for her at all then.

Shivering, she dismissed the thoughts as the maids came in and helped her finish her bath and dress. She didn't know whether to take it as a good sign or not that they merely brought the things needed to dress her instead of her entire wardrobe.

She was told when her toilet had been completed that she was expected to present herself in the great hall for supper.

She'd been wondering what the empty feeling was all about. Until she received the message she hadn't realized that she actually was hungry.

Nerves still made her feel faintly ill at the thought of eating though, and truth be told, she was far more tired than hungry. She glanced longingly at the bed but she thought it might be best not to test Daigon's patience further. He would no doubt consider a refusal as direct defiance of his wishes and he was already unnervingly furious about her suspected part in Gerard's theft of the treasury.

If was unjust, of course. She'd had nothing to do with it and Gerard would certainly not have listened to any demands she might have made concerning what he considered to be his even though he had in effect ceded the right to it the moment he'd abandoned his people to flee--it was taxes for the maintenance of the kingdom after all. But she had said nothing about it either, which had allowed Gerard a good lead in his escape with it.

She had not thought of it. She doubted anyone would believe that, but her thoughts had been centered on her fears at the moment, not coin.

Sighing, she straightened her spine and left the king's chambers, ignoring the guards as they fell into step behind her.

So much for the question of whether or not she was actually a prisoner!

* * * *

Hunger could be an inconvenient and embarrassing state, Rhiannon reflected wryly. She had presented herself for the meal as ordered, but she'd intended to maintain the air of a martyr at her treatment at the hands of the warlock. The problem with that amiable resolve was that she hadn't eaten all day and the emotional shock had worn off enough for her body to begin clamoring for food almost as soon as the servants had brought the dishes in and the delicious smells had assailed her nostrils. She'd been seated beside the warlock, which should have been enough in itself to wind her stomach into a bundle of nerves. It hadn't. Instead her stomach had begun to churn ominously, threatening to growl like a starving beast.

Pretending to have no appetite while her stomach got louder and louder in its demands wouldn't have impressed anyone with anything except that she was being silly and childish, so she'd decided to pick at her food, hoping she could appease the beast and still appear put upon. From the looks of amusement the warlock kept casting her way, she couldn't say that she'd carried even that off very well, though.

And when she'd expressed her desire to retire when she'd finished eating, the warlock had had her escorted back to his apartments.

She looked around the room uneasily when the door had closed behind her. She'd refused to allow her ladies to prepare her for bed, hoping that, at least, would give the gossip mongers pause, but she didn't have a great deal of faith that it would.

The door still vibrated with their departure when the manacles appeared on her wrists once more and Rhiannon's heart skipped several beats as she glanced around the room expecting to see the disembodied eyes again. She relaxed fractionally when she didn't, testing the manacles. They didn't feel nearly as heavy as they looked and she was certain they should feel, but they were solid enough, she discovered.

Dismissing them finally, she looked around the room uneasily, but with curiosity. Not surprisingly the royal apartments were even more opulent than the remainder of the castle, she saw. The bed chamber was enormous and the sitting room that opened off of it on one side larger still. Besides the bed chamber and sitting room, the apartment consisted of a dressing room and large closet where the royal wardrobe was kept. Doors that looked as if they'd been fashioned for giants opened from the bed chamber onto a wide balcony, which might have diminished the apartment's security, but added much to the graciousness of the apartments.

The walls and ceiling were lavishly ornamented with scrolling, flowering woodwork that had been leafed with gold. The upper portion of the walls were covered in dark silk, the lower portion whitewashed. A number of heavy tapestries hung along the walls, depicting scenes of battles that may or may not have ever been fought. Thick rugs woven of sheep's wool and died to match the silk on the walls were scattered about the planked floor.

The bed was perhaps twice the size of her own and she'd thought her own bed huge. Dragging her gaze from the bed, she glanced toward the spot where the tub had rested at its foot.

The tub had been removed and the room cleaned while they had dined, she saw. She stared at the damp spot on the floor for several moments while her mind recalled the incident between her and the warlock earlier with such vivid detail that she began to grow increasingly uncomfortable.

Irritation surfaced. Her impatience was directed more at herself than the warlock, but she nursed it anyway, trying to dredge up enough righteous anger to chase away her uneasiness. Giving the bed a wide berth, she began to pace the room, absently examining the furnishings while her mind wandered at will, but she very quickly found her thoughts turning from the warlock and his dastardly deeds to her uncle.

Almost with a sense of surprise, she realized she was far more than upset and angry at Gerard's denouncement and desertion. She hated him. He'd been affectionate when she was a child, at times too affectionate for her comfort, but that had only made her more uneasy about him, not less and she could not recall that she had ever felt any sense of affection toward him, even before her father's death. She remembered Gerard's anger and determination to dominate her and the cruelties he practiced with unnerving frequency against the people under his rule far better than any kindness toward her, even though she could not say that he had been particularly cruel to her at any point.

She supposed, even if not for that, Gerard had given her reason enough to despise him now.

What was to become of her now? Particularly since Gerard had thumbed his nose at the warlock and stolen the treasury when he escaped, making her an accessory? Would the warlock decide to retaliate against Gerard by having her executed? Imprison her for the remainder of her life?

He could not ransom her, though he might think it a possibility. Gerard had denounced her. He would certainly not part with any of his precious coin to buy her back, whatever the warlock threatened to do with her.

She had thought it bad to be no more than a pawn, but being of no use at all, she realized, was far worse.

And how much did the warlock know? She'd seen what he was capable of, but were those things he'd done merely a very limited range of magical tricks he'd learned? Or was he as powerful as he made himself appear? And, if the latter was true, how could anything be kept from him?

He'd seen her in the caverns. Had he seen everything that had transpired?

She frowned at that, pausing beside the bed in her pacing, but she couldn't believe that he had since he'd said nothing to indicate he thought she was worthless to him.

Several moments passed before she realized she was staring at the warlock's staff.

She had never seen one so close. The staff itself appeared to be made of horn. Curious, she moved toward the staff, peered at it more closely, wondering if it was indeed horn and if so what kind. After a moment it dawned upon her that no beast had that peculiar swirling sort of fluting beyond the unicorn.

Her heart skipped a beat.

Was that the source of his powers? Or only what he used to focus them?

Her gaze leapt to the crystal mounted on the top of the staff with silver talons. The stone didn't appear to be anything more than ordinary crystal and not particularly fine crystal at that. The crystal was murky, almost opaque.

Throwing an uneasy glance toward the door, Rhiannon returned her attention to the staff, lifting her hand to touch the crystal. Her fingers were only inches from it when the staff abruptly bounced upward and sideways, landing on the bed.

"I must insist that you refrain from touching my--uh--staff. You might not care for the results."

Rhiannon uttered a squeak of fright, jumping almost a half a foot off the floor and whirling.

The warlock stood at the foot of the massive bed. She'd been staring at him for nigh a full minute with her mouth agape and her eyes as wide as saucers, wondering if he had simply appeared there in a puff of smoke, before his comment finally made its way through her shock to her brain. Color started at her breasts and climbed upwards toward her hairline. She closed her mouth abruptly, studying him suspiciously for any sign that the comment had carried a double entendre.

The gleam of amusement in his eyes assured her it had and wasn't merely the product of an overly fertile imagination and her fears. Embarrassment spawned irritation and fear fanned it rapidly to anger. "I had no intention of ... of doing anything with your staff! I was merely curious... That is, I merely wanted to examine ... uh..."

His dark brows rose almost to his hair line, but the amusement in his eyes deepened. "You are certainly welcome to examine my staff, but you may only look. Touching it, as I said, could have consequences you are not prepared for."

Rhiannon's lips tightened. "I can see this sort of sword play amuses you!"

His lips curled upward at one corner. "I readily admit I find sword play very much to my liking."

"I meant verbal!" Rhiannon snapped testily.

"That, too."

Realizing that she was no match for him, at the moment and under current conditions, Rhiannon changed the subject abruptly, stalking away from the bed. "Why are you keeping me here?"

The amusement vanished. He studied her thoughtfully for several moments and finally settled on the foot of the bed. "You seem intelligent enough. I would've thought that much was clear."

Rhiannon blinked several times rapidly as the realization sank in that he'd misunderstood her. She did not want to get into any discussion regarding his purposes for coming to Aradan or her role in his quest for revenge. It was a cowardly attitude, she knew, and yet she didn't think she was prepared at the moment to know what his long range intentions were. She had merely intended to challenge his careless regard for her reputation.

"You are hostage for your uncle's behavior," he continued after several moments.

Nausea washed over Rhiannon. If he thought for one moment that Gerard would be the least concerned for her treatment and safety he was very much mistaken. Torture and slow, agonizing death blossomed like a dark cloud in her mind as she imagined the two men taunting each other over her corpse. "I meant here--in your apartments," she said a little weakly.

The amusement returned. He leaned back on the bed, smiling faintly. "Why? Did you have something particular in mind?"

Rhiannon stared at him, trying to command her mind to rational thought. Was he merely toying with her? Or did he actually have some interest in her body? And if he did, could she bring herself to use the only weapon she had to protect herself?

Should she offer?

Or would he spurn the offer, having merely been trying to goad her into making it?

She didn't know whether to be more disturbed by the realization that she was not entirely repelled by the thought of lying with him, or that the thought of rejection bothered her more than actually yielding up the use of her body to put herself in his good graces.

She reddened. "I cannot stay in your apartments without my reputation being shredded by the gossips," she said finally.

He frowned. "I could remove a tongue or two. That should quiet the rest."

Rhiannon stared at him in horror, wondering how she could have so completely misjudged the man. "That would make you no better than my unc...."

His brows rose, but his expression was thoughtful. "Would it appease your sense of propriety to be housed in the dungeon then?"

Rhiannon stared at him in dismay, realizing martyrdom didn't seem nearly as appealing as she'd thought it might, not when faced with the possibility of becoming a permanent resident of the underworld of the castle. "Could I not be imprisoned in my own apartments?" she asked a little weakly.

His lips tightened. "Either you have a much higher opinion of your charms than I do, or you think I am a fool to be so easily charmed by a pretty face and a pretense of innocence."

Rhiannon gaped at him. "I only thought...."

"That I, ruler of a conquered people, would be so arrogant as to think none would defy me by helping you to escape?"

Rhiannon was embarrassed, not the least because she realized that his keeping her in his apartments had nothing at all to do with an interest in her personally, but also because she'd been so focused upon her fears that she'd not considered there might be another, perfectly reasonable motivation, for his behavior.

She decided, after several unnerving moments, that she was going to dig her grave with her tongue if she didn't gather her wits about her. "I beg your pardon, Sire. I did not think that at all. It is only--I am naturally fearful of what you intend...."

His irritation vanished. "Have I offered you any harm?"

It was early days yet, but she decided not to point that out. "No, Sire."

"Then you have no reason to fear."

"And none to trust that there is no reason for fear!" Rhiannon snapped before she thought better of it.

To her surprise and relief, although anger sparkled briefly in his eyes, he seemed to have it well under control. "And I have none to trust you either."

It was a very good point, but she refrained from expressing her feelings on that matter. The truth was, she didn't trust him and she was fearful, but neither emotion had so completely obliterated good sense as to encourage her to think she had any chance at all of slaying him in his sleep or getting away with it if she managed the deed. Instead, she merely nodded and looked around the room. "Where shall I sleep then?"

Amusement instantly gleamed in his eyes again. He patted the bed beside him. Rhiannon gave him a look. "I would rather not, Sire," she said stiffly.

"Daigon."

She blushed, but using the title 'Sire' kept her a comfortable distance from him. Using his given name seemed too intimate by far. "I would prefer the floor," she said stiffly, although she didn't prefer the floor at all. Not that she expected him to give up the bed for her, but she rather thought he might at least make some arrangements for her comfort if he meant to keep her in his apartments.

"I thought we'd established that you need have no fears of ravishment," he said thoughtfully. "But I see your mind is still fixated upon it."

"It is not!" she disclaimed. "But I see no reason to test your ... uh ... restraint!"

He chuckled out loud at that. "You have no confidence that I can control my lust for you? You are fully clothed. Surely that is armor enough?"

Her lips tightened, but she refrained from pointing out that a gown was hardly 'armor' when all he would have to do was to toss her skirts over her head. She might be a maiden still, but she was hardly ignorant. Gerard had been a lecherous rogue and his court had followed his example. It would have been easier to count the number of times his feasts had *not* degenerated into orgies of the flesh than the times it had.

"I've no reason to believe *any* man can control his lust and every reason to believe that convenience can be, and often is, taken as an invitation!"

Chapter Six

Daigon sat up abruptly, and this time there was absolutely no doubt in Rhiannon's mind that he was angry, very angry.

"And why is this?" he asked, his voice a soft, menacing purr that sent prickles of uneasiness chasing each other along Rhiannon's spine.

"What?" Rhiannon asked blankly, her mind scurrying around in circles while she struggled to figure out exactly what she'd said that had set him off this time.

"You have experience of this?"

Visions of having her chastity thoroughly inspected instantly swamped Rhiannon in a rush of horror. "Not ... not personally," she said faintly, feeling her color fluctuate madly. "But you could not have failed to have heard that Gerard took much pleasure in matters of the ... uh ... flesh and his court was no different."

Daigon did not look particularly pleased by the information, but after studying her for several moments, he seemed to dismiss it. Rolling from the bed, he stalked toward the wardrobe in one corner and examined the contents. Apparently he did not find what he sought, for he closed it again and moved to the chest that stood at the foot of the bed. Dragging a heavy blanket from the deep chest, he tossed it to her. Rhiannon was too surprised to catch it and the blanket merely hit her squarely on the chest and fell to the floor. The pillow he dragged from the bed and tossed at her went the way of the blanket.

Without a word, he began to disrobe while Rhiannon merely continued to gape at him in stunned dismay. When he was completely naked, he climbed onto the mattress and composed himself for sleep.

The veiling of his stunning body by the coverlet he dragged across his waist broke the spell of stupefaction at last and Rhiannon dropped her gaze to the bedding on the floor at her feet as the candles in the room were abruptly extinguished as if by a gust of wind.

Feeling entirely disconcerted by the turn of events, Rhiannon finally knelt to make a thin pallet and settled on it.

Despite the fact that the results were less than wonderful, Rhiannon slept like a rock when she'd finally managed to find a reasonably comfortable position. Her ladies woke her the following morning when they came in bearing her personal belongings. Disoriented, Rhiannon merely watched them sleepily for some time, wondering why they were moving her things around. Their curious glances finally penetrated the remnants of sleep, however, and a thought occurred to Rhiannon that had not the night before--the pallet on the floor would not help her reputation if she was to sleep in the same room with the warlock. Almost as bad, maybe worse, the fact that she was on the floor, and not ensconced in his bed, made it look as if he had no interest in her.

He'd said he didn't, and she was actually quite glad that he wasn't interested, but in retrospect she didn't particularly care for the idea of everyone snickering behind her back because he'd relegated her to the floor.

The manacles, she discovered with almost a sense of dismay, had vanished as before and she did not even have the comfort of that evidence to show that she was being held against her will, or to help her to win her ladies' sympathy.

The wily bastard!

With that thought, she rose stiffly to her feet, brushed as many wrinkles from her gown as she could with her hands and headed for the garderobe. She was escorted by the guards stationed outside the door, which put her in a foul mood--or, more accurately, a worse mood.

She was halfway through her toilet and still wearing nothing more than her under-shift when the warlock, Daigon appeared in the room. Her heart fluttered uncomfortably when she looked up to see his reflection. The maids gasped and twittered nervously at his sudden, silent appearance, like a flock of startled birds, but Rhiannon found she couldn't comfort herself with the thought that her own reaction was entirely from surprise--some of it, yes. Part of it, though, was because it was the first time she'd looked at him without fear, distress, and anger clouding her vision and she saw that the impression he had made upon her was not false. He was an extraordinarily attractive man. No doubt his parents had been quite nauseatingly well favored to have produced such a splendid specimen.

She wasn't particularly happy that she'd noticed.

"As you see, I am still here," she said sweetly.

His dark brows rose. "I hadn't expected otherwise. It is my men who guard the door."

Her lips tightened, but he turned away and moved to examine the items the maids had brought in. "You might as easily have them guard the doors to my own apartments," she pointed out.

"I might--if I wished it."

Rhiannon swiveled around on the bench to stare at him, struggling with the impulse to demand why he'd kept her in his apartments when his primary argument had been to make certain the castle folk didn't help her to escape. She'd been tired indeed the night before not to have considered it. She finally decided, though, that arguing with him in front of the maids probably wasn't wise. He had been amazingly patient with her temper. He might not feel nearly as inclined to be patient if she challenged him in front of others.

Instead, she summoned the maids to help her into the over gown she'd chosen, examining her reflection in the looking glass critically while they tightened the ribbons.

She'd never actually studied herself with any curiosity about how others perceived her, particularly not men. It had not mattered. She was Princess Rhiannon. That was enough in itself to make her extremely desirable if she'd had a squint, a pitted complexion and a gimp leg. Very few of the men who'd petitioned for her hand had ever set eyes on her beforehand. They had always seemed pleasantly surprised at her appearance, though--as if they'd expected her to be an eyesore. But did that mean they had actually thought her pretty? Or just that she didn't look as bad as they'd expected?

Daigon had said she had a pretty face--not in those precise words, of course. At best, it had been a backhanded compliment, but nevertheless he had seemed sincere.

He had also said she was not to his taste, though, so perhaps he didn't think she was pretty after all?

Whatever he thought, she considered her figure good. Perhaps she wasn't as voluptuous as he liked, but she was nicely rounded in all the right places and hardly a stick.

"If you've finished admiring yourself, perhaps you would join me?"

Rhiannon reddened. "I was checking the fit of the gown," she said stonily.

"It has shrunk since last you wore it?" he asked politely.

She didn't know who she wanted to slap more, him or the maids, who were trying not to look amused. Shooing the maids away, she decided to ignore the provoking remark. "I am ready. Where are we going?"

He offered his arm and when she'd placed her fingers upon it, escorted her from the room. "The men have returned with the treasure. I would like you to check to see if they have recovered it in its entirety."

"Oh," Rhainnon responded, feeling curiously deflated. "I have not broken my fast."

"Then I suggest you rise earlier tomorrow. It is nigh noon."

Startled, Rhainnon glanced up at him. "So late?"

"Yes."

"I--didn't sleep well."

"No doubt the bed would have been more comfortable."

Rhainnon glanced around self-consciously but saw that they had left the guards behind when they had left Daigon's apartments. "*My* bed would be more comfortable."

"Would you prefer that we remove to your apartments then? I'd thought Gerard had appropriated the best for himself."

"You know that is not what I meant," Rhiannon said somewhat sulkily, realizing that it was no wonder the man found her so unappealing. To his mind she was stupid, self-indulgent and lazy to boot to sleep till nearly noon.

"I do, but I intend to keep you close so you waste your breath arguing the point."

Uneasiness lodged in Rhiannon's chest. She couldn't help it. The suspense of not knowing was beginning to weigh upon her. "What do you intend to do with me?"

"Truthfully? I haven't decided."

That wasn't very comforting, particularly when she couldn't imagine *any* use he might have for her. He might not know she was useless as a pawn, but she certainly did--unless her uncle found it useful to bargain with some wealthy powerful lord to have her in exchange for help in recovering his kingdom and she somehow doubted she would be extraordinarily valuable in that sense. She didn't delude herself into thinking she was such a prize that there would be many willing to expend so much only to have her, particularly when she would be the only prize, not her and the kingdom.

The warlock did not seem to have any interest in her on a personal level, even for his comfort. And she could not think he would be terribly pleased to have her uncle laugh in his face when and if he tried to use her to control Gerard.

That thought made her feel a little ill and she wondered if she should give some consideration to trying to escape after all. It would be dangerous, all the way around, but would it be *more* dangerous to stay? Or more dangerous to risk the hazards inherent in an escape attempt?

"I'm not--I'm not at all certain that I can tell just from looking if anything is missing. I've only ever been in the vault once and if I had not seen my uncle and his men loading the bags I would not have known anything at all," she confessed in a rush. "I feel sure there are records somewhere. Uncle Gerard was not terribly meticulous about most records, but he did have someone who kept accounts of taxes and so forth."

"Nevertheless."

She tried not to look as dismayed as she felt. She sensed a test was in the offing and she was bound to fail it simply because she truly did not know what her uncle had had before. If she said it was all there and it transpired that it wasn't and her uncle had managed to keep enough to hire an army, it was bound to enrage the warlock that she had 'lied' to him. If she said it was not all there, he would send more men out and, once they'd tracked her uncle down, he might discover that she was wrong and decide she'd lied then for some nefarious purpose.

She didn't think he would readily accept 'I don't know' since he was determined for her to look when she'd already told him she didn't.

She was cold with nerves by the time they reached the vault. When the guards had stepped aside and Daigon had unlocked it, he grabbed a torch from the wall nearby, pushed the heavy door open and ushered her inside. The gleam of precious metal and jewels nearly blinded her. Dazzled, she stood rooted to one spot as Daigon settled the torch in a wall sconce. Realizing finally that he was waiting, she shook off her stupor and looked around. The room seemed full almost to overflowing. It hadn't looked this way by the time she'd arrived. Her uncle and his men had already stuffed much of it into bags.

Frowning, she studied the accumulated wealth of the kingdom, trying to recall the scene as it had been that day when she'd arrived. When she was fairly certain she had a good picture of that which had remained in the room, she tried to calculate the number of bags and the amount each might have held. Moving around the room, she made a mental note of the things she recalled as opposed to the things she didn't remember seeing.

On her second circuit of the room an object caught her attention that rooted her to the spot. Her heart skipped a beat. Without thinking, she reached for the small pendant and picked it up.

It had been her mother's. As hazy as her memory was, she recalled her father telling her the story of the pendant's history when he had given it to her. The pendant had been a wedding gift from her grandfather to her grandmother and meant to be passed down from daughter to daughter.

Her uncle had told her the pendant had been buried with her father.

What else had he lied to her about if he would lie about something that was so insignificant to him? It was of no great value. The beauty of the pendant lay in the cunning workmanship.

Feeling a lump form in her throat for the mother she couldn't even remember, Rhiannon carefully set the pendant down again and cleared her throat. She saw when she glanced at the warlock that he was watching her. "I cannot say for certain because they had ransacked the room already when I arrived, but ... I do not think it has all been recovered. There were six men with him. Each carried two bags filled quite full, and my uncle, as well. The gold is heavy, and would have been awkward to carry and to hide, but jewels would have been another matter."

Daigon's lips tightened. Instead of commenting, however, he merely nodded, grasped her elbow and escorted her out once more. When he'd secured the room, he led her toward the receiving room. Rhiannon's uneasiness increased with each step, becoming full blown fear long before they reached the chamber. "I am only guessing," she said a little breathlessly, partly because her stride was so much shorter than his and she was having to race to keep up with him and partly from fear. "I was not in my uncle's confidence and certainly not allowed to go into the treasure chamber. It might well all be there."

"And it might not," Daigon said grimly.

Rhiannon knew she was white faced with fear by the time he settled her in a chair near the throne for the simple reason that she was feeling distinctly lightheaded. It took all she could do to concentrate on not embarrassing herself further by fainting and sliding to the floor, but she heard Daigon's sharp command that Captain Bryon be sent for. Nausea washed through her, adding to her distress. She hadn't considered that someone's life besides her own might hang in the balance.

Captain Bryon looked distinctly uneasy when he arrived.

"You sent for me, Sire?"

"Princess Rhiannon tells me that there are jewels missing."

Rhiannon glanced at Daigon sharply at that, for she'd said nothing of the kind, merely that there was the *possibility* that some of the jewels were missing. When she glanced at the captain she saw that his face was no doubt as white as her own. His expression was carefully guarded but she felt accused because she felt as if she'd betrayed him. She might have leapt to her feet then except that Daigon's hand came down over hers, pressing her hand tightly into the armrest of the chair in a silent command to remain seated.

"I took what we found, Sire--all that they carried and returned it all to you. I swear it! Ask your own men if you do not believe me! We searched everyone, including Gerard."

"A few jewels would have been easy enough to conceal," Daigon said pensively.

Captain Bryon's face reddened. "I am no thief to take that which does not belong to me!"

Daigon's eyes narrowed at the outburst, but instead of responding directly to Captain Bryon, he sent a messenger to bring the rest of the party before him. When they had assembled, Rhiannon was almost as frightened as they were, certain he was about to order them all summarily executed, and only because she had not adequately considered the consequences of trying to be as truthful as possible--to protect her own hide.

When Daigon had finished questioning all of the men, he settled back in his throne, studying them thoughtfully. "You have failed me," he said finally. "Your primary objective was to see to it that Gerard did not carry away what he would need to finance an army. You will try again. If you catch him, bring him back. If not, you are to search their trail for where they might have hidden the jewels."

The men glanced at each other in dismay. "Gerard and his men have had more than enough time to cross the border, Sire," Captain Bryon said finally.

"Then you will have to cross it, as well. Alternately, you may want to consider stationing men to watch them return. If they did hide the jewels and have not had the time to retrieve them, then they will want to do so as quickly as possible, don't you think?"

Captain Bryon looked shaken. He merely nodded, however, and took his leave.

Rhiannon expelled a relieved breath, but she was still so shaken from the incident that it took an effort to fight her emotions into abeyance. “Thank you, my lord,” she managed finally.

His dark brows rose.

She bit her lip. “I would not like to think that I had cost those men their lives.”

His face hardened. “This was a quest for the truth. If I had found that they had lied to me, their own lies would have cost them their lives, not your suppositions.”

Rhiannon swallowed with an effort. “All the same....” Gerard, she realized abruptly, would have had them flayed alive if he’d even suspected they might have lied to him. As relieved as she was that Daigon had shown restraint, she realized she should have considered her answer to Daigon’s question more carefully. A thought occurred to her just then. “You knew it was not all there.”

“Yes.”

She felt her color fluctuate. “Did I pass the test?” she asked stiffly.

“You surprised me,” he responded.

It wasn’t until Rhiannon had returned to the apartments that she realized he hadn’t actually answered her question.

Chapter Seven

Rhiannon found that she was still in a state of nerves when she reached the apartments once more. Daigon had not condemned the men to death for failing him, but the realization that he might have was enough to throw her in a state of nerves and she had no way of knowing if they had merely been given a reprieve. She knew very well what her uncle would have done, that there would not even have been a reprieve, a chance to redeem themselves, but that didn't make her feel one whit better.

It would almost have been a relief if Daigon had been of the same ilk as her uncle. At least then she would have known what to expect. As it was he had kept her in a constant state of dread and hope from the moment he had appeared at the gates of Aradan Castle and she wasn't certain she could endure a great deal of hovering on the brink of disaster without becoming a raving lunatic.

After pacing the room for a time trying to ignore the chatter of her ladies, she sent them away. The moment they left the room, the manacles reappeared on her wrists and she stared at them blankly, not nearly as surprised and upset by their appearance as before, but confused that they appeared at any time she found herself alone in the King's apartments.

It was some sort of spell, she realized, and not actual manacles of the physical world, but she couldn't seem to think what sort of spell would make them appear only when she was alone.

After a moment, her thoughts turned from the manacles to the problem that had so disturbed her.

The quiet, she discovered, did not aid contemplation as she'd hoped.

All she could think was that she deeply regretted that she hadn't simply struck off behind her uncle, whatever his orders. She could not have hoped to keep up on foot, but she would have been miles from the castle by now--alone in a frightening wilderness, of course, but the distant threat of wild animals, hunger and thirst, did not seem nearly as unnerving as the game of cat and mouse the warlock was playing with her.

Grudgingly, she admitted that he had every reason to distrust her and none to trust. She was the daughter of his father's killer as far as he knew, the niece of the king he had deposed. If their positions had been reversed, she would not have trusted him either. She would have expected treachery of some kind behind every word and gesture.

It did not help her that she could see to realize that, except to build a growing sense of futility.

Dismissing that thought for the moment, she began to try to think where she might go if she could escape. There seemed little point in trying to think of a way to do so unless she had somewhere to go.

King Linea popped into her mind. Shuddering, she dismissed the possibility, but her mind kept going back to that possibility over and over. As revolting as she found the notion of turning herself over to him, she knew he was the only one of all of her suitors who had had more interest in her person than her dowry. He was in desperate need of an heir and she was young, healthy, and a princess.

She set that aside. It was a possibility--not a particularly pleasant one, but a place that she might go to seek shelter. His kingdom was many days' ride and across the sea of Midae, and she had no idea what length of time it would take to walk such a distance, but she began to think she might catch a ride with travelers going that way. She might prevail upon some fisherman to carry her across the sea.

Would her uncle have gone there? It seemed probable. Across the sea, he would be able to raise an army with the jewels he'd stolen. Those who ruled the kingdoms around Aradan were either his enemies or simply indifferent to Gerard, certainly not allies and it seemed doubtful he would be so misguided as to go to any of them.

He would not be pleased that she had followed. More likely, he would be furious, particularly if he was hoping for help from King Linea.

She decided she didn't care. He wouldn't dare do anything to her for fear of displeasing King Linea.

Escape was the problem. In time, Daigon might cease to have her watched so closely, but she did not want to wait for some distant possibility that might never materialize. There had to be a way around the guards.

It occurred to her in a blinding flash of insight that the tunnels below the castle might be more significant than she'd previously considered. The castle was centuries old. It had weathered many tumultuous reigns and there could be little doubt that the original ruler had had his hands full or he would not have seen the need for a subterranean escape route. And if he had seen that need, then he would almost certainly have devised some way to reach it if he found himself cornered in his keep.

Rhiannon stopped pacing and looked around at the walls. As far as she knew, this suite of rooms had always been used as the royal chambers. That didn't necessarily mean that it always had been, but there was at least a chance that there were hidden doors leading to secret passageways--for that matter, the very fact that someone had managed to murder Daigon's parents while they slept seemed to indicate that there was a way into the suite besides the corridor.

The warlock might know. She knew of no way to prevent him, however, and she decided to try anyway. If she found the secret way, and if she managed to do so without him discovering that she had, then she might have a chance to escape.

There were a lot more ifs, but if she allowed herself to dwell on them she would loose her nerve.

She spent days searching every inch of every wall and even the floor for signs of a trap door. A week passed and hope began to dim. If there was a secret passage it had begun to seem that she could search forever without finding it.

The warlock had begun to watch her broodingly. She didn't know if that was because he suspected, because he knew what she was up to, or if it was merely because he expected treachery from her. She slept fitfully at night if at all. She'd begun to have dreams she didn't entirely understand--or perhaps didn't want to understand. In those dreams Daigon touched her in ways that stirred the fire in her blood as he had the day he had fondled her breasts and kissed them until she'd felt faint. She often woke damp and excruciatingly sensitive, as if she had a fever of the blood, sometimes with the certainty that Daigon was actually there. At others, she knew that she was dreaming and almost allowed herself to follow where he led her to discover what it was she ached for.

The dreams made her more self-conscious in his presence, so that even though she became accustomed to him on one level, on another she only became more leery. She more than half suspected he had had some hand in the dreams, that he'd placed some sort of spell on her, but he never indicated such a thing by word or deed. He always behaved toward her with utmost courtesy, but with a coolness that not only implied that he truly had no interest in her as a woman, but also underscored his distrust.

Rhiannon was actually glad of it. If he had seemed to unbend toward her, if he had set out to try to charm her, she wasn't confident she would have been able to resist. She was as drawn to him as she was distrustful of him and she was fairly certain that she could not trust herself to offer any resistance if he kissed her like that again.

Not that resistance had been a possibility for her.

And truthfully, she wasn't even certain any of it had happened anymore. He had not seemed the least affected by it, and she found it very hard to accept that he could have had such an impact on her without experiencing something himself.

It made it worse that she suspected she was fantasizing about him. Whether he had offered her any harm or not, he was still her enemy, most likely would always be. She could not change who she was, or whom he thought she was, and he wasn't likely to believe her if she said she was not the daughter of his parents' murderer. The worst thing she could possibly do would be to fall for a man who hated her and saw her only as a means to exact the revenge that had been denied him upon her father's death.

Those thoughts drove her to renew her search.

She found the door almost by accident. It hadn't occurred to her before to check the great fireplace, more because she knew that would be the worst possible place for a secret door than any other logic. She'd exhausted every other possibility, however, and finally began to go over the ornate carvings on the fireplace surround and mantel piece. She bumped the latch with her knee as she stretched upward to check the carvings above the mantel. Silently, the door slid open, as if it had been well maintained--which it no doubt had since her uncle was obviously very familiar with the castle's secret passages.

The whisper of sound alerted her just as a chilling breeze blew across her skin. Feeling the hair at the base of her skull prickle, Rhiannon leapt back. The opening was barely wide enough for a man to squeeze through sideways. It yawned into a blackness so profound it seemed almost solid.

She stared at the opening, feeling nothing that she'd expected to feel, feeling fear more than anything else, as if, having found it, she no longer had an option but to try it. After a moment, she examined the fire place surround for the trigger. Even knowing the general area to look it took her nearly ten minutes to locate it and close the door. By the time she had closed it, she was trembling with reaction. Weak in the knees, she moved to the sofa nearby and sank down on it, trying to decide what she should do.

She could escape.

Should she though?

Would she be better off? Or worse?

If she was caught in the attempt she would almost certainly be worse off.

Daigon, as he so often did, simply appeared while she was arguing her mental debate. Rhiannon nearly jumped out of her skin when she looked up to discover him watching her. Guilt, no doubt, was written all over her face. His brows descended, his eyes narrowing speculatively.

"Now what, I wonder, have you been up to?"

Rhiannon blinked several times, trying to think up a believable lie. Nothing came to mind. "Nothing."

A hint of amusement entered his eyes. "Why, I wonder, don't I believe that?"

Rhiannon reddened. "I don't know," she said stiffly. "Because you don't trust me?"

"Have I reason to distrust you?"

Rhiannon looked down at her hands. "No. Did you want something?" she added, trying to change the subject. She got to her feet abruptly, unable to sit still under that penetrating stare any longer.

Daigon frowned. He ignored the question. She could not have more blatantly changed the subject if she had tried. Moreover, he had not really had a reason for coming beyond the desire to see her and he certainly had no intention of allowing her to know that.

Uneasiness had set off alarms but he could not quite pinpoint the source beyond Rhiannon's guilty expression and nervousness. He finally decided that she had done nothing--yet. She was planning something and he was fairly certain it wouldn't be something he would like.

Frustration surfaced as he watched her nervous pacing. He was becoming obsessed with her. If he had not known better, he would have suspected that she had placed some spell upon him.

He did know better, though. He had not had to consult his own magic for that answer because as powerful as her affect upon him was he knew the difference between magic and the natural.

It was incomprehensible to him that he could desire the seed of the murderer of his parents, a woman whom he would not have trusted even if that were not so, for she was the niece of the man whose throne he had taken even if not for the other. His dark side toyed with his mind, though, encouraging him to slake his lust, to consider it revenge, to consider it a means of meeting out his own brand of justice. His rational side argued that he was only seeking excuses to do what he wanted to do and that there was danger in it. He could not take what he desired without opening a door to her that he might not be willing, or able, to close once opened because he also found himself wanting to believe she was exactly as she seemed--an innocent caught in the webs of others.

It seemed far more likely, however she appeared, that the seed had not fallen far from the tree from which she had sprung. Her façade of innocence was just that, a shell to hide the dark, treacherous thing inside. Deception, treachery, and cowardice were her birthright and he would find himself defeated as his father had been, by stealth, by trusting where he should not have.

He had something his father had not had, however. He had his magic from his mother, honed and fine-tuned by the grandmother who had snatched him from his dying mother's womb.

Unfortunately, he did not dare use it to probe her mind for the truth. To do so could cost her her sanity or her life, and he was not willing to risk that so long as doubt existed in his mind.

He was not above using it to take her will, however, and use whatever persuasions came to mind to try to coax the truth from her, for he was well aware that she was far from immune to him--and therein lay a good deal of the danger in that type of persuasion for he could as easily catch himself as her.

Rhiannon looked at Daigon uneasily several times when he did not answer her question of what he'd come to speak to her about and she decided she disliked the look in his eyes. "It must be nigh on time to sup," she said abruptly as she glanced out the window and saw that dusk was falling. "I should summon my ladies to dress."

"Not just yet."

Rhiannon glanced at him uneasily over her shoulder and reached for the bell pull anyway. In the next moment, she found herself plastered against the wall as she had been before, held there by invisible threads that prevented her from moving so much as an inch in any direction. The warlock now stood mere inches from her, his eyes dark, gleaming with something that was neither anger nor amusement. “You did not answer my question,” he said coolly, “but I confess I’m fond of this game myself.”

Rhiannon licked her lips. Her heart was pounding so hard in her ears that it distorted his voice. “What game?” she asked uneasily.

His lips curled into a smile. “What will it take to loosen your tongue?”

His gaze skated downward, lingered for several moments on the mound of her breasts pushed up by her tight stays and then dropped lower. The girdle separated and fell to the floor at her feet. Rhiannon gasped, but the absence of the girdle made it no easier to drag air into her lungs, nor chased away the faint lightheadedness that had begun to assail her the moment she felt his nearness.

“I told you--nothing,” she said a little desperately as he calmly proceeded to scoop her breasts from the neck of her gown.

“Precisely. You told me nothing.”

He’d begun tracing a pattern lightly across her breasts with one finger. His touch, light though it was, stirred heated currents that seemed to ripple outward from her breasts until they washed through her entire body. Her nipples puckered and stood painfully erect long before he neared them. Something tightened abruptly inside her when he began to trace a narrowing circle around the peaks of her breasts.

“Because it was nothing,” Rhiannon managed to say on a breathless whisper.

“Nothing? You were pale as ghost and shaking like a leaf.”

Rhiannon swallowed with an effort. “You startled me.”

He studied her a long moment. “I did,” he said finally, “but that had nothing to do with your state before I arrived.”

Rhiannon’s breath caught in her throat as he cupped one breast and lowered his head. She stared down at him, waiting, wondering if it would feel as strange and wonderful as it had before. Her heart jerked several times, almost painfully, as his tongue glided across the sensitive nipple. She lost her breath when the heat of his mouth settled over the tip. For several moments she thought she would faint at the exquisite sensations his mouth created inside of her. Closing her eyes, she struggled to catch her breath, but that only seemed to make the sensations more intense, seemed to focus her entire being on that one point of delirious pleasure.

A war of emotions erupted. She wanted nothing so much as to close her mind to everything except the fever of need that exploded inside her with the first touch of his mouth and built like wildfire until she was trembling with it. At the same time, she felt her vulnerability to his will and that of her own body's craving for more. Reason was rapidly vanishing. She hardly knew where she was or what she was doing now. If he continued, she was liable to tell him anything. Summoning what little wit she still retained, she searched her mind for something to prick his hide. "You are no different from any other man save that you use your magic to take my will and give you the illusion of willingness, instead of the brutish force of a mortal man."

He released her abruptly--completely released her. Rhiannon was so weak from the fever in her blood that she nearly slid to the floor. Her heart was still pounding with excitement, but it almost stood still in her chest when she saw how furious he was. Before she'd completely assimilated the fact that the 'prick' she'd used had been more like a blade in his ribs, he slipped his arms around her, dragging her up tightly against him. Threading the fingers of one hand through her hair, he tugged, tipping her head back. His lips covered hers then and the heat of his mouth decimated what little wit remained to her. A thrill of heady excitement rushed through her. Unconsciously, she lifted a hand to steady herself against the whirlpool threatening to drag her down, clutching a fistful of his tunic. The rough caress of the fabric of his tunic against her bared breasts added another dollop of dizzying sensations as she leaned against him, mindlessly stretching upward to give him better access to plunder the amazingly sensitive inner surfaces of her mouth with his tongue.

As wonderful as his mouth had felt on her breasts, it felt even more wondrous against her own. His scent and taste filled her with both delight and an unidentifiable hunger for more.

Disappointment filled her when he broke the kiss, but vanished when he tilted her head further and traced a path down her throat to capture the breast he'd neglected earlier. An explosion of delight quaked through her when he suckled the tender nipple that set her to trembling.

She'd only begun to nurture the enchanting sensations when he released her. This time, he moved away. She saw when she managed to lift her heavy eyelids that his breathing was nearly as ragged as her own. "I do not need magic," he said harshly. "Your body sings to my touch."

Rhiannon blinked at him, steadying herself with an effort, curbing the urge to demand to know why he'd stopped. The realization that she hadn't wanted him to stop coupled with his comments finally penetrated the heated fog that her brain had become, but before she could think of a suitable set down, he vanished.

Stunned, Rhiannon looked around the room for several moments in disbelief while her throbbing body beat out want, need and finally anger at being denied. "Bastard!" she snarled at the empty room. "You delude yourself! That was the most disgusting thing I've ever experienced in my life! You just *thought* I liked it because you were enjoying it so much!"

He reappeared. "Is that a challenge?"

Rhiannon gaped at him for a split second. Abruptly, she gathered her skirts and made a dash for the wardrobe. Slamming the door firmly behind her, she slumped to the floor and covered her face with her hands.

Chapter Eight

Rhiannon didn't know whether to be more relieved or more sorry when the warlock allowed the matter to drop. She was certainly not up to challenging him, or making a liar out of him if he tried anything else.

Embarrassed by her own lack of control, she was very tempted to remain in her room and not present herself for the evening meal. The reflection that she would only be feeding his erroneous belief that she didn't trust herself around him forced her to straighten her spine and go anyway.

To her relief, he behaved as if nothing had transpired between them. He was so distant, in fact, that it became obvious to her even in her disordered state that he was still furious. Briefly, she wondered if she might have wounded him and if that would explain his cold behavior toward her, but she decided that was too egotistical on her part to seriously consider.

She told herself she was glad, but she discovered she wasn't particularly happy about being relegated to the status of distant stranger. As disconcerting as it had been for him to tease her, she hadn't realized how much she'd actually enjoyed it until he stopped.

Several days passed before it occurred to her that she'd succeeded far better than she'd anticipated when she'd insulted him. Not only had he forgotten to question her further, he did not bring it up again.

Regardless, it dawned on her that his certainty that she had offered a challenge made it imperative that she seriously rethink the idea of escaping. If he caught her, and she knew he very likely would, and he decided to use his peculiar method of inquisition she had no doubt that her shaky defenses would crumple to dust. Perhaps even worse, he might get the mistaken notion that she had orchestrated the entire thing just to push him to that point.

That thought naturally led her to question her own motives, to wonder if, deep down, she actually *wanted* to push him into doing something she both craved and dreaded at the same time, freeing her from responsibility of the results. She decided not to delve to deeply into the darker side of her nature, however.

Directly after the incident, she'd been so shaken it was only fear and the realization that lack of planning would doom her attempt that kept her from lighting out immediately. After several days of more calm reflection, she began to realize that the entire plan was insane. Daigon was a scary man when he bellowed in anger, and even more scary when he spoke with soft menace, but he had done absolutely nothing to indicate that he was a monster or that she need fear him so long as she behaved within reason. He was not the sort of man one would consider betraying and she did not doubt that, given the right provocation he could be extremely dangerous, but he was not cruel. He was not without mercy and he treated everyone, from the lowliest servant to the highest in position, with respect for them as a human being.

Two weeks into the reign of Daigon, son of King Rhainor, everyone began to feel a ray of hope that fate had smiled upon them the day that the warlock had come to their gates. As terrifying as the sacking of Castle Aradan had been, Daigon had offered quarter to everyone who'd lain down their arms and he had done nothing since to indicate he was not sincere in his determination to restore order and prosperity to Aradan. His justice was often harsh and swift, but he showed every sign of being scrupulously fair. Unlike Gerard, his predecessor, his justice did not seem to revolve around whim, or his disposition at the unfortunate moment that petitioners came before him seeking justice. He listened with attention to every detail of every case presented to him, questioned everyone involved thoroughly, and based his decisions upon the facts presented, and his punishment upon the crime. Fines were commonplace for smaller infractions, but so it had been in Gerard's time, and Daigon rarely ordered a fine *and* corporal punishment and everyone was inclined to count their blessings.

Rhiannon's own fear and confusion abated after a while into mostly confusion. Despite the intimacy of their close proximity and the 'games' he'd instigated to bend her to his will when he'd questioned her, he made no further attempts to break through her resistance. He displayed no interest in taking her to his bed nor did he oust her from his room to take another woman to his bed, which shattered all of her preconceived notions about men in general and him in particular.

At first, she was simply glad--a little disconcerted that he seemed to have no interest in her as a woman despite those moments that had so completely disrupted her senses, but on the whole, she was relieved. However tarnished her reputation might be because her presence in his room made it *appear* that she was his layman, she at least had the comfort of knowing it was not so. And since he was so obliging as to pretend nothing intimate had ever transpired between them, she worked hard to follow his example and made it a point to seek her pallet and pretend sleep before he retired for the evening. As the days passed into weeks and she became more accustomed to his presence and less unnerved, though, she began to become more curious than cautious and after a while it began to prey upon her nerves in an entirely different way to be so close to him.

She'd seen him completely naked and she had liked what she had seen. She had felt wonder at his touch, and she discovered that no matter how tightly she closed her eyes, or how determinedly she tried to focus her mind elsewhere, she was acutely aware of his movements in the room with her at night and that was enough in itself to make her restless with need.

She rather thought if the first incident had been the only time he'd touched her she might have been able to dismiss it. She might have been able to convince herself that he had used magic against her and that the feelings he'd evoked had simply been some sort of spell. He had not allowed her to comfort herself with that, though. He had removed the spell that had prevented her from actively resisting and forced her to see that the only 'magic' was his touch and the way he made her feel.

She was contemplating that state of affairs one day and working half heartedly on her needlework when she heard a commotion outside that drew her attention. At first, she thought perhaps some accident had occurred. The men had been working assiduously at repairing the damage to the keep during the assault, restocking the arsenal, and training for battle. There was nothing in the shouts to indicate such a thing, however, and finally, when the noise continued instead of abating, she lay her needlework aside and moved to the door that opened out onto the balcony and peered down at the exercise field.

The archers, she saw, were practicing. Rolling her eyes at the things men found so entertaining, she had already prepared to step away when Daigon strode into view. Her heart skipped several beats.

He was bare to the waist and the sun glistened off of the moisture that had gathered on his body. She watched as he retrieved a handful of practice arrows and disappeared from view again. After standing at the door for several moments, debating with herself, she finally yielded to temptation and strolled as casually as she could across the balcony for a better look.

She knew very well that she could not have possibly made enough noise to attract notice, and yet as casually as she had made her appearance, gazed into the far distance for some moments, and finally nerved herself for a better look, the warlock was staring straight at her when she glanced his way. Startled, she jumped and was thrown into such a state of disorder to have her curiosity about Daigon instantly noticed that she retreated into the apartment in complete confusion without considering that that behavior was enough in itself to give her intentions away.

Daigon remarked upon it at dinner.

Rhiannon reddened. "I'd only thought to get a breath of fresh air. I didn't know it was forbidden," she responded tartly.

Daigon darkened at her tone, his lips tightening. "Since you cannot fly, I certainly have no objection. I would imagine the view from the northern side of the balcony would be far more interesting, however, than a view of the men working in the keep."

Rhiannon stared at him blankly for a full minute before it dawned upon her that Daigon thought she'd gone out to watch the men and had been startled to discover that he was among them.

It took no great leap of imagination to get from that point to one she found highly intriguing. He was jealous! Sucking her bottom lip in to hide the smile that threatened, she looked away quickly.

"There is something in that to amuse you?"

He didn't miss much. "It was a grimace," Rhiannon lied, focusing her attention on her trencher of food. "I caught my lip with my teeth."

To her relief, he seemed to dismiss it. After glancing at him several times, Rhiannon decided to see if she could appease some of her curiosity about him. Beyond his assertion that he was the son of King Rhainor and the fact that he was a powerful warlock, she knew almost nothing about him. He was surprisingly reticent about himself, which she found refreshing in a way, having been accustomed to men who liked nothing better than to talk about themselves, but it was annoying to have to try to wheedle the information out of him when she didn't particularly want him to know of her interest. "I have wondered why it is that you only came now to reclaim the throne of Aradan?" she said on a questioning note.

"Have you?"

Irritating man! "It just seems curious that you would wait until you are quite--uh--young men tend to be so hotheaded. I was only curious to know why you had not tested your metal sooner."

She saw he was looking annoyed.

"Old?"

"Well, I am certain you cannot be above five and thirty summers," Rhiannon said, yielding to the impulse to be deliberately provoking.

"It relieves me that you think so, particularly when I am not above thirty summers," he said dryly.

Rhiannon did not try to hide her smile that time.

"You are a provoking creature."

Rhiannon saw when she glanced at him that his eyes were filled with amusement now. "And you are not?"

His dark brows rose. After a moment, he signaled for a servant to remove his trencher and settled back in his seat, sipping at the wine in his goblet. "What would you like to know?"

She would have liked more subtlety, Rhiannon thought with more than a touch of irritation. She had wanted to appease her curiosity without appearing to be too pointedly interested. "The sacking of Aradan?"

He shrugged. "I grew up in a land far from here."

Rhiannon frowned. That told her next to nothing. "You said a witch had rescued you? She traveled so far with a newborn infant?"

He frowned. "Zella was my grandmother--mother to my mother. As my mother lay dying, she begged Zella to take me and carry me to safety--which she did, but she considered the further the better. She was well known in Aradan and many of the surrounding kingdoms. An infant would have been noticed if she had lingered anywhere for long this side of the sea of Midea and it would not have taken a great deal of intelligence to figure out where the infant had come from. So she traveled until she came to a land where none knew her or had heard of her.

"Zella told me the story when I was still a young child--she never spoke of it again."

Rhiannon digested that for several moments, suddenly seeing it not as a story, but as hurtful events to real people. Empathy swelled tightly inside of her. "It must have been painful for her--the memory of having to do such a thing when she was grieving for her daughter."

When Daigon said nothing, she glanced at him. He shrugged. "Mayhap. She was not prone to expressing her feelings."

She was cool and distant--like Daigon, Or perhaps vice versa would be more accurate? He had not grown up with affection. For that matter, neither had she, but she at least had a handful of memories from before. The witch, Zella, was the only parent Daigon had known.

"She still lives in that faraway land?" Rhiannon asked hesitantly.

"Nay. She was old when I was born. She died many years ago when I was still a youth."

Rhiannon gaped at him in dismay, wishing she hadn't asked. "I'm so sorry to have brought up painful memories. I shouldn't have asked that."

He shrugged, but it was impossible to tell from his expression whether the reminder bothered him or not, if he grieved still, how painful it might have been at the time. However lacking the woman might have been in motherly love, she had nurtured him from an infant--and he was not an unfeeling man. He must have loved her and it would have had to be hurtful to him to lose her. "How did you--I mean, did you live with someone else then?"

He grimaced. "Nay. I stayed at the cottage. I didn't have a great deal of choice. Zella was a determined woman."

"How so?"

"She placed a holding spell upon me. I could not leave until I grew strong enough to break the spell."

Rhiannon was horrified and made no attempt to hide it. "But--how could you survive under such circumstances?"

"The spell was upon me--I could not leave. There were servants to attend my needs. And I did not say that others were prevented from coming to me. She--arranged a thorough education, an education befitting the king I was to be, but she also saw to it that the hotheadedness of youth did not lead to my downfall even though she could not stay with me to protect me from myself. The spell could only be broken by me, and only when I had become powerful enough to ensure a victory in my quest."

"Oh," Rhainnon responded, mulling over what she'd learned of him, trying to imagine the sort of life he'd had. It defied her imagination, but it sounded like it must have been terribly lonely.

Another thought occurred to Rhiannon presently, one that should not have and would not have if she had not been so keenly interested in Daigon personally. If he had been so confined, what sort of experience would he have had with women? She reddened at the thought and glanced at Daigon self-consciously.

Amusement gleamed in his eyes. The threat of a smile curled the corners of his lips. "She insured that I have a very *thorough* education, and she was a most practical woman." He leaned close, whispering in her ear. "There were--women from the village."

Embarrassment flamed in Rhiannon's cheeks. "That was--most improper," she said faintly. "And not something I particularly wished to know." It had been, though, and she could tell when she risked a glance at him that he knew very well that she'd been dying to know. "I believe I'll retire now," she said stiffly, getting to her feet abruptly.

It wasn't until she'd reached the king's apartments that it occurred to her that Daigon's upbringing had very likely deprived him of one thing, regardless of what he'd said. He might well have had a parade of prostitutes, and she didn't doubt his experience in that way, but he would not have had any opportunity to form any sort of relationship. It seemed unlikely that he would have any idea of how to woo, or court, a woman when the only women he was familiar with were paid for their services.

No wonder he had been so angry when she had accused him of using magic to give him the illusion of willingness!

It was absurd that she found that thought so intriguing, but somehow it made her feel less inadequate in dealing with Daigon. Before, the fact that she had knowledge but no first hand experience in matters of the flesh had made her feel completely out of her depth beside Daigon's superior age and experience. She had had the opportunity to engage in more than one flirtation, however, and as minute as that experience was, it had still given her some understanding of the mating dance. As with matters of the flesh, she knew much more from observation than actual experience, but she had certainly had plenty of opportunities to observe. She doubted very much that Daigon would have had such opportunities in the life that he had described.

It shouldn't have made any difference to her at all, of course. She knew very well that Daigon could not have, in just a few short weeks, set aside his animosity toward her family sufficiently to look upon her as anything but an enemy. But she could not deny that she *was* intrigued by that one, tiny possibility of vulnerability in an otherwise impregnable fortress of a man.

She might also be entirely wrong. Just because she had put the thoughts together from what he had said did not make it so. He had, in truth, given her very little--far more than she'd known previously, but still not much.

It was possible, maybe even likely, that she had done precisely what she had accused him of--interpreting his behavior according to what she wanted to believe rather than looking for another explanation that might not be as palatable.

Pure imagination or not, the possibility of it being true was intriguing enough Rhiannon found it very difficult to resist the temptation to test her theory. After pacing near the open door to the balcony for several days, straining to hear what was being said by the men in the keep, and more specifically straining to hear one voice in particular, she finally nerved herself to venture out once more.

Oh so casually, she glanced down at the keep, but all pretense of subtlety abandoned her the moment she spied Daigon. He was bare to the waist and laboring in the sun. The sunlight gleaming off of his glistening torso was mesmerizing. The flexing and bunching of his muscles as he moved and lifted entranced her so deeply that she became transfixed and completely unaware of anything else, including the passing of time, until she finally became aware that Daigon had stopped what he was doing and was staring back at her.

Chapter Nine

Captain Martunae stepped back to appraise the wall they'd just finished repairing, wiping the sweat from his eyes. "Good as new," he finally pronounced.

Daigon sent him a wry look. "Repairs are never 'as good as new.' The wall is weak here."

Captain Martunae shrugged. "I doubt we'll be able to do any better shy of taking the wall down completely and starting from scratch and I'm thinking this probably isn't the best of times to consider it. Ye might've done better with a bit o' your magic, and saved us weeks of hard work to boot," he said, grinning.

Daigon smiled grimly. He didn't have to look around to know the men, the Aradan men in particular, were listening to the conversation. "I might have, but I see no reason to expend myself when there are plenty of able-bodied men to do the job."

Chuckling, Captain Martunae shook his head. "Ye don't call that expending yerself? Ye've worked as hard on the wall as the lot of us."

Daigon shrugged. "Laziness can make a man soft and vulnerable to his enemies. In any case, a good day's work ensures a good night's rest."

"I can think of a more pleasant way to ensure that," Captain Martunae said, grinning as he glanced upward at the balcony off the king's apartments. He saw when he looked at Daigon again that his eyes had narrowed and his smile vanished abruptly. "A tankard of ale'd do it," he added a little uneasily.

Daigon smiled thinly. "Alas, I'm not a drinking man."

Clearing his throat, Captain Martunae instructed the men to hurry with clean up and report to the field for an hour's practice before sunset.

When the men had moved away, Daigon turned toward the well in the center of the keep. Hoisting a bucket up, he splashed the cool water over his head and chest to rinse off the worst of his labors. Sloughing the excess water from his body, he glanced toward the balcony once more.

She was still there, making no pretense this time to be looking at anything other than the keep, and more specifically, him. His fastidious soul was offended by the thought of approaching her in his current state, but his curiosity got the better of him. On impulse, he used a spell and joined her.

One moment the warlock was standing by the well, the next he wasn't. Rhiannon glanced around to see where he'd disappeared to. When she discovered he was now standing less than an arm's length away from her, leaning against the wall of the castle, her heart seized painfully and she let out a yelp of surprise. The fright, coupled with his knowing expression was enough to send her temper soaring. "Showing off your magic tricks to the men again?" she snapped irritably.

The comment effectively wiped the pleased expression from his face, replacing it with irritation of his own. "As it happens, that wasn't my intention, but then I don't consider it 'showing off.'"

"What do you consider it then?"

His eyes narrowed. "Saving myself from the necessity of killing any of them. Dead men are far less productive and fearful men less likely to consider treachery. Taking the air again?" he changed the subject abruptly.

Rhiannon gaped at him in silence for several moments, wondering if the comment about treachery had been aimed at her. It would certainly not be the first time that he had pointed out that he expected such a thing of her. Swallowing her fright and anger with an effort, she turned away, strolling toward the far side of the balcony. "I was bored," she hedged, refusing to look at him.

"What did you do with your time before?"

Rhiannon glanced at him in surprise, but she saw only curiosity in his expression, not judgment. She shrugged, smiling wryly. "I was bored then, too," she confessed. "It can be very tedious to spend the whole of every day with nothing but my needle and a gaggle of chattering females. I preferred to stay as far from my uncle as possible, though."

"Did you?"

Rhiannon studied him for several moments. "It may come as a great surprise to you, but I am not and have never been terribly fond of Uncle Gerard."

"But blood is still thicker than water, yes?"

The impulse arose to tell him there was no blood bond between them. She curbed it, feeling a coldness sweep over her the moment she realized how close she'd come to confessing it. She looked away, chastising herself for being a complete fool. When had it become so important to her that Daigon not see her as his enemy? She wasn't certain, but she feared it was a dangerous state. She knew little more about him now than she had before, not enough to know how he would react to that information.

The men he'd sent to search for her uncle had been gone for weeks without word, but even as ignorant as she was in matters of war, Rhiannon could see that Daigon was preparing to defend what he'd taken. He expected her uncle to try to regain his hold upon Aradan. Very likely, he saw her as his trump card.

He would certainly not be pleased to find himself holding a joker.

Instead of answering him directly, she simply stared off toward the distant horizon, watching as it slowly changed colors. "When I was a little girl, I used to wonder what my life would be like if I'd been born to another family," she said musingly. "In those days, we had fairs at least twice a year, and everyone would come from miles around to visit and I would envy the families I saw. I knew they were poor, and often hungry. I knew their lives were hard, but they always seemed so happy when I saw them, so excited by all the sights. And I would think 'they are serfs, but they are still more free than I will ever be.'"

"You were wrong."

She glanced at him. "Yes, but the point is no one ever really knows what another person's life is. They are on the outside looking in. They may see only the best moments, or the worst, and they judge from that and a glimpse is not enough to make a judgment."

"Meaning I have misjudged you?"

Rhiannon sent him a look from beneath her lashes.

Frowning, he moved away from her and stood watching the men below.

Rhiannon debated with herself for several moments and finally joined him. The men, she saw, were setting up for archery practice. "Tell me what you know of these men," Daigon said.

Rhiannon glanced at him in surprise. "You probably know them far better than I," she responded.

He lifted his dark brows and a touch of irritation surfaced. He must know she had little contact with the common soldiers--very little with the knights if it came to that. He had worked alongside them for weeks, practiced war with them--fought against them. What could she possibly add that he would not already have discovered for himself?

She looked away, staring down at the keep below them. "Many are mercenaries, though most were hired by my uncle three summers past when war seemed likely with Caracco. Captain Bryon seemed to have few complaints of them, nor the people, so I would be inclined to say that they are good men and trustworthy. The others are of Aradan and have families here."

"And their loyalties?"

Rhiannon glanced at him again. "The mercenaries are hired--their loyalty lies with whoever pays them. The others, like Captain Bryon--they are loyal to Aradan and fight to protect their families."

"Not Gerard?"

She frowned. "He was not a beloved king if that is what you are asking."

He fell silent, watching the men practice. "You have some knowledge of archery, do you not?"

Rhiannon glanced at him and saw that he was studying the mark on the palm of his hand. She could hardly claim that as proof of her accuracy, even if she'd wanted to. She'd been aiming for his heart and they both knew it. "I can usually hit what I shoot at," she said.

He nodded. "But you are not up to a contest."

Obviously there was no question in his mind that her abilities were extremely limited or there would have been a questioning note to the comment. Rhiannon suspected that she was being played, but the comment pricked her anyway. "I have not the strength for distance shots," she said tartly, "but my accuracy at short range is good."

"Good enough that you would consider wagering on it?"

Something tightened in her belly at the expression on his face. "I have nothing to wager," she responded a little breathlessly.

"The question is, are you certain enough of your skill to wager?"

Rhiannon wrestled with the cowardly urge to say she wasn't and the unwise impulse, she feared, to say that she was. The teasing light in his eyes was enough to push her toward the latter impulse. "Yes, but...."

He grinned. Before she had quite grasped his intention, he caught her and pulled her tightly against his chest. The feel of his body pressed tightly against hers, his heat and scent wafted over her, leaving dizziness in its wake. She gasped as the sensation engulfed her completely and she felt as if she were falling into a chasm.

She became aware of sound first, confused by the nearest of the voices of the men, the smells of the keep. When she opened her eyes, she discovered that she was standing in the keep. Disoriented, she simply stared, unmoving, at the men who were gaping at her. Finally, when it occurred to her that the hard surface she was plastered against was moving, she lifted her head.

The warlock, Daigon was looking down at her with an unreadable expression. Disconcerted to discover that she was still wrapped tightly around him, especially since she didn't remember hugging herself to him to start with, she let go of him and stepped back.

"Are you all right?"

"How did I get here?" The words were scarcely out of her mouth before she realized exactly how she'd gotten from the balcony above them to the practice yard and she sent Daigon an accusing look.

His lips twisted wryly. "I see you've remembered. Are you still up for the contest? Or are you going to beg off now?"

She sent him a resentful glare, well aware that he'd deliberately asked loudly enough for everyone to hear. She had not, precisely, agreed to the contest and he knew it, but she saw from the expressions of those around her that if she said no they would think her a poor sport. She shouldn't have cared, but she did. It was bad enough that they thought so poorly of her uncle. She didn't want that low opinion reflected upon her. "I was only a little dizzy," she said pointedly. "I am fine now."

Triumph gleamed in his eyes. A smile tugged at one corner of his lips, but her expression obviously gave him pause for the smile never entirely materialized. He looked away. "A bow for the princess. She has challenged me to a contest of skills."

Rhiannon gave him a look. "I did no such thing!" she whispered irritably. "And what is more, I have no idea what the wager is and I will not go one step more until I am certain it is something I am willing to agree to!"

Daigon chuckled and leaned low. "It is not something you will miss having given it."

Rhiannon blinked at him, feeling her jaw go slack and a dark tide of color rushing upward from her breasts to her forehead.

Her reaction obviously struck him as funny, for his chuckle became an all out laugh that startled her almost as much as the suggestion he'd made. Regardless, it warmed her, lightening her spirits. She saw that it had had a similar effect on the men around them and it occurred to her abruptly to wonder if that had not been at least a part of the reason Daigon had suggested the contest, to boost the morale of the men. They looked as if they'd been offered a rare treat.

"Princess Rhiannon has wagered one kiss, freely given, upon the outcome of the contest."

The color that had only begun to fade returned with a vengeance as the men, after a stunned moment, laughed heartily at that announcement.

"You have not told me what you mean to put up against that prize," Rhiannon said, smiling with an effort.

His dark brows rose. For several moments Rhiannon felt almost faint at the possibility of what he might offer. She didn't know whether to be relieved or indignant at the prize he *did* offer.

"Why, I will give you one kiss, freely given, if you should best me!" he said with a chuckle, his eyes fairly dancing now with such mischief Rhiannon had the feeling he knew very well what had been running through her mind while she waited for him to offer his 'prize.'

The men found that even more uproariously funny.

As charmed as she was by his teasing, Rhiannon wasn't amused. "I had something else in mind," she murmured.

He gave her a look that had the men making wolf whistles and cat calls. She glared at him, feeling her cheeks flamed again. "Not what you're thinking, obviously," she snapped.

A faint grin curled his lips. "But then you don't know what I'm thinking."

"I can guess," she responded tartly. As irritated as she was for his risqué innuendo, she wasn't altogether displeased that his mind seemed to be wandering down that path. But then, he might be doing it to deliberately mislead the men, she reminded herself, since his objective seemed to be to divert them from their own troubles.

That possibility made her uncomfortable with the idea of demanding to be freed as his part of the wager--from sharing a room with him at the very least. It was bound to put a damper on the jovial atmosphere.

She would have preferred, of course, that their amusement wasn't directed at her, but she couldn't bring herself to ruin their enjoyment whatever her discomfort. "You will grant me one boon, of *my* choice--if I win."

He distrusted that. His smile did not waver, but his gaze became far more penetrating. "Granted--if you win."

"Without knowing what it is?"

He shrugged. "I do not expect to lose."

Rhiannon gave him a piercing look at that, wondering if he would cheat if necessary. Somehow, however, she did not believe it of him. Everything she had learned about him seemed to indicate that he was a man of honor.

She was on edge regardless and wondered what had possessed her to agree to the wager. The idea of kissing Daigon made her breathless in so many ways that she felt faintly dizzy.

Trying to calm her nerves, she turned to watch the men scurrying about to set up for the 'contest.' When they'd set the targets and paced off the distances agreed upon, they gathered on the sidelines, jesting with each other about how far they should pull back for safety's sake when the princess took her turn.

She smiled thinly, trying to take the teasing in good part, although she found it highly irritating.

Daigon bowed, indicating that she was to go first. She looked at him unhappily, so nervous by now she wondered if she could hit the target at all. Since there seemed no hope for it, she notched the arrow and focused, steadying her breathing with an effort. Despite her shakiness, she not only managed to hit the target, the arrow pierced the edge of the inner ring.

A sense of relief and pride washed through her when the men, after a stunned moment of silence, applauded her enthusiastically. Curtseying for them, she turned to look at Daigon expectantly.

"You are a worthy opponent," Daigon said, smiling with genuine warmth.

The praise, and the smile that went with it went a long way toward easing Rhiannon's nervousness. "Thank you."

Notching his arrow, Daigon took aim and released the shaft. It flew straight and true, burrowing into the target virtually on top of hers. Captain Martunae and two seconds stepped forward to study the shots and finally announced that Daigon had taken the advantage by a hair's breadth.

Rhiannon frowned in disappointment, but she felt more confident now, less nervous as she and Daigon moved back to the next line. The men, thankfully, were more cooperative, holding silent as she took aim and fired her arrow into the air. Her second arrow landed almost in the center of the target and the men cheered louder and longer. When they had finally begun to calm down, Daigon stepped up to the line and fired his second arrow. As before, his arrow struck the target almost directly beside hers, but slightly closer to the center.

Rhiannon eyed him suspiciously.

He gave her a look all innocence.

Grinding her teeth, Rhiannon grasped her skirts and marched to the next line back.

Chuckling, Daigon followed.

Rhiannon's third arrow embedded itself into the target almost beside the first. Dismay and dread filled her as Daigon took her place and fired his own. It landed dead center.

He was proclaimed the indisputable winner of the contest and the men cheered him with more enthusiasm than they had her and began to chant for her to pay the forfeit. Rhiannon reddened. Stalking toward him in irritation, she went up on her tiptoes and gave him a chaste peck on the cheek.

He caught her around the waist before she could escape. "That was not the agreed upon forfeit."

Rhiannon lifted her brows. "Of course it was--one kiss, freely given. You did not specify what type of kiss or where to plant it."

His eyes narrowed, but his gaze was more speculative than annoyed. "You stuck to the letter of the wager, then, but not the spirit."

She gave him a look. "And you did?"

The annoyance in his eyes became more pronounced at the accusation. He released her. She'd just gathered her skirts to flounce off when she heard a gasp behind her. The sound halted her in her tracks. When she turned she saw that everyone was focused on the target--and that Daigon had just loosed an arrow that had split one of those protruding from the contest. In swift succession, he split three others. "*That* is skill," he said grimly when she met his gaze.

Before she could respond, he dropped his bow to the ground. Pulling an arrow from his quiver, he tossed it toward the target like a spear. The shaft shot straight toward the target and then abruptly executed a 90 degree angle and shot skyward. Above their heads, the arrow performed a series of loop de loops, and then shot downward once more, plowing into the dead center of the target. "*That*," he said, "is magic."

Chapter Ten

Any reservations Rhiannon had that it was purely her imagination that the sympathies of the men had shifted to Daigon on the 'dueling' field vanished when she presented herself for supper. Everyone was as polite as could be, but she could see from the expressions of those she passed that they'd condemned her unsportsmanlike behavior.

She'd been embarrassed and angry about his display at the time. She'd resented the fact that he'd made it so abundantly clear to everyone that any 'cheating' he'd done was to handicap his skills to keep her from feeling so inadequate and that he was a far better marksman than she could ever hope to be.

It had made her feel very mean-spirited and she'd resented that, too.

Later, she'd realized that it was her accusation that had goaded him into showing her how wrong she was and that he was probably more angry that he'd let his temper get the upper hand than he was at her for her behavior.

Taking the seat reserved for her at the high table, Rhiannon sighed inwardly. She couldn't even summon resentment. After Daigon had stalked off and left her standing in the keep, she had felt pretty mean-spirited without any help from anyone else. Their feelings on the matter only made it that much worse.

After sending a few glances in Daigon's direction and studying his carefully neutral expression, she decided to concentrate on her meal. It might have been sawdust for all she tasted of it, or enjoyed it.

She would have to apologize, she decided. It wasn't enough to simply act contrite, she'd accused him of cheating at a contest of skills. It didn't matter that she'd been subtle about it. She'd left him in no doubt of what she'd meant, and since she had goaded him in to that display, the men would also have surmised that she'd accused him of cheating.

That was probably the root of their condemnation--not her unsportsmanlike behavior, though she didn't doubt they had a poor opinion of that, too.

She should never have put herself in such a position to start with, but, in all truth, she knew very well she hadn't tried all that hard to avoid it. She'd been titillated at the prospect of kissing Daigon and having an excuse to do it. And while she was being honest, she knew it had been cowardice that had prompted her accusation. She'd known he hadn't cheated. She'd just been embarrassed at being faced with the results of the temptation she hadn't been able to resist.

For once she didn't have to work at pretending she had little appetite. She was picking at her food absently when a commotion at the back of the room near the doors drew everyone's attention. Little by little, the room fell silent as the messenger pushed his way toward the high table and bent low to speak with Daigon. Daigon frowned, his lips tightening. Finally, he nodded.

"Inform Captain Bryon that he's to clean the muck of the trail off and present himself as soon as possible."

The messenger bowed and withdrew, leaving the great room as hastily as he'd entered it.

A low buzz began in the room as everyone speculated on the meaning of the interruption. Rhiannon lost what little interest she'd had in her food and had difficulty maintaining even a pretense of eating while she waited to see if Captain Bryon would come at once.

Perhaps ten minutes passed and the sounds within the hall were rapidly returning to normal when another commotion at the rear of the great room drew everyone's attention. Captain Bryon, looking gray with fatigue, his hair slicked back on his head from a quick bath, strode across the room and bowed low before the high table. "Sire!"

"You have news?"

Captain Bryon lifted his head. "Aye."

Daigon's eyes narrowed as he studied the man. Finally, he rose from his seat. "We will withdraw so that you can give me a full report," he said.

Relief passed across Captain Bryon's face, but also fear. Nodding, he rose to follow Daigon from the room. Rhiannon discovered when she looked up at Daigon that he was holding his hand out to her. Surprised, she laid her palm in his without even considering if she wanted to go with him, or why he had decided to include her.

They'd reached the corridor leading to the reception chamber before it occurred to her that she might have reason to fear. A coldness washed over her. When Daigon gently squeezed her hand, she looked up at him. There was nothing in his expression, but it occurred to her after a moment that he'd intended the tightening on her hand as reassurance and she managed a faint smile.

Once they had settled themselves in the receiving chamber, Captain Bryon knelt before Daigon. "As I had feared, Sire, Gerard and his men had crossed the border before we could catch up to them. He has sought sanctuary in Rottham. I left three men to wait and watch in case they returned and took two with me into Rottham. We had no trouble following him as far as Rotthamburg, where King Saliem's palace lies. Once we reached the city, however, we could find no news of him at all at first. We mingled with the townsfolk, however, and learned that he had stopped to petition the king's aid. King Saliem refused it, but allowed him refuge.

"Almost a week passed before we discovered where he was staying, and only then because word had begun to circulate that he was hiring mercenaries. I sent Lark, one of Captain Martunae's men, to sign up and learn what he could since I would have been recognized.

"From what Lark learned, there can be little doubt that Gerard managed to cross the border with the jewels, for he has been to no lenders and the king had refused to offer anything more than shelter."

Captain Bryon paused and lifted his head. "He has sent men to secure the services of the Wizard Climaus."

Rhiannon felt a pain stab into her chest at that, for the Wizard Climaus was renowned as one of the most powerful wizards of all. When she glanced fearfully at Daigon, however, she saw that he was merely looking at Captain Bryon with interest, his dark brows raised as if in polite surprise. "And what is the word on that?"

Captain Bryon reddened. "We did not stay to hear more. I thought that you would want to know so that you could prepare to fight the army being raised against you. I was recognized as we left, however, and we were ambushed near the border. Two men lost their lives. Of the others, two more most likely will not last the night."

Daigon's lips tightened. "I will see them myself. Ordinarily, I do not claim much skill as a healer, but I can hardly do worse than Aradan's resident healer, Mikla."

Captain Bryon nodded, looking relieved, but he did not rise. "They are good men."

"You had something else to add?" Daigon asked when Captain Bryon did not rise at once.

The captain cleared his throat. "I--regret that I failed you once again, Sire."

Daigon propped an arm on the arm of the throne, dropping his chin to his hand. "You consider your mission a failure?"

Captain Bryon blinked, looking as if he feared the warlock was toying with him. "I failed to retrieve the jewels as commanded."

Daigon nodded. "But then we can neither of us be entirely certain that he had them with him."

Captain Bryon frowned, thinking that over. "You think that he had hidden the jewels before?"

Daigon shrugged. "He did not strike me as a man who trusted overmuch--quite possibly for very good reason since he was not a well loved king from what I understand. I do not say it is so, only that the possibility exists and that I cannot pass judgment when I do not have all the facts. I will reserve judgment. If it transpires that the news you have brought to me is reasonably accurate, then I will consider that you did just as you should have."

The captain looked so relieved that he looked almost faint. When Daigon waved a hand in dismissal, he rose shakily and retreated from the room.

Rhiannon watched his departure with a good deal of dread. Fear had spread icy fingers through her and it took an effort to still the trembling that seemed to have begun in her belly and radiated outward. She saw when she looked at Daigon at last that he was studying her. "What will you do, my lord?"

He looked surprised that she would ask. "Prepare for war."

With that, he rose from his seat and held his hand out to her. She took it, allowing him to help her to her feet. "You tremble," he observed.

She was having difficulty keeping her teeth from rattling together. "Do you... do you know the Wizard Climaus?" she managed to ask.

He lifted his brows. "I cannot say that I do."

Rhiannon bit her lip. "He is renowned as the most powerful wizard of all."

"Truly?" Daigon asked with little interest, leading her from the receiving chamber. "Then I should certainly have heard of him."

Rhiannon stopped when they'd reached the corridor and she saw that he would leave her there. "Do you think that he will not come then?" she asked a little hopefully.

Daigon shrugged. "I've no idea, my dear."

Rhiannon stood where she was, watching until Daigon had disappeared down the corridor--to check on the wounded men, she supposed. Finally, she turned and, ignoring the guards who fell into step behind her, headed for the king's apartments. She was almost tempted to rejoin the folk in the great hall, for she wasn't certain she wanted to be alone with her thoughts. A very little consideration convinced her, however, that it was doubtful the noise of the hall would divert her and would likely only make matters worse since she would have to pretend to be undisturbed by the news Captain Bryon had brought.

She settled on a couch and tried to focus on her needle, but after stabbing herself a half a dozen times, flung the needlework down and rose to pace. Her thoughts were chaotic and she could bring no order to them at all. Finally, she left the room and moved out onto the balcony to stare into the dark night. The cool night air chilled her, but it was no colder than her fear.

After a time it occurred to her that she should be elated to know that her uncle would be returning to take the kingdom, and thus free her, as well. She had every reason to be fearful, regardless. A war was brewing, perhaps one that would encompass the entire kingdom this time, and not merely the main keep, Castle Aradan. Men, women and children died or were maimed, were left homeless and starving in these wars the men fought for power. Her own life was in as much danger as anyone else's, perhaps more because she was at the heart of the dispute.

She found that she was far more fearful of the news of the wizard, however, and it did not take long to figure out why.

She was afraid for Daigon, not for herself.

Daigon didn't understand the threat to him. He couldn't when he knew nothing about the wizard Captain Bryon had spoken of. If it came to that, she knew very little herself--only what she had heard, but she feared he was too powerful for Daigon to be a match for him let alone win any contest between the two.

If it had been otherwise, she would still have been anxious, but not nearly so fearful, for she knew that Daigon was a powerful warlock, and also that he was a warrior of considerable skill. Under ordinary circumstances, she would have felt that he would almost certainly be victorious over any army her uncle might raise, but there was nothing ordinary about the possibility of having to face the Wizard Climaus.

The chill of the evening and her thoughts finally drove Rhiannon inside once more. Feeling curiously drained, she settled on the couch with her needlework and found, once she'd focused on it for a time, that her nerves had ceased to jump and her chaotic thoughts calmed.

It occurred to her then that she had been, and still was, overly concerned about the welfare of a man who was her enemy. She couldn't delude herself that it was personal fear that had upset her so, and it was certainly not anxiety on her uncle's behalf.

Unwilling to examine her feelings too closely, she dismissed them with an effort and returned to worrying over the possibility that her uncle's plans would come to fruition. She did not doubt his determination, but did he actually have sufficient funds to hire an army of the size that he would need? Or had he, despite what Captain Bryon had heard, managed to convince King Saliem to aid him? And what of the Wizard Climaus? What might Gerard offer him that would interest him in helping? The possibility of pitting his powers against a potential rival in the art of magic?

Feeling a headache brewing, she set the needlework aside after a time and summoned her ladies. She did not allow them to linger, but sent them on their way as soon as they'd helped her change and combed out her hair.

She was tired, but not sleepy and found it difficult to compose herself for sleep after she'd settled, despite her determination to avoid any uncomfortable conversation with Daigon by being conveniently asleep when he returned to his apartments. After tossing and turning for a time, she finally abandoned the hard pallet again, crossed the room, and went out onto the balcony once more.

She thought perhaps that she had been listening unconsciously for his return, for she knew the moment Daigon appeared in the doorway behind her and felt none of the surprise she generally felt when he simply appeared without a whisper of warning.

"I would think it is far too chill outside to have much appeal."

Rhiannon turned at the sound of his voice. "How are the men?"

His dark brows rose. After studying her for a moment, he merely shrugged. "I have done what I can."

Rhiannon nodded, wrapping her arms around herself and rubbing the chill from her shoulders. "You seem--unsurprised by the news Captain Bryon brought."

"Because I wasn't."

Rhiannon frowned. "You had foreseen this?"

"Not in the sense that you mean, no."

She thought that over for several moments. "Then, why did you allow him to leave? If you knew that he would return with an army, why did you not simply settle it then, when you first came?"

He eyed her thoughtfully. "I cannot quite figure you out."

Rhiannon looked at him in surprise at the comment, trying to decide whether he had simply changed the subject or if the comment was leading somewhere. "I'm not sure I understand what you mean."

"You have asked your enemy why he did not kill your uncle, but allowed him the chance to live, and you can't understand what I meant by the comment?"

That question threw her into complete disorder and she realized that she hadn't considered that her remarks might be interpreted as a suggestion that he should have slain her uncle. She hadn't intended that at all. She disliked Gerard. There had been times when she had felt she hated him, particularly when he had abandoned her, but she had never wished him dead.

Or maybe she was saying exactly that? Because her uncle was a threat now that he had not been before and that, of the two men, she preferred if one would die that it be her uncle?

She rubbed her temple as her headache intensified. "I am--grateful, naturally, that you showed mercy. It's only--if you expected that it would come to this, it seems that you would have finished your enemy before he could cause you more grief. Many more will die now, if Gerard brings an army into Aradan and you are forced to meet him."

Daigon's face hardened with anger. "And I could have prevented the death and suffering of many if I had used better judgment to begin with?"

"I am worried for yo...." Rhiannon broke off her impulse outburst abruptly, staring at him in distress. "I didn't mean it that way. I didn't--I wasn't accusing. I am only trying to understand you. And I am afraid--of what will happen now."

"Worried for ...?" he prompted, tilting his head questioningly.

Rhiannon shook her head, glad for the darkness that concealed the blush that rose in her cheeks, and the chill breeze that cooled them.

"You were waiting for me. Why?"

Rhiannon stared at him in dismay, wondering how she'd managed to work herself into such a corner. "I was concerned about the men who were wounded," she said finally. It wasn't a lie. She was concerned.

"But that isn't the reason."

Abruptly she remembered her decision before Captain Bryon had arrived and so disordered her thoughts. Under the circumstances, it seemed poor timing for an apology, but she thought any distraction better than allowing him to pursue the course he was on. She knew him well enough to know by now that he wasn't easily distracted. "I wanted to apologize--for what I implied this afternoon. I didn't mean it. I only said it because I felt I had been tricked--not that you had used magic to win," she added hastily.

"Tricked?"

"Not--not that--exactly." She sighed. "It was not at all sporting of me to evade the forfeit."

He smiled faintly. "No, it wasn't. But then it wasn't at all sporting of me to manipulate you into agreeing to it."

"All the same," Rhiannon said, trying to gather her nerve, "I don't feel right that I didn't ... uh ... pay when you won the contest."

He held out his arms at his sides in a gesture of surrender. "So--pay."

Chapter Eleven

Rhiannon felt as if she'd suddenly found herself standing on the edge of a precipice--breathless, fearful, giddy, as if only a single step more would take her world out from under her. Her body felt heavy and at the same time weak.

Breathless with anticipation, she waited. At last it dawned upon her that he was waiting, as well, that the bargain had been 'freely given' and he expected her to fulfill every nuance of the wager.

It took a tremendous effort to move, to close the distance between the two of them. When at last she found herself toe to toe with him, she felt as if a giant hand were squeezing the air from her lungs. Unable, at first, to lift her head to gauge his reaction, she stared at his upper chest, watching the rise and fall as he, too, struggled for breath. A pulse beat rapidly in his throat, she saw as she lifted her hands, palm outward, like a sleepwalker and gingerly placed them over the hard mound of his male breasts.

His heat filtered through his shirt almost at once, penetrating the cold that had turned her hands icy, traveling along her arms and evoking a shiver that made her belly quiver and tighten. Dragging in a difficult breath, she slid her palms upward to steady herself on his shoulders, curling her fingers around the hard ridge of muscle, tendon, and bone. Almost as slowly, she lifted her gaze to look up at him.

He stood rigidly straight, unbending, refusing even to meet her halfway. After a moment, she leaned closer, pushing upward on her toes until her mouth hovered a mere inch from his.

She hesitated there for a handful of heartbeats, gathering her nerve as she felt her resolve waver, unnerved by the welter of chaotic sensations and emotions creating havoc within her. Curiosity and the desire to discover more finally impelled her to move closer still. Her eyelids slid closed of their own accord as she brushed her lips lightly against his to test the texture and firmness of his mouth.

His lips were as hard and unyielding as the rest of him and delight fluttered through her as she explored his lips with her own. He sucked in a sharp breath as she plucked at his lower lip with her own, running her tongue smoothly over the surface she held between her lips, sucking lightly.

As if he could no longer keep still, or feared she might take flight and end her tentative exploration, he caught her upper arms in a tight grip, drawing her closer as he dipped his head to give her better access. Her heartbeat trebled, but with a thrill of excitement. Any anxiety she'd felt had vanished almost the moment she touched her lips to his.

Her thoughts, her entire being was centered on the wondrous sensations pelting her from everywhere at once from Daigon's touch. Blood engorged her nipples as his hard chest brushed teasingly against her breasts with each shaky breath of need they dragged into their lungs. Each brush touched off a wave of stinging sensation that cinched around her lungs a little tighter and made breathing more difficult, surrounding her in waves of vacillating darkness. The feel of his lips against hers seemed to magnify the other sensations so that the muscles low in her belly clenched, as well. Heat and moisture gathered there as she molded her lips at last against his, matching surface to surface, drawing his breath into her mouth to mingle with her own scent and taste until they were entwined and inseparable, as one.

Dragging in a shaky breath, she allowed her lips at last to part from his, slowly, regretful at the loss of contact, the loss of his heat and touch. He refused to allow the retreat. As she drifted away, he moved a hand upward to spear his fingers through her hair, curling his long fingers against her scalp.

Sluggishly, as if waking from deep sleep, she lifted her lids, gazing up at him. The night cast his face in shadows. Light spilling from the room behind him and the stars above them glinted in his dark eyes and brightened slashes of flesh along the narrow blade of his nose, his high cheekbones, and his aggressive chin. The effect of light and shadow emphasized his dangerous allure and sent a shiver of nervous anticipation through her as he moved imperceptibly closer.

Rhiannon sucked in a shaky breath as his lips brushed hers again, allowing her eyes to drift closed in tacit surrender. Her heart jolted almost painfully in her chest when after the briefest of explorations his mouth opened over hers. His heat scorched her. His essence invaded her even before she felt the aggressive assault of his tongue along the seam where her lips met. Without a whimper of protest, she yielded to the demand, parting her lips and allowing the invasion to overwhelm her shaky defenses.

For a multitude of frantic heartbeats, she held perfectly still, so enraptured by the faint roughness of his tongue as it stroked ravenously along hers, exploring the cavity of her mouth with a thoroughness that seemed to leach the last ounce of strength from her body, that she could only feel, not react. His retreat touched off a wave of anxiety, however, that he would withdraw altogether.

She closed her mouth around his tongue, sucking, coaxing him to explore more, to give her more of the delight. A tremor went through him. His fingers tightened against her scalp. Exhaling a groan of need, he thrust again, touching off new waves of pleasure.

Mindless, she entwined her tongue with his, offering pleasure for pleasure, touch for touch. With each thrust and retreat of his tongue, she felt herself sinking deeper and deeper into a quagmire of sensation she had no desire to escape.

She was so deeply under the spell of his touch and taste that she scarcely registered the first sounds that erupted in the room beyond the balcony. It seemed doubtful that she would have noticed at all except that, imperceptibly at first, with obvious reluctance, he withdrew. She would have followed when he lifted his lips from hers save for the fact that he held her so tightly she couldn't move.

"Sire?"

The voice penetrated her mind as if from a great distance.

"What is it?" Daigon demanded, his voice harsh, sounding strangely hoarse.

"You asked to be informed when the men were ready to leave."

That comment from the disembodied voice beyond the door of the balcony punctured Rhiannon's euphoria at last and she opened her eyes to look up at Daigon. He was staring down at her, his face taut. When their gazes met, some of the tension seemed to leave him. "You have done so. Await me below."

Confusion filled her. "You are leaving?"

His gaze flickered over her face. "I must check the defenses of the castles that guard Aradan's borders myself." He lifted a hand that shook slightly, caressing her cheek. "It is--tempting to ignore my duties when I want nothing so much as to bury myself so deeply inside of you that no thought but me exists in your mind."

Rhiannon swallowed with an effort, fighting the wave of need that rushed through her at his words as the image filled her mind of his body entwined with her own, the hard flesh of his manhood thrusting into her as his tongue had claimed her mouth.

Daigon smiled wryly, without humor. "It's the strength of that desire that concerns me." He released her, setting her slightly away from him, but captured her face in one large hand. "Know this, I will redeem the promise your body made to me when I return."

A shiver skated through Rhiannon when he stepped away from her and through the open door into the main room of his apartments once more. Numbly, she followed him, almost like a sleepwalker. It was only as she stared down at her hands that a thought finally surfaced.

"The manacles are gone," she murmured in surprise.

Daigon halted at the door and turned. "There never were any manacles--except of your own making."

Rhiannon frowned, staring at him in confusion. "But--I could not break them."

His eyes gleamed with something akin to triumph. "Because your fear and distrust of me forged them."

He had been gone for some time when Rhiannon finally became aware of her surroundings once more and looked around the now empty room. Her body still hummed with need, however, and she found her mind as empty of thought as the room was of his presence. Finally, she moved to her pallet and stared down at it. After several moments, she lifted her head to study the bed and then moved toward it, climbing up on the high mattress. His scent lingered, seeming to envelope her in an embrace as she settled her head against his pillows. She gathered one against her belly and pulled the coverlet over herself.

The manacles were gone because her fear had fled, but was the emotion that had taken its place far worse, she wondered?

* * * *

Daigon's thoughts should have been focused entirely upon the task at hand by the time he passed through the gates of Castle Aradan and into the cool spring night. Instead, they lingered on the balcony with Rhiannon when they did not dwell on the images his mind conjured of her naked and writhing with need beneath him as his hands skated over the silky skin of her thighs and belly and breasts.

Time and again he banished the images, but they returned persistently to plague him until fatigue and the chill of the night wind finally cooled the fire in his blood.

Other thoughts swarmed close to vex him then.

Why had she tormented him with her cool distance until the eve of war? Why choose this time, on this day, above any other to decide to boil his blood in his veins with her yielding body and fevered kisses?

The answer seemed self-evident, and yet he distrusted it almost as much as he distrusted his reflexive urge to dismiss it.

Or, perhaps, he didn't distrust his logical conclusion so much as he desired to dismiss it?

He shook the thought off, but he realized that he had no hope of cool headed logic at the moment. He could not think of Rhiannon at all without his blood heating to the boiling point and frying his brain, and his groin throbbing painfully for the succor he had denied himself.

Or would she have called a halt herself if they had not been interrupted? Would she have teased him to the point of madness with the illusion of her own desire and then refused to allow him more than a taste of the feast so that she could coil him about her finger inch by excruciating inch?

The possibility infuriated him. At the same time, most reluctantly, he admitted to himself that, like mist, she had breached his defenses long since, so long ago he wasn't even certain when she had done it, perhaps from the very beginning? Perhaps that was why it had taken no more than a glimpse of her upon the wall to instantly redirect the focus of his conquest from her uncle to her? Perhaps even his motives for granting leniency to her uncle were tarnished by a desire to find favor?

He rubbed his aching head, cringing inside at those thoughts. It made him feel like a moonstruck calf to think that he'd been so smitten on first sight that the arrow she'd aimed at his heart had seemed more like cupid's dart than the lethal missile it was intended to be. And yet, as much as he would have liked to deny it, there was no way to deny that she had so disrupted his concentration that he had allowed her arrow to pierce his palm when he had reached to snatch it from the air.

Fool! The voice in his head carried the ring of Zella's voice, not his own.

Daigon was startled, for she had not come to speak to him in many years. He recovered quickly from his surprise, however, goaded by her tone as much as the insult itself. *To a degree, granted,* he growled back at her, *but not entirely. She does not know and cannot use it against me.*

That is a matter of opinion--and a matter of time. Even if she does not know now, she will find your chink when she sorts through her own feelings.

She is--not certain? He ground his teeth at the note of hopefulness that had invaded the thought.

The powers of darkness preserve me! Zella exclaimed, plainly exasperated. *You behave like an untried boy! Did you learn nothing from the women sent to you?*

All that they could teach me, he responded, struggling not to sound like the sulking child she'd called him as he strove to tamp his anger.

The voice remained silent for many moments, chastising him. *Distance and time will cool your blood and give you a clear head for reason, if you will only use the opportunity fate has granted.*

Wry humor welled inside him. *Only you, Zella, would consider a call to war an opportunity.*

Each turn fate takes opens a door of opportunity and one that leads to failure. You must see clearly in order to know which door to step through.

Unconsciously, he rubbed his throbbing loins. *I left her untouched,* he pointed out irritably. *Is that not proof enough to you that I am still capable of making a rational decision where she is concerned? You know as well as I that I must maintain some tie to have the vision.*

And what has your vision shown you lately of the uncle?

Daigon frowned, shaking his head. *Nothing.*

"Sire? Is there a problem?"

Surprised, Daigon glanced distractedly at his captain. "Nay. I am but speaking with my grandmother," he muttered.

Captain Martunae's eyes widened. The hair on the nape of his neck lifted even as the color was leached from his face by fear. It did not abate when he'd glanced quickly around Daigon and seen no sign of the dead woman the warlock conversed with, for he didn't doubt the presence of the witch, Zella, whether he could see her or not.

"Pardon, my lord," he said shakily and pulled back on his reins, dropping back to ride with the knights that followed at Daigon's heels.

"There is a problem?"

Captain Martunae glanced at the man who'd spoken to him, and then at those around them, but shook his head. It would be far better, he thought, if they didn't know Daigon spoke with the dead. They'd been unnerved enough when they'd seen the army of specters he'd raised, but those, at least, had been mere puppets and he wasn't sure the men realized that it actually *had* been an army of the dead, and not merely an illusion. "Wake up Lars and Angus before they fall off their horses."

Daigon frowned at the distracting murmur of voices behind him, summoning his grandmother to him once more. *You know something I do not?* He demanded.

You are puzzled. You have not ferreted out the reason? Or has that female so bewitched you you cannot think?

Daigon's lips tightened. *If you have solved the riddle, then speak.*

The simplest answer is usually the correct one.

Which is?

There is no blood bond between the girl and your enemy.

Daigon's heart seemed to jolt to a halt in his chest. *She is not the daughter of Nordain?*

If she were, a link to her would give you a strong link to her blood kin, would it not?

Daigon considered that for several moments, wondering why he hadn't realized it before. Was it because she had so successfully distracted him? *Does she know?*

You will have to find your own answer to that, but I cannot see that it is of any importance. The only thing that is of importance is that she is a distraction you cannot afford and of no value to your efforts.

Anger surged through him at the direction of her thoughts. *Beware, old woman! Grandmother or no, I will not allow your interference in my affairs.*

A prolonged silence greeted that thought. *But you do not object to my help, or my advice, so long as it coincides with your wishes?*

I did not ask for either! I have spent many years learning my own way and depending only upon myself. I can damned well manage without your help, or your interference, Zella!

The Wizard Climaus will join forces with your enemy. You may need me more than you think.

Impatience surged through him. *You have so little faith in my abilities?*

It is more a matter of the faith I have in his than a lack of faith in yours. He is a very real threat, mistake not!

My thanks for the warning then, Zella. I still cannot see why he would make Gerard's battle his own.

He does not. He had only to learn that you were my grandson. His weakness is that he doubts you are a worthy adversary.

The voice fell silent then, leaving him with only his own thoughts for company as he guided his men through the predawn darkness and came at last to the crest of a hill that overlooked the castle guarding his northern boundary.

Captain Martunae nudged his horse until it came abreast of Daigon's mount. "Do ye think they've heard the old king is making a fuss?"

Daigon smiled grimly. "Word has a way of traveling on swift wings--especially if the news is bad."

The captain frowned. "I should approach the keep first, just to be certain their loyalties have not shifted since the last time we were here."

Daigon shook his head. "We will approach as if we expect to be welcomed, with banners flying. If there is treachery afoot, I will know it long before we reach the walls."

Chapter Twelve

Time weighed heavily on Rhiannon's hands with little besides her thoughts for company. On one level, she was anxious for Daigon's return. On another, anxious of *when* he would return. Naturally enough, he had told her nothing about his plans, but it had been no great difficulty to learn that he had gone to visit each of the keeps that guarded Aradan's borders, to make certain of their loyalty and make plans to repel the army Gerard was building.

She should not have worried for the safety of a man who was her enemy, but she did, because she could no longer think of him as her enemy, however he might feel about her.

He was a powerful warlock and a skilled warrior. That should have been reassurance enough to keep her from biting her nails and standing watch for his return on the balcony for much of each day.

He was not immortal, however, and she could not convince herself that he would not run afoul of the vanguard of Gerard's army, or even men who were supposed to be loyal to him. Regardless of what had been said, and left unsaid, there was a chance that those holding the keeps, having heard that Gerard meant to return, might decide to curry favor with the returning king by turning on the man they had so recently given fealty to.

The moment those thoughts would enter her mind, she would immediately begin to envision Daigon and the handful of knights he had taken with him lying dead or dying in some field or ditch or wood and a coldness would sweep through her. Pain would follow closely on the heels of that horrible image, for she couldn't bear to think of Daigon's bright eyes dimmed or his great body cold and still with death.

The vow Daigon had made caused her almost as much turmoil. She didn't doubt for a moment that he'd meant it. What she couldn't decide was whether she was more anxious to receive him or more unnerved by the prospect. She could not think of that vow without remembering the kiss they had shared the night he left and the distress she'd felt afterwards that he had not fulfilled the promise of pleasure her body had craved. And each time she remembered, she felt the same, as if it had been no more than moments before that they had shared the intimacy of their mouths instead of days.

Despite that, her knowledge of such things was limited to what she'd seen and heard, not experienced. She worried that he would not be pleased with her, that she would fail in some way because of her ignorance.

Contrarily, she worried that it would take no more than his possession to deprive her of her own will altogether and what she would do when he tired of her and cast her off.

When she was not mooning dreamily over Daigon's kisses and caresses, she was worrying herself sick over imagining Daigon wounded or killed. And when neither of those anxieties plagued her, she was agonizing over the situation and wondering if there was any way to divert Gerard from his plans.

It seemed unlikely that anything she might say or do could sway him, even if she had some means of speaking with him, but she couldn't help but worry the thoughts over in her mind, looking for a way out of the tangle that would not include so much bloodshed.

Of all the things she fretted over, she supposed that that was probably the most useless. She had not been able to sway her uncle when she had been in 'favor.' He had disclaimed her, abandoned her to what might well have been her death. There could be no doubt in her mind that he cared less than nothing for her, which left her nothing to barter with.

Or did it? Gerard had wanted to use her to gain power in Midae. He was raising an army already. Was it possible that she might convince him to target Midae instead for its riches?

She supposed there was at least a slight possibility of it, particularly since King Linea was old and less a threat than Daigon.

But then, if Gerard had managed to secure the services of the Wizard Climaus, he would not be so fearful of Daigon. Without the wizard the chance of convincing him to conquer Midae were probably good--with the wizard, probably not nearly as good. And it was the wizard she was most worried about.

In any case, she supposed the question was moot. Gerard would be on her doorstep before any opportunity arose for her to speak to him. Daigon was not likely to allow her to go to her uncle to beg for peace. He would not trust her even if he was interested in bargaining for peace.

Before she'd managed to go completely mad from all the things that were worrying her, Daigon returned, eliminating most of her anxieties, but she knew the moment she met his gaze that something had changed between them.

* * * *

It wasn't merely happenstance that Rhiannon was on the balcony, gazing off to the south of Aradan when Daigon and his men crested the rise at the far end of the field. Since he had left the keep, she had spent many hours gazing into the distance, thinking, waiting, wanting to believe that something had happened between her and Daigon the night they kissed that went beyond the needs of the flesh.

She could no longer deny to herself that she had changed. More accurately, she supposed, she had experienced enlightenment. In the days since he had left, she had finally had to admit that she did not just desire Daigon. She cared for him. She had ceased to see him as her enemy, ceased to fear him, and come to admire and respect him. When coupled with everything else she had come to feel about him, it was useless to try to tell herself she didn't love him, madly, deeply.

She had spied the party even before the watchers, who had immediately sounded the horn signifying that riders had been spotted. Breathless moments passed while she watched the dark shapes resolve themselves into a small party of mounted riders. She recognized Daigon at the forefront even before she recognized the banner they flew.

Doubt assailed her as they crossed the field, however.

What if what had transpired between them had meant nothing at all to him? What if he had felt nothing but desire? She *wanted* him to desire her, but that was not enough when compared to the way she felt about him.

That fear spawned a wave of fearful indecision and she retreated inside. She'd been pacing the room anxiously for several minutes before it occurred to her to check her appearance in the looking glass over the dressing table.

She was not happy with what she saw. The color of her gown was flattering, her hair still neatly arranged, but there were dark circles beneath her eyes from many restless nights and strain, as well, from the anxiety. She bit her lips and pinched her cheeks to bring color to them, but she was dismayed at the results. Deciding that the spots of color, her pallor, and the dark circles combined made her look more like she'd been beaten than anything else, she moved to the wash stand and splashed cool water over her face.

Should she go down, she wondered?

She was not his wife, not even his woman--and she certainly wasn't the chatelaine of the keep any longer. Greeting him on the steps like a welcoming hostess probably wasn't the best of ideas.

She glanced at the door to the balcony as she dried her face, partly because she could hear the sounds that told her the troop was entering the gates, and partly in debate of whether to walk out again or not.

But what if he hadn't missed her as she had missed him? What if he ignored her? Did she really want to be seen by all the castle folk, leaning out over the balcony like a common woman?

Unhappy with her thoughts, she finally decided to compromise. She would only go out onto the balcony a little ways and take a peek. If she saw that he had glanced up to look for her then she could allow him to see that she was glad that he had returned. If he didn't look around for her, then she would only have to retreat a few steps and very likely no one--most importantly Daigon--would have noticed her at all and she would not have to feel like a complete fool.

Her heart was hammering so hard in her chest as she stepped through the door, she felt almost faint. Nerving herself, she glanced down at the grounds near the stables to see if the men had dismounted while she had wrangled with herself. To her disappointment, she saw that the men had already dismounted and disappeared. The stable hands were leading their mounts inside.

Sighing in regret, she moved to the edge of the balcony and looked down to see if Daigon had entered the castle yet. Almost as if he sensed her presence, Daigon paused on the steps and lifted his head to look up at the balcony. For a handful of heartbeats their gazes met. There was no welcome in his expression or his eyes, however.

To say that Rhiannon was disappointed would have been an understatement. Guilt instantly swamped her at that look, although she had no idea at all of what she might have done or what she was being accused of. Fear, naturally enough, followed guilt in quick succession.

She tried to dismiss both as she retreated inside the apartments once more and glanced around a little frantically, as if there was actually some possibility of hiding.

She took herself to task when it dawned upon her that she'd actually been contemplating flight. She hadn't done anything. There was no reason for her to feel any guilt aside from the look Daigon had given her and she might easily be reading far more into it than there was.

Uneasy still, she finally moved to the couch and settled with her needlework in her lap. She simply stared at it though, without making any pretense of actually working on it since she was shaking so badly she was fairly certain she couldn't do so without butchering her fingers with the needle and bleeding all over the tapestry she'd been working on for months.

She jumped, dropping her needlework to the floor when Daigon strode through the doors to the apartments like a windstorm. It would almost have been less of a jolt if he had simply appeared as he habitually did. She found the deviation most unnerving.

He looked exhausted, she saw when she had recovered enough to steal a glimpse in his direction, and achingly handsome despite the soils of his travels and the day's growth of beard on his face. She rather thought it surprisingly appealing, for he was an extremely fastidious man and she'd never seen him other than neat and clean as if he had only just stepped from his dressing room.

Anxiously, she watched as he paced the room restlessly, trying to think of something to say. Nothing came to mind, however, that didn't ring of domesticity and she wasn't comfortable with the idea of assuming a role she had not been invited to take upon herself. 'You are back!' rang even worse in her mind as it sounded vacuous and inane. "There was trouble?" she finally asked, hoping to get some hint of what was bothering him, for it was obvious something was, whether she'd misinterpreted the look he'd given her or not as the source of disturbance.

He glanced at her coolly. "Nay."

Irritation surfaced. He might at least aid her attempt to converse, she thought with some dudgeon. What was she to do with a single word response?

She cleared her throat and decided she was more uncomfortable with the silence than the possibility of setting his back up by mouthing the sort of domesticity she'd previously rejected. "You look exhausted," she observed.

He lifted one black brow at her.

Rhiannon reddened and set her needlework aside. Before she could formulate another question, however, the door to the apartments opened and servants began to troop in with the bathing tub and accoutrements of a bath. She watched uneasily as they set the tub up and began to fill it.

As anxious as she'd been previously to take up where they'd left off at his departure, she didn't currently feel up to it and she knew better than to think she had any chance of fending him off if he decided to pursue the matter.

"I will leave you to your bath," she said, getting to her feet abruptly.

"Sit!"

Rhiannon sat before she even had time to consider whether she meant to obey the order or not. The uneasiness returned, but anger matched it. Picking up her needlework once more, she began to stab her needle into the fabric jerkily, paying little attention to what she was doing. A splash of water dragged her from her mental rant some time later and it was only with a tremendous effort that she quelled the instinctive urge to look up.

The splashing continued for some time. Tiny beads of perspiration broke from Rhiannon's pores at the images running through her mind, but she resolutely refused to glance toward the tub.

"Wash my back."

The demand brought Rhiannon's head up with a jerk of surprise. She met his gaze for several moments, considering what her chances were of simply jumping to her feet, making a dash for the other room, and bolting the door. Not good, she finally decided, and worse than that, the door would not prevent him from coming after her.

Slamming her needlework onto the couch, Rhiannon got to her feet stiffly and stalked toward the tub, extending her hand for the cloth he held out to her. It was a shame, she thought as she settled on her knees on the floor behind him, that she wasn't manacled still, with *real* manacles. She could have used the chain to choke the life out of him.

The anger behind the thought dissipated almost the moment the idea popped into her head. Why, she wondered, was she so angry? He hadn't done or said anything to provoke her anger except that he had not behaved as she had expected.

She was disappointed, because she had thought he might care for her, at least a little, and she would see some sign of it upon his return, something in his eyes to show her that he'd missed her as much as she'd missed him even if he had not gone so far as to profess some feeling for her. She was also anxious, fearful because it seemed to her that the reverse was true. He not only did not display any affection for her, he had distanced himself from her since she had seen him last. That might mean that he had learned something that had caused the change, and it might not. She was allowing her imagination to upset her.

Thrusting the thoughts off, she lifted the dark tendrils of hair from his back and pushed the wet mass over one shoulder. There was some relief that she saw no sign of new injury as she began to scrub his back. She could not pretend she had not worried about him only because she was disappointed that he didn't seem to return her affections.

"A thought plagues me," Daigon said pensively when she had begun to rub the soapy cloth in small circles over his shoulders.

Rhiannon hesitated, but she was almost more relieved that he seemed inclined to address what was bothering him than she was unnerved to be summoned so close before he did so. "What teases you?" she asked finally.

"I cannot see Gerard."

Rhiannon registered absolute blankness at the remark. "I don't understand."

"When he had stolen the treasure, I had no difficulty summoning the vision. The link was strong, the vision sharp and clear."

Enlightenment dawned, but Rhiannon was still confused. "You mean when you used the staff to bring forth an image of Gerard and his men in the woods?"

"Precisely."

Rhiannon considered that, trying to figure out what he was getting at. She sensed that this was what the silent condemnation was about, but turn it though she would, she couldn't figure out what it had to do with her, at least not directly. It occurred to her that it might be merely accusation by way of extension--she was Gerard's niece and he blamed her because Gerard was not handy to blame. Somehow, though, she did not think the answer was as simple, or petty, as that. "Do you think, perhaps, the wizard has conjured some spell to prevent it?" she asked a little fearfully as that possibility occurred to her.

He shifted, twisting his head to meet her gaze for several long moments. "No," he said finally. "The link grew too weak to be of use long since--well before any possibility that Climaus might have had a hand in it. At first I believed that it was my own doing, that I had allowed too much distance between myself and the link."

"But you do not believe that now?" Rhiannon asked slowly. "What is the link? Perhaps if I understood that, I would have a clearer understanding of what you are asking me."

This time when he swiveled toward her, Daigon removed the cloth from her hand and caught her arm, drawing her around to the side of the tub so that he could study her face. Unnerved, but more curious than afraid, Rhiannon made no attempt to resist.

"You."

Rhiannon felt her heart jerk painfully. Blood flooded her cheeks and washed away again so rapidly and drastically that she felt a wave of dizziness. "Me?" she asked a little weakly.

"Even with magic, there must be a chain," he said coolly. "My link to use is--should be--weakest, by no more than--touch, your proximity--even desire. The one that has vanished altogether is the link between you and--your uncle. Why is that, do you think?"

Rhiannon found that she could not maintain eye contact when it struck her like a tone of stone what he was hinting at. She swallowed with an effort, feeling sick. "Because--because I had no affection for him?" she asked shakily.

He caught her jaw in the palm of his hand, forcing her to look up at him. "Is that what you believe?"

Rhiannon stared at him while a dozen thoughts collided in her mind all at once, making it nigh impossible to sort through them. One thing emerged with crystal clarity, however, the reason Daigon had kept her close, and she didn't know whether she was more devastated by that realization or fearful because of it. Lying seemed pointless. To her horror, she felt tears filling her eyes so that his image wavered before her. "I was afraid to tell you he was not truly my uncle," she said with an effort because her lips felt strangely stiff and awkward in trying to form the words.

"Because you were afraid of me?"

"Yes! You said that--that you had come to avenge your parents' murder and that you would take the seed of your enemy since you could not have him. If I had tried to tell you then, you would not have believed me. Later, when I saw you did not mean to kill me, I thought that you kept me here to barter me with my unc--Gerard, and I was afraid of what you might do if you learned that I was of no use to you."

She blinked the tears from her eyes to see him, to see if she could discover any chink in his expression that would tell her she need not fear now that he knew. His expression was hard and uncompromising, however, giving nothing away save the anger he felt because she had lied to him by maintaining his belief that he held a pawn within his grasp.

"When did you learn this?"

It took several tries to dislodge the knot in her throat so that she could answer. "When he left. I followed him ... hoping to reason with him, I suppose. I just couldn't believe that he was abandoning us all to die, fleeing to save himself instead of trying to lead those who were fighting to preserve his kingdom for him. He said that it would help more to keep his life and fight another day. I pleaded with him to take me, but he refused. He said that you would certainly come after him for you had demanded me in his stead." She paused, trying to remember the whole of the conversation, but it was no use. She'd been too upset at the time to recall the episode with any clarity. "I think I asked him if there was any truth to what you had said about my father. He said that it *was* true, that Nordain had done just as you had claimed, but that Nordain was not my father. I didn't know whether to believe him or not, but I knew my life would certainly be forfeit if I was of no use to you."

He released her chin after a moment. He was frowning, she saw, but more thoughtful than angry. "It didn't occur to you that it might be safer if I had believed you weren't the daughter of my enemy?"

Rhiannon sniffed. "Of course it did! I wanted to tell you, but then I realized that you would only think I was lying to protect myself."

Agonizing minutes passed while Rhiannon waited to see what he would do, or say, now that he knew. When he said nothing at all, she got to her feet hesitantly. He caught her wrist just above her hand before she could move away from him. To her surprise and consternation, he pulled on her arm so that she toppled into the tub on top of him with a resounding splash that sent a wave of water cascading over the side and across the floor.

Chapter Thirteen

Before Rhiannon could do much more than gape at him in stunned surprise, Daigon captured her face between his palms, studying her piercingly. He shook his head finally. "I cannot tell if you are lying to me still, or telling the truth. I find I don't particularly care at the moment," he murmured, slowly closing the distance between them. "But you are wrong in one respect. I can certainly think of a very good use for you."

Rhiannon didn't have time to consider the nuances of that last remark. He captured her lips beneath his then and all possibility of thought fled as his heat instantly seared through her. A sound of surrender escaped her as his mouth moved over hers hungrily. Dismissing her tumultuous emotions of before, the discomfort of wet clothing, the heat of the water seeping into her clothes and the chill of cool air on damp skin and clothing above the water, Rhiannon looped her arms around his neck, surging closer to the source of heat she most desired. Enraptured by the thrust of his tongue inside her mouth, her senses filled with him, Rhiannon lost all touch with the world around her, focusing completely on Daigon, returning his caresses feverishly with caresses of her own.

Her reaction seemed to surprise him. He stiffened, but only for the briefest of moments. Pulling her more snugly against his chest, he released her when she tightened her arms around him. Dimly, she was aware of the tug of his fingers as he loosened the ties of her clothing, tugging her corset off and tossing it onto the floor, but she could not have cared less if everything she owned was ruined. The only thing that mattered was his mouth on hers, his lips and tongue creating the magic mating dance that she had yearned for so desperately for so many days.

His touch felt far better even than she remembered, whisking her so abruptly from despair to the heights of desire that she felt faint with the swiftness of her ascent, murmuring a sound of complaint when he ceased tugging at her bodice and caught her arms, disentangling himself from them and pushing her slightly away. Stunned by the move, Rhiannon opened her eyes to stare at him blankly, confused.

Frowning in concentration, he struggled with her soggy clothing for several moments and finally managed to push the sleeves of her overgown and undergown from her arms, baring her to the waist. Relief and desire flooded her as he pulled her close once more and settled his mouth over hers, kissing her deeply. Her bare skin against his chest felt delightfully wicked. She wrapped her arms around his neck again, rubbing her skin along his experimentally. The touch of skin to skin combined with the slickness of the water felt indescribably wonderful, touching off waves of sensation that felt like fire as it crawled through her.

He rose from the tub abruptly, taking her with him. Startled, Rhiannon had to force herself to relax her grip on him as he set her on her feet on the floor beside the tub. Climbing out, he tugged her clothing from her waist so that it landed with a soggy splat around her ankles. Her pantelettes followed and then he scooped her up and strode to the bed with her, placing her on the mattress and following her down.

The chill of the sheets on her wet skin caused an eruption of goose flesh, elevating her entire body to a state of excruciating sensitivity. As he sprawled on top of her, the skate of his damp skin against hers swamped her senses. Darkness encroached along the fringes of her consciousness, focusing her entire being on the only source of awareness and sensation, Daigon. The hardness of his flesh, the sharp contrast of silky slick skin and slight abrasiveness of his body hair as it rubbed against her evoked heady delight.

He caught one breast with one hand, massaging it gently even as he covered the tip of her other breast with his mouth. She realized she had forgotten how mind numbingly wonderful his caresses felt on that sensitive bud of flesh. She gasped as the heat of his mouth invaded her, inundated her with fresh waves of aching, torturous pleasure. She held perfectly still as long as she could, fearful that he would stop, holding that pleasure to her, drawing it deeply inside, struggling to draw breath. She quickly found that she could not remain still, though. The fever was upon her. She began to thrash with the building of tension inside of her, moaning incessantly.

When he moved to her other breast to tease that nipple as he had the first, she flinched all over, uncertain that she could bear more, certain that she was going to die if he stopped. Mindlessly, she wrapped her arms tightly around him, arching upward to meet the torment of his mouth.

Within moments her body had reached a point of desperation. The tension had coiled so tightly that she felt she couldn't bear it if he continued to tease her. "Daigon," she gasped desperately. "I need. I need."

What?

She wasn't entirely certain of what she needed to find relief, but she knew she didn't want him to stop. He hesitated, lifting his head to look up at her. "Please," she murmured desperately.

After a moment, he shifted upwards until he could cover her lips once more in a deep kiss. Wedging one knee between her thighs, he grasped her leg. Instinctively, she did as he urged, spreading her thighs wide for him. When he had settled between them, he arched against her. The turgid flesh of his man-root plowed along her cleft, touching off sizzling jolts of desperate need that took her breath for several moments.

Feeling almost ill with yearning, she arched her back to meet him when he thrust against her again. His shaft parted the nether lips of her womanhood, rubbing along the sensitive inner flesh and she tore her lips from his, groaning. "Daigon," she gasped in acute distress, digging her nails into his shoulders where she gripped him tightly.

He reached between them, aligning his body with hers and burrowing into her.

Her eyes widened in sudden shock and fear at the invasion, but her body clenched around the head of his shaft, demanding more. She caught her breath, held it as he thrust again, sinking more deeply inside her. Despite the resistance of her flesh to his conquest, or perhaps because of it, she was enraptured by the feel of him inside of her. When he thrust again, she met him with more certainty, moaning in delight as she felt him sink almost painfully deeply inside of her.

He captured her mouth once more as he began to move, slowly at first, matching the thrust and retreat of his tongue inside her mouth with the thrust and retreat of his shaft along her passage. Understanding dawned and she began to counter his movements, awkwardly at first, but then with more surety as he groaned in pleasure. Tightening her arms around him she bent her knees, digging her heels into the mattress to give her more leverage, widening her thighs further still to ease his passage so that he could thrust deeper still.

The coil of pleasure grew more and more taut with each thrust until, suddenly, it seemed her body could contain it no longer. It shattered. Her muscles clenched, spasmed as purest bliss exploded, spread outward through her body in a hard wave that made her cry out at the intensity of it.

He stiffened. A tremor went through him and then he began to move inside her harder and faster than before until, abruptly, a low growl of satisfaction escaped him and he shuddered as she had and finally went still.

Dazed, so weak she could hardly move, Rhiannon felt as if she were melting into a puddle of supreme satisfaction. With an effort, she stroked his back as he lay gasping for breath on top of her, glorying in the wonder he'd shown her, reveling in the knowledge that she had given him pleasure, as well. She was disappointed when he gathered himself at last and rolled off of her. Briefly, coolness replaced his warmth, but then he slipped an arm beneath her and pulled her close once more. Snuggling contentedly against him, she gave up the effort to fight off the weariness of the expenditure of so much energy and drifted away.

Need of a different kind woke her. Hazily, she lifted her head and glanced around. Daigon had rolled away from her in his sleep. He was sprawled bonelessly on the bed beside her, sleeping the sleep of the truly sated--and the truly exhausted, she mentally added wryly.

She propped her chin on one hand, studying him to her heart's content as she had not dared to do before. A faint smile curled her lips as it occurred to her that he looked every bit as dark and dangerous in his sleep as he did when awake. It was the eyebrows, she decided, resisting the urge to trace them with her finger with an effort, and his hard, uncompromising mouth.

Just looking at his mouth was enough to evoke memories that made her body clench and her breath grow short.

She settled her head on a pillow once more, trying to ignore the demand of her bladder. She had not had the chance to study him before. She was reluctant to chance waking him.

Something began to tease at her mind as she studied him, though. What was it that he'd said just before he'd kissed her?

He had a use for her.

Rhiannon struggled without success to ignore the meaning that most readily came to mind. It settled in the pit of her stomach like a rock, though, indigestible, painful.

She was not a princess. She was a bastard. What possible use could a man like Daigon, a man of royal bloodlines, have for a woman like her when she was of no use to him as a bargaining tool, or even a link to his enemy?

He had amply demonstrated that, hadn't he?

It was unreasonable of her, she knew, to feel hurt. She had not discouraged him in any way, quite the contrary. She had behaved as if she was nothing more than a common whore, begging, demanding.

Color flooded her cheeks at the thought. It receded with a vengeance when another thought occurred to her abruptly.

Their coupling had been staggeringly wonderful.

And she had felt no discomfort at all. None.

Even she knew that wasn't right. She was not experienced--she should have felt discomfort at least, pain at worst. She'd overheard women talk of their first time with a man.

How could she *not* be a virgin when she knew she had never been with a man?

Sudden, icy fear, clenched painfully around her heart.

More importantly, had Daigon noticed?

He hadn't seemed to, but perhaps he had been too caught up in the moment to realize that something wasn't quite as it should have been? Maybe he didn't *know*, never having been with anything but prostitutes?

Then again, maybe he did.

And maybe it didn't matter anyway. If she was nothing to him but a whore, why would he care if he had not been first?

She cared.

She loved him. It mattered.

She was too distressed over the collapse of her girlish dreams to feel like worrying over it until, and unless, she had to, she decided, fighting the urge to burst into tears. Easing her way off the bed with great care, she glanced at Daigon again to make certain he was still deeply asleep and moved as quietly as she could to the wardrobe that held her clothes.

When she was dressed, she tiptoed into the outer room and left the suite. The guards, as usual, escorted her to the garderobe and waited outside. She was too upset for that to bother her as it generally did, though.

Doubt and anxiety assailed her anew as she left the garderobe. She did not want to face Daigon in the worst sort of way, but she knew she could not avoid a confrontation indefinitely, whatever she decided to do. Perhaps, she thought, it would be best to get it out of the way at once rather than have to dread it?

Reluctance dragged at her as she headed for the king's suite, but she did her best not to look like a prisoner headed for the headman's ax.

The moment the doors to the apartment closed behind her, someone seized her from behind, clapping a hand so tightly over her mouth and nose that she thought for several terrified minutes that she would suffocate. Mindlessly, she clawed at the hand over her face and the arm squeezing the breath from her lungs as the man lifted her clear of the floor and half dragged half carried her across the main room and into the bed chamber.

Chapter Fourteen

"You stupid whore!" Gerard growled, releasing Rhiannon so abruptly that she sprawled on the floor.

Despite the struggle to catch her breath, recognition was almost instantaneous. Rhiannon's head instinctively swiveled toward the sound of his voice and she stared up at Gerard in absolute stupefaction, unable at first even to accept that he could possibly be standing over her.

He was glaring at her furiously, however, examining the wounds she'd inflicted with her nails and that look was all too familiar to her.

Before she had even completely grasped that Gerard truly was standing before her, her mind leapt toward Daigon and she whipped her head around fearfully to find him. He was standing beside the bed, as if he had only just leapt from it to face his foe, so perfectly still he might have been a statue. Acute pain erupted inside her. Dead? Although she strained, Rhiannon could see no sign that he was breathing.

A knot formed in her chest, making it a struggle to breathe. It was even more of a struggle to gather her wits, but she fought the fear and pain, trying to think what to do, trying to figure out if there was anything she *could* do.

She saw then that a gnarled old man dressed in elaborately ornate robes stood before Daigon, his wrinkled face puckered speculatively as he leaned toward him, studying him curiously.

"Merciful gods!" Rhiannon gasped the prayerful oath without even realizing she'd spoken aloud.

The old man glanced at her at that, favoring her with a jagged toothed grin. "The gods had no hand it this simple spell. I confess, I'm disappointed. This warlock is known far and wide for his command of the dark forces, reputedly stronger even than his grandmother, whom I knew personally--well enough to know that *her* powers were not merely childish tricks to impress the ignorant. I had not expected he would be no challenge at all."

Terror and indignation collided inside of Rhiannon that he dismissed Daigon's powers so easily. He was lucky he had caught Daigon completely by surprise, so exhausted from his travels--

and their lovemaking--that he had not had the chance to grab his staff before they were upon him.

Climaus was as cowardly as her uncle to cut a man down from behind without challenging him fairly!

"Is he aware of us? Can he hear us?" Gerard asked quickly, almost breathless with anticipation and glee as he circled the bed and came to stand beside the wizard.

The Wizard Climaus rubbed his beard thoughtfully and finally shrugged. "I cannot say. Perhaps. It depends upon how deeply the spell holds him." He paused for several moments. "You are certain this is the warlock, Daigon?"

Gerard looked at the wizard curiously. "So he claims. Why?"

Climaus stroked his beard again, plucking a little nervously at a scraggly thatch and twirling it between his fingers. Finally, he clapped his hands loudly in front of Daigon's face, poked him with his index finger a couple of times. "That *was* a powerful spell I cast--truthfully I'm amazed he did not block it--but even so." He shrugged, apparently deciding to dismiss his misgivings. "I can see no sign that he is playing us."

"He is not dead?" Rhiannon asked fearfully, climbing to her feet with an effort.

Gerard grinned at her. "Not yet."

Rhiannon felt a wave of agony wash through her. She beat the fear and pain back, trying desperately to formulate a plan. Daigon was alive, but helpless. If she could do nothing for him, he would die. Naturally enough, her first thought was to summon the guard. She hesitated, realizing that that was not likely to avail them. The Wizard Climaus could certainly dispose of the threat of the guards swiftly if he had not already cast some sort of spell to keep them out, and crying out would relieve Gerard of any doubts he might retain that she was very much his enemy now.

Climaus lifted his head abruptly, as if he could hear something they could not. "The army approaches the gates. Time to remove the cloaking spell and open the gate to them," he muttered, almost to himself. Crossing the room, he opened the door to the balcony and stepped outside.

Gerard sniffed, drawing her attention back to him. "The scent of copulation fills the air. Did you enjoy it my dear? Or has it finally occurred to you that the only thing you have to bargain with is your body?"

Rhiannon reddened, but wisely kept her tongue between her teeth.

"Did he question you about who had plowed those rows before?"

Rhiannon gaped at Gerard in shock. Unable to resist, she glanced at Daigon. She could see nothing that indicated he was aware of anything any of them said, and a measure of relief filled her. "You are wasting your time to taunt him with that lie. He cannot hear you and he wouldn't care if he could. I am only his layman--one of many," she lied.

Gerard's brows rose. He eyed her speculatively for several moments. "You really don't remember, do you? I believe I am insulted. A woman should always remember the man who plucked her."

Nausea washed through Rhiannon. She felt the color leave her face in a dizzying rush.

"Ah--it's coming back to you now. I see it in your face." He shrugged. "Maybe it's only that you were so young at the time that you have trouble remembering," he said speculatively, "in your very first bloom of womanhood. I'm sorry to say it wasn't that memorable for me either. I was sorely disappointed. You put up such a fight in the beginning I'd expected a more exciting ride, and then, at the moment of truth, you simply lay there like a dead thing."

Bile rose in Rhiannon's throat. He was wrong. She still didn't remember. She only remembered that she'd been afraid of him when she was young, repulsed by his displays of affection and spent much of her time hiding from him.

It didn't matter. She fought the nausea back, forced a smile as she watched Gerard draw his knife from his belt and test the edge with his thumb. Dimly, as if from a great distance, she heard the alarm sound. They could not know that Gerard had already breached the king's chambers, she realized almost at once. The alarm must be the army Gerard had brought with him.

Consternation filled her. They needed Daigon.

With an effort, she dragged her mind from the turmoil outside to focus on the only problem she felt she had any chance at all of solving, slim though that might be. "I'm older now, more experienced."

He glanced at her in surprise. His eyes narrowed upon her speculatively as he examined her from head to toe. "You're a bit--overblown for my tastes now," he said dryly.

Rhiannon swallowed with an effort, ignored the slight. "But--I could make it good for you. And--and think how much pleasure you could have with the warlock watching," she added on sudden inspiration. "He is no threat to you now. Let him live so that you can take a full measure of revenge, enjoy it in leisure."

She could see the idea appealed to him. Before she'd quite managed a sigh of relief, Climaus spoke.

"Not wise. The spell will deteriorate in time and if his mind is not as frozen as his body, he could discover a way to break the spell."

Gerard looked torn. Rhiannon used his indecision to place herself between Daigon and Gerard's knife. "But there is no rush, surely? We have now," she said with an effort, lifting her hands to skate them over Gerard's barrel chest in imitation of a caress.

His eyes narrowed. He reddened with anger. "You think me such a fool, so taken with your charms, that I would ignore the warnings of Climaus?" he growled.

Despair filled Rhiannon when she saw that her ploy had been for nothing. "Have mercy then!" she cried. "Please--don't hurt him. I'll do whatever you like," she babbled in desperation. "Anything!"

"It will please me most for you to join him in death, you treacherous harlot!" Gerard howled, swinging the knife blade so quickly toward her throat that Rhiannon didn't even have time to flinch.

The hand that shot over her shoulder and grasped his knife hand was little more than a blur. It took Rhiannon several heartbeats to realize that she felt no pain.

She'd barely assimilated that when Gerard thrust her so roughly to one side that she sprawled on the floor, skidding several feet before she came to a stop. A roar of sound filled her ears.

* * * *

Consternation filled Daigon when he heard the sounds behind him that told him Rhiannon had returned. With an effort, he closed his mind to the sounds of struggle, focusing on the counterspell he'd summoned to break the spell Climaus had trapped him with.

It had been a calculated risk to allow Climaus to bespell him at all, but one he had been willing to take when he realized that Rhiannon was safely out of their reach. Zella had said Climaus' weakness was his arrogance, his certainty that Daigon could not match him and to use that advantage, he had thought it best to allow Climaus the first strike while he gauged the old man's strength.

Now he had to wonder if his own arrogance would be his downfall--his arrogance and his inability to focus upon anything but Rhiannon and the fear for her that began to gnaw at his concentration the moment he realized she was in trouble.

Briefly, relief flooded him when she moved within his view and he saw that she was unhurt, but before he could focus once more on the task, Gerard distracted him once more with his bragging and a jolt of shock went through him followed almost instantaneously by rage.

The rage was nearly his undoing. It boiled inside of him like acid as Gerard taunted Rhiannon with his misdeeds.

Emotions! Zella spat angrily as she entered his mind. *You cannot summon the forces if you allow them to rule you! I knew that woman would be your downfall, whether she wills it or not.*

He knew she was right. Blinded by his emotions, he lost control and without control of himself he had no control of the forces. He gritted his teeth, abandoning the spell he'd sought to free himself and summoning a protection spell for Rhiannon.

Fool! Focus upon the wizard. Forget the woman!

Nay!

Then I will protect her! Free yourself! You cannot help her--or any of your people if you do not dispose of Climaus!

Swear to me that you'll protect her! He demanded.

She was silent in her anger for several moments. *I will let no harm come to her*, she said finally. *I swear it on the body of your mother!*

Relief flooded him and still it took more effort than he would ever have thought possible to ignore Rhiannon's pleading and focus upon the task at hand. The spell gained strength, however. With agonizing slowness, he felt the hold begin to fall from him, felt his muscles begin to relax. The moment he found a fault in the spell, he reached through it and touched Climaus.

Startled, Climaus whirled to face the threat he hadn't even suspected. For a split second, their gazes locked as Daigon's holding spell stole over Climaus, freezing him to the spot. Daigon smiled grimly, but before he could finish the wizard, Gerard's voice, high with fury, brought his attention instantly to Rhiannon. It was instinct that guided his hand to catch the blade Gerard wielded before it could pierce Rhiannon's throat. A cold sweat broke from his brow when he realized how nearly Rhiannon had come to death. Fury followed the fear in quick succession as Gerard shoved Rhiannon from his path, thinking no doubt that he still had a chance to kill Daigon before he completely emerged from the spell Climaus had cast upon him.

He was wrong, dead wrong. Pursing his lips, Daigon summoned another spell and blew a puff of air in Climaus' direction. It struck the wizard with hurricane force, tossing him about like a leaf and carrying him clear across the distant sea of Midae.

His gaze met Gerard's horrified one before Gerard was sucked away by the tail of the winds that had carried Climaus to the sea.

* * * *

In shock, Rhiannon pushed herself upright to look just as the Wizard Climaus flew backwards off the balcony. His mouth gaped in surprise as he disappeared. Gerard screamed in pure terror as the same invisible hand snatched him from his feet and swept him through the door behind Climaus.

Numbly, with great effort, Rhiannon dragged her gaze from the horrifying sight to look at Daigon. She saw that he was frozen no longer. His gaze was unreadable as he stared at her for a long moment and then abruptly vanished.

Dazed, still too stunned to actually absorb what had happened, Rhiannon remained where she was for some time, listening to the sounds erupting through the open door grow louder, building ominously.

Finally, as much to assure herself that she had not merely imagined that Daigon had escaped the trap sprung upon him as to see what was transpiring, Rhiannon got to her feet and moved to the window. Below, she saw the keep rapidly filling with a tangle of struggling men as Gerard's army clambered over the walls and through a v shaped crevice that had opened along one wall. Daigon now stood on the top of the wall, his dark hair and cape swirling and snapping about him as the wind rushed around him. As she watched, the sky darkened until it almost seemed a premature night had fallen. Lightning flashed, adding a fearsome noise to the already near deafening roar of shouting men, clanging swords, and screaming horses. The wind spun more tightly, following, she saw, the movement of Daigon's staff, which he held toward the sky. Faster and faster, he twirled it, almost seeming to coil the wind around it.

When he released it at last, the funnel of air slammed into the ground beyond the gates. Men, horses, wagons, cannons, and cannon balls were plucked from the ground, spun wildly in the churning winds for many moments and then flung like flecks of sand across the field.

As horrified as Rhiannon was, she discovered she couldn't look away. As she watched in terrified fascination, the winds pounded the army at the gates like a great fist, decimating all in its path.

Below, the men who'd charged the keep slowly became aware that their numbers were dwindling. When they looked about them and discovered their comrades had not followed them inside, they began to cry out for quarter.

Daigon, who'd turned from his contemplation of the destruction beyond the keep walls to assess the progress of his men below, merely watched for many moments. Finally, he called out to his own men. "Give them quarter!"

The mercenaries, one by one, threw down their swords. Before a full hour had passed, the sounds of clashing swords was replaced by the cries and groans of the wounded.

A sob escaped Rhiannon as relief washed over her. Covering her mouth with her hands, she turned away from the window at last, sliding down the wall until she was huddled in a tight ball on the floor.

She'd barely gotten her sobs under control when two boots appeared before her. With dread, Rhiannon lifted her head to look up at Daigon. "By the gods!" she cried out. "I didn't know! I swear it on my mother's soul!"

Something flickered in Daigon's eyes but Rhiannon was afraid to hope.

"You didn't know about the secret passage that led directly to these chambers?"

Rhiannon bit her lip, but she knew it was useless to lie. "I found it one day when I was searching for a way to escape. I never dreamed that Gerard would use it to catch you off guard. It was stupid, I know, not to tell you, but I...." She broke off, realizing that it would sound no better to tell him she had not warned him because she had thought to use it herself in case of need.

"You didn't want me to know because you thought you might have need of it?" he asked, finishing the sentence for her.

She nodded, mopping the tears from her cheeks with her hands.

After studying her a moment, Daigon approached her, squatting down in front of her so that his face was almost level with hers. "No more lies."

Rhiannon's chin trembled. "I didn't mean for anyone to get hurt."

"I know that."

Rhiannon sniffed. “Then--you’ll forgive me?” she asked tentatively.

He tilted his head, studying her. “Will you give me your word that you will not lie to me again, by commission or omission?”

Rhiannon nodded readily, too desperate to win his forgiveness to give any thought to the future.

“Then tell me why you tried so hard to convince Gerard to spare my life.”

She stared at him in dismay, but she had given her word. “Because--because I couldn’t bear to see your life taken.”

He cupped her chin in his hand. “Is it so hard for you to say, then?” he asked quietly.

Rhiannon’s face crumpled. “You will laugh.”

“I will not. I swear it.”

“Because I love you,” she wailed.

Daigon chuckled, but caught her arms, pulling her to him. “There, that was not so difficult, was it?”

Rhiannon struggled to free herself from his grip. “It was not hard at all for you!”

His arms tightened around her until she gave up on the possibility of escaping. “It is every bit as hard for me. I have never been in love before.”

Rhiannon’s breath caught in her throat, but she could only stare at him speechlessly.

His dark brows rose. After a moment, he loosened his grip on her and traced one index finger along her lower lip, smiling wryly. “I’m no good at pretty speeches, my love. Will it content you to know that I love you more with every breath I take? To know that I desperately want you for my wife?”

Rhiannon burst into tears, but flung her arms tightly around his neck. “Yes!” Doubt shook her. “Should you? You know I’m no princess and--and I was not a--You were not the first.”

“If he is fool enough to allow that to dissuade him, then you should count yourself well rid of him, my dear.”

Rhiannon jumped, jerking away from Daigon and glancing quickly around the room.

An ancient woman stood perhaps ten feet from where she knelt on the floor next to Daigon. Daigon turned to look at the woman. His eyes narrowed. “You!” he snapped angrily, surging to his feet. “You almost cost her her life! You swore to me on my mother’s soul that you would protect her!”

The old woman shrugged. “She is alive.”

Daigon ground his teeth. "Because I managed to break free in time to prevent Gerard from cutting her throat, not because you kept your word."

The old woman's lips tightened. "I would have cut her throat myself if I had not been reassured that she truly loves you--enough to give up her own life to save yours. Nothing less would do."

"I warned you once before to tread warily where Rhiannon is concerned. Do not make me chose between you two, old woman."

Stunned by the exchange, Rhiannon got to her feet slowly. "Daigon! This is--this is your grandmother? Zella? But--you said she was dead."

Zella and Daigon exchanged a look. "I crossed over," Zella said finally. "But I had to keep a watchful eye on my boy. I promised his mother."

Daigon reddened. "I am no boy, grandmother."

"Pish!"

As unnerved as she was at the thought that she was staring at a ghost, Rhiannon had trouble accepting it. It was hard to doubt, though, that the woman stood in the place of mother considering the way she spoke to Daigon--and his response. She bit her lip in amusement. "You should not speak so disrespectfully to your grandmother," she chided him.

He turned a dark glance upon her, but after a moment a gleam of amusement replaced it. Ignoring the old woman, he caught her arms and dragged her against his chest, dipping his head to silence her with a leisurely kiss that made her temperature rise.

"You should wait till you're wed, else she'll be dropping your heir before a decent interval."

Breaking the kiss reluctantly, Daigon murmured, "Go away, Zella. Rhiannon and I have much to--discuss."

She sniffed. "It won't bother me. In my time we knew how to have fun."

"Old pervert!" he muttered, dragging kisses along Rhiannon's throat.

"Fine, randy young buck! But don't say I didn't warn you! A pretty sight she'll be waltzing down the aisle with a swollen belly. I'll just go see if Climaus managed to break your spell in time to save his winkled old hide. If he wants to duel, I'm game."

Daigon broke off long enough to fix his grandmother with a glare. "I don't suppose it's possible to send you back?"

She snorted, but then smiled wickedly. "You'll figure it out--eventually. You always do."

The End

BLOOD MOON

Prologue

The persistent, escalating commotion in the courtyard finally roused Aslyn from sleep. Alarm should have jolted her awake, should have galvanized her into instant action. At any other time, her mind would instantly have responded to the sounds that could mean nothing but danger. Instead, a heaviness pervaded her senses, as if she'd drank too much wine or mead.

Her sluggish mind connected with that thought, meandering along it until she recalled the celebration the night before. Her father had announced her betrothal to Wilhem of Leitsey Marr.

She had been reasonably satisfied with her father's choice of husband. He was an older man, nearing thirty, but not so old that she felt repelled by his age, and he had attained some note as a warrior. He was not hard on the eyes, either, for which she was grateful.

Twenty-six did seem a little old to a fifteen-year-old girl, particularly since she'd hoped to make a match nearer her own age, but she was certain she had not imbibed more than she should have, either from excessive delight or anxiety.

The direction of her thoughts finally roused her sufficiently that she pushed herself upright and looked around. The tower room was dark still, barely lighter than it had been when she'd doused the candles and climbed into her bed the night before. The sun could not have risen.

Why then did it seem the entire keep was aroused and moving about as if they were well into the new day's activities?

As she was striving to puzzle through it, she realized she was covered in a chilled, sticky wetness. She looked down at herself then and a new wave of confusion swept over her.

She was nude. What had happened to her gown? More importantly, what was the substance she was coated with?

Her hands, her entire body was splotched with the sticky residue. She held out her hands, peering at them in the dim light. Slowly, her eyes focused. Slowly the dark patches attained a rusty hue.

Blood.

Her heart lurched painfully in her chest. Stumbling from the bed, she staggered toward the reflecting glass that was perched upon her dressing table.

Streaks of the same sticky substance smeared her forehead and cheeks. It was concentrated, however, around her mouth and throat. Instinctively, her hand went to her throat.

It wasn't hers. She had no injury.

She stared at her hands, her arms, looked down at her body in dawning horror, trying to grapple with possibilities.

How could she be soaked in blood when she was not injured?

Some nameless fear seized her and she stumbled to the wash stand. Dashing water from the ewer into the basin, she began scrubbing herself frantically. She had to get rid of it. She had to remove the evidence....

She broke off the thought, paused in her task. The evidence of what?

She couldn't grasp it. She couldn't seem to move beyond the need to bathe. Dismissing it, she concentrated on cleansing herself. When she'd finished, she stared down at the filmy water in revulsion, realizing she could not leave it for the maids to find. Lifting the basin, she stumbled awkwardly with her heavy burden to the window, then set it down on the floor to unfasten the scraped hide that covered the opening.

Below, chaos reined. People were dashing hither and yon; women screamed; horses reared as her father's guard fought to bring them under control; the dogs from the kennel bayed as if they had the scent of death in their nostrils.

Aslyn grasped the bowl and tossed the contents from the window.

She'd barely done so when her door exploded inward with a force that slammed the wooden portal back against the stone wall with a sharp crack of splintering wood.

"Lady Aslyn! Oh! Thank the saints you are here and unharmed!"

Aslyn stared at her nurse wide eyed. "Where else would I be at this hour?"

The nurse burst into wails. “My lady! My lady! I don’t know how to tell you this terrible thing!”

A wave of dizziness washed over Aslyn. “My father?”

“No, no! My poor child! I did not mean to frighten you for your father! And your mother gone these many years, I know how dear he is to you. I should have thought! I should have realized....”

Aslyn strode toward the woman, grasped her shoulders, and gave her a shake. “Cease your babbling and tell me! You are frightening me to death! What has happened?”

“Your betrothed! Lord Wilhem, my lady! He has been found....” The nurse broke off, clutching her chest, gasping.

“For mercy’s sake, tell me. Do not leave me to wonder what ill has befallen us. I shall go mad! Has he attacked us? Has he fallen ill? What?”

The nurse clutched her, her fingers curled like claws, digging in to Aslyn’s flesh painfully. “It’s horrible. I shall carry the image to my grave. Some beast fell upon him last eve and ... and it must have been a wild beast or some evil thing. No man could have done to him what was done. I would not have recognized him but for the ring he wears. His face was torn away, his body ripped apart, his entrails scattered, as if wild dogs had fallen upon him and fought over his remains.”

Aslyn felt the strength leave her knees. She wilted to the floor, her thoughts chaotic.

One thought pounded through her mind over and over, however. The blood-- She had been covered in blood and she had no idea how she had come to be covered in blood.

She very much feared, however, that she might remember.

Chapter One

The dream was the same as it had always been, so far back into her memory that she could not remember when it had first crept into her sleeping mind to frighten her. She was a young child. She knew this somehow, though she had no idea of how old she was, small enough to hide under the benches in the great hall and creep away unnoticed ... less than five, she was certain. She was afraid and triumphant at the same time. She'd escaped nurse's watchful eye. She'd managed to slip through the garden and out the postern gate.

Someone had left the gate ajar and the outside world beckoned. Her sense of happy adventure had lasted until she realized she was lost. When had the meadow given way to wooded lands? She couldn't seem to remember anything except that she had chased a rabbit, round and round, enjoying the pursuit and far more interested in running that in actually catching the poor creature.

She heard voices calling to her. They were fearful, angry. There were many voices, as if everyone from the keep had come to look for her. The idea frightened her almost as much as the fact that she was lost. She didn't want to be punished. Instead of answering them, she ran and hid. As she crouched beneath the tangle of brush, however, darkness began creeping through the leaves of the trees, closing around her.

Finally, her fear of the dark woods had overcome her fear of punishment. She'd crawled from hiding, begun to run toward the voices that still called her name, though anger had given way to their own fears. Even as she ran, however, she heard the voices become louder, closer--she realized that something was running behind her, giving chase as she had pursued the rabbit before. Quite suddenly, it had bounded from the brush and pounced upon her, knocking her to the ground, its sharp teeth bared in a snarl, its golden eyes gleaming in the light of the full moon.

She threw up her hand in an effort to protect herself. Pain flooded through her as she felt its teeth sink into her flesh. She screamed in terror and kept on screaming as the pain filled her shocked mind.

Aslyn woke, still caught in the grips of her nightmare, still struggling to scream.

As it slowly faded, she realized she was cold, so cold her teeth were chattering. Dazed, her mind still sluggish, it took her some moments to assimilate where she was.

With the dread of recognition, her gaze finally focused upon her hands, curled inward toward her palm, almost like claws. They were bloody. She needed no mirror to tell her that her face and neck were covered with it, as well. She'd shifted in the night, fed upon ... some hapless prey. The time of the moon was upon her.

Shuddering, she rolled over, sat up abruptly and looked around. She was naked, lying in the snow. Small wonder she felt as if she would freeze to death.

There was no escaping the nightmare world she had descended into in her fifteenth year, although, in the beginning, she had lied to herself that she would find a way.

Fearful that she would harm someone she cared for, or that those who loved her would discover her affliction and be forced to destroy her, she'd fled her home after the death of her betrothed. But she had told herself that she would discover a cure. She would find a way to lift the curse, or affliction--she wasn't even certain of which it was. Over the past three years since her quest had begun, she had acquired a good deal of knowledge in the healing arts, and even discovered others on her own, but she had never come close to curing her own malady.

Each time the moon waxed full, the madness seized her. She wasn't certain whether it was a blessing or a curse that she could never remember what she'd done. She remembered feeling a darkness churning to life within her as she gazed up at the full moon, a throbbing to life of something primal--and then she remembered nothing more, awaking each time naked and bloody and certain only that she had savagely killed again.

In truth, she supposed it was both blessing and curse. It was hard enough to deal with the knowledge that she had killed without having to bear the weight of the memory of the kill. And yet, how was she to find a cure when she didn't know with any degree of certainty what was happening? Somewhere in the knowledge that eluded her lay a piece of the puzzle. She was as certain of that as she was certain that the nightmares that had plagued her these many years were not nightmares at all, but memories.

Whatever had happened to the child she had been was at the root of her curse.

Forced from her contemplation finally by physical distress, Aslyn focused on scrubbing the blood from herself with snow. There was no water and in any case she was half frozen already. Using snow would not make her any colder. She had to rid herself of the blood before the stench made her ill.

It was far from ideal, however, in the sense that it was impossible to cleanse herself thoroughly with the icy crystals. Finally, satisfied that she'd removed as much of the drying blood as she would be able to until she found running water, she stumbled to her feet and looked around.

Scraggly, winter bare trees dotted the area around her. Here and there a craggy knob of rock poked through the white blanket, however. She frowned. She'd sought shelter in a cave when the snow had begun to fall. Turning in a slow circle, she finally spied a dark crevice some little distance from where she now stood. Relief flooded her. She'd returned to her burrow.

She had learned that she could, generally, count upon that, at the very least. Whatever madness seized her in the night and sent her scouting for a kill, she usually returned to whatever shelter she'd sought for herself when morning chased the night shadows away.

With an effort, she stumbled toward the narrow opening, tripping in the shifting, almost knee deep snow drifts. Her clothing littered the entrance of the tiny cave. Shivering, she lifted the coarse gown that lay closest to examine it.

There had been a time when the lowest scullery maid in her father's castle had worn more comely gowns that the one she now held, when nothing had touched her own skin save the finest of silks and satins. She had learned in the time since to be grateful only to cover herself.

However thankful the poor were for her services in healing their sick, they had little to give. Beyond that, she could not bring herself to accept more than what it took to survive. The work she did in healing others was a form of penitence for the evil she did when seized by the madness. She knew that it was her only hope of salvation for her soul.

Not surprisingly, she saw that the gown was ripped into tatters. It had been repaired many times, until it was a crisscross of stitches, but only a part of the repairs were from the normal wear and tear one could expect in so old an article of clothing. Her first act upon assuming her other form was to rend the clothes from her back. She had learned only to wear loose clothing. The more restrictive the gown, the less usable afterward. As if being trapped in clothing was sufficient to send her into a mad frenzy in and of itself, anything that could not be discarded with relative ease was shredded to ribbons by either razor sharp teeth, or claws, or perhaps both.

Sighing, she moved to the bundle that lay near the back of the cave, untied it and unrolled her 'second best' shift and gown. She could repair the other later. The moon had begun to wane. She was reasonably certain she was safe from her curse for a few weeks. Right now, she needed to dress herself and move on. She had made it a practice to move as far away from an area as possible after she'd killed.

Bundling her belongings, she wrapped her worn cloak tightly about her shoulders, pulled her hood close around her face and left the cave. To her relief, she discovered her boots within a few yards of the cave. One had somehow landed upright when she'd 'lost' it. It was filled with snow. She upended it, struck the sole to loosen the ice crystals. When she'd emptied it, she brushed the snow from one stocking, stood on one leg and tugged the boot on, then repeated the process with her other foot.

Her feet felt like blocks of ice.

If she were still human, frozen feet would mean more than discomfort.

But she had ceased to be human years ago.

* * * *

Aslyn had not traveled more than a mile when the distant wails of a distraught mother reached her. She froze, lifting her head to listen, turning slowly until she could distinguish the direction.

Her heart seemed to drop to her frozen feet and freeze itself into a hard, suffocating knot.

She hesitated. It would be wiser, she knew, to run the other way. Some instinct told her that she had more to do with the woman's grief than she ever wanted to know, that her evil deeds would catch up to her, at last, if she didn't flee while she had the chance.

She found that she couldn't.

She could not know that she was responsible. If she fled, without offering her services as a healer, then she would most assuredly be guilty.

Hurrying toward the sound now with a sense of urgency, she came upon a small rise. When she'd struggled up it and reached the summit, she saw that she was looking down upon a narrow road. Debris littered the rutted track behind a cart that lay drunkenly upon its side. An ox, struggling to right itself, added its own mournful bellows in counterpoint to the woman's wails. The woman, Aslyn saw, was sitting on a bank of snow nearby, a child clutched to her breast, rocking back and forth.

Relief flooded Aslyn. It was an accident then, not some horror of her own making.

She stumbled as she hurried down the slope, nearly falling flat, but managed to catch herself. "Madam," she called a little breathlessly as she neared the woman. "What has befallen? Is the child ill?"

The wails ceased as abruptly as if they'd been choked from the woman by a tight fist. Her head whipped around, stark terror in her eyes. It faded slowly as she focused upon Aslyn. "She's dying. She's wounded unto death. My poor babe. My sweet angel."

Aslyn reached the woman, grasped her shoulder. "Let me see her. I'm a healer. Perhaps I can help."

The woman sniffed, studied her suspiciously. "You are young to be a healer. You are scarcely more than a child yourself."

Aslyn's lips tightened. "Nevertheless, I know my craft. I have been practicing for several years now, learned the secrets of the herbs when I was but a child in truth. What have you to lose by allowing me to see to the child's hurts?"

Reluctantly, the woman loosened her grip on the infant. Aslyn whipped her cloak from her shoulders, folded it and laid it upon the snow, then took the baby and lay it carefully on her cloak. "What happened?" she asked as she checked the child's injuries, noting with a great deal of concern that, while the child still breathed, its heartbeat was faint.

A sob tore from the woman's throat. "A beast attacked us. It was not good day ... still too dark to see clearly. I scarcely caught a glimpse of it, but I think it was a wolf."

Fear clutched Aslyn's heart. She felt the blood drain from her face in a dizzying rush. "A wolf, you say? The child's not been bitten. I can see no signs."

The woman shook her head. "Nay! It attacked the ox. The poor thing was terrorized and bolted, crashing the cart. I tried to shield the baby, but she was ripped from my arms when we struck the boulder and flew from the cart."

Aslyn nodded, checking the child's head carefully with her fingers. A knot the size of a goose egg had risen on the baby's forehead, but she could not detect any other injuries to the head. She carefully rolled the baby onto its side and ran her fingertips along its spine, checking each tiny vertebrae. They seemed intact. She could not detect any notable breaks, at any rate. Until, or unless, the baby awoke, she could not be sure the child had not injured her spine or neck.

She sat back and glanced around. She hated to expose the child to the elements, even to check her injuries, but she saw no hope for it. There was no shelter. She looked at the woman, who seemed more in possession of herself now. "Gather close and spread your cloak so as to block the wind as much as possible. I must undress the baby to examine her and I don't want her to catch a chill."

The girl child woke as Aslyn unwrapped its swaddling and removed its gown. The child's mother made an abortive movement to gather it into her arms once more, but Aslyn forestalled her. "No. It will cause her no harm to cry. She should not be moved again, however, until I have determined if she has broken any bones. The crying is a good sign. Such strong, lusty wails could mean she is not so badly injured as you thought."

It could also mean she was in terrible pain, but Aslyn didn't voice those thoughts aloud. She closed her mind to that anxiety and concentrated on the task at hand. Bruising had already begun to develop. She counted a half a dozen that looked fresh enough to be the results of the crash. Except for the knot on the baby's head, however, none seemed swollen, nor could she detect any other areas that had swollen, indicating deeper injury. The child's frantic wriggling seemed to belie the possibility of broken bones.

Aslyn dressed the child once more and carefully wrapped her. She smiled faintly as she handed the wailing child to its mother. "I do not believe she has sustained lasting hurt. You must watch her closely throughout the day, however." She removed her pouch and carefully spread it upon the cloak, examining the herbs in the tiny bundles inside and selecting small portions of several. These she bundled together in a small scrap of cloth. "If she appears dazed or confused, sleepy when she should not be, in any way not her usual self, powder these herbs, take one fourth of them and feed them to her in a cup of tea or warmed milk. I do not believe you will need it, but it is better to be safe than sorry."

The woman nodded and took the pouch. "This is for...?"

"Swelling. If her brain has been bruised, it could swell and ... cause her to be very ill. These herbs are known to reduce swelling and should help. But do not give her anything at all unless she seems strange to you. It is not a good idea to give medicine where it is not needed."

A look of fear flickered through the woman's eyes, but she nodded jerkily that she'd understood.

Aslyn rose a little stiffly, shook her cloak out and donned it once more, carefully pulling her hood over her head, as much to hide the red hair she despised as to ward off the wind.

The child's wails had quieted to a snuffling whimper as her mother put her to her breast to pacify her. "What do I owe you?"

Aslyn glanced down at the woman. "Nothing."

The woman shook her head, a look of obstinateness hardening her features. "We are poor, but we are not beggars. My man will insist upon paying you for your services when he returns."

Aslyn glanced around the area.

"He ran after the beast. He will be back soon, likely with the dead beast. We have no money," she added. "But I can at least offer you something to chase away the chill. For the rest, we can haggle on something at a later time."

"That I will gladly accept," Aslyn said, smiling. "But I offered no charity. The babe was not in need of my attention. I did nothing but look at her. What do you call her?"

Pulling the babe from her breast, the woman held the child up and bounced her slightly, smiling. A look of uncertainty crossed her features, whether because her tit had been so rudely taken, or because she didn't care for the sense of falling, it was difficult to tell. "She is called Bess. Aren't you, my beauty?"

Bess offered her mother a wavering smile. Her mother's smile widened to a grin.

She tucked the child close to her again, settling her in a sling of fabric tied crosswise around her neck and over one shoulder. When she was certain the baby was secure, she smiled at Aslyn. "I am Enid. Come 'round to this side of the cart. Perhaps it'll block a bit of the wind and I can get a fire started."

Aslyn wanted to be on her way. However, she could not dash off into the wilderness without arousing unwanted suspicions. She subdued her sense of urgency to depart, went to gather some sticks, and helped Enid to build a small fire. Relief had loosened the woman's tongue. Or, perhaps, she was merely starved for company. She chattered animatedly as she set up a small tripod over the fire and set a tin packed with snow over it to boil for tea. As she moved to the cart and dug out a couple of earthen mugs and a jar that contained, Aslyn supposed, the promised tea, she explained to Aslyn that she and her husband had been on their way into the small, nearby town of Krackensled in hopes of finding shelter there for the winter. They had a tiny farm, but, naturally, could do little with it in winter time. Ordinarily, they would merely have settled themselves in for the winter and waited for spring thaw, but there were rumors going about that had made them uneasy enough they'd decided to seek safety in town.

Aslyn's brows rose. "Rumors of what sort? I confess I've not heard much news of late, but ... our land has not been invaded?"

The woman crossed herself. "Don't even say such. It tempts the fates. Nay. Wolves. Not more than a month ago a stranger passed through and told us there'd been attacks, and not only upon livestock. And then, only a few days ago, our nearest neighbor came huffing up to our door at dawn, white as death, and babbling about some great beast trying to tear his door down and set upon him and his family. I decided right then that that was enough for me, but Jim--that's my husband--he wasn't so easy to convince. I suppose he's convinced now, though," she finished, looking pleased about the matter as she handed Aslyn a cup of the tea she'd brewed.

Aslyn took it and glanced at their wrecked cart. "I would think so."

"Where are you off to then?"

Caught off guard, Aslyn stared at the woman blankly a moment.

"You said you'd not heard the rumors." She paused, frowning, then looked around as if she'd only just then realized that Aslyn was alone. "And traveling alone? That seems a bit strange, even for a healer."

Aslyn stared into her tea, trying to quiet her pounding pulse. "I'm on pilgrimage. I travel with others as I can. Only this morning, I parted company with the group I'd been traveling with, for they were headed west and I north."

The woman nodded, apparently satisfied. "You should come with us. It isn't at all safe to travel alone just now. And lone travelers this far north are like to be viewed with suspicion. Not so likely when you're a woman, but still.... We could introduce you around. I know for a certainty they've no healer in Krackensled. The old woman, Gershin, died nigh six months ago. We heard of it the last time we were there."

Aslyn looked at her, torn. In truth, she would have far preferred to part company with the woman altogether, but she was weary from her travels and needed to find a place to stay for a while. She would have to move on before the moon completed another cycle, but the chance to rest awhile, and the comfort of a cottage were too great to resist. "You don't know me. I couldn't ask it of you," she said a little hesitantly.

"You didn't, did you?" Enid responded tartly. "I offered. Besides, I figure one good turn deserves another. Anyway, I can see you've a good heart."

Aslyn might have argued further, but she was distracted by the sounds of approaching riders. Enid looked up, as well, rose slowly to look down the road. "Soldiers," she gasped, her eyes widening. "The king's men by their banner. Should we hide, do you think?"

Aslyn moved a little closer to the woman. "Too late," she murmured. The riders were already bearing down upon them and had almost certainly spotted them. They couldn't outrun mounted horsemen in deep snow anyway, no matter how fleet of foot and, in any case, Enid was burdened by her child. Aslyn would have little chance. Enid none at all. As strong as the urge to flee was, Aslyn found she simply could not run off and abandon the woman.

The man leading the group was not dressed as a soldier but rather wore the garb of huntsman. Long and leanly muscular, his build seemed to bear up the image of hunter. She had no difficulty imagining such a man moving invisibly through the forest.

His face, she saw as he came closer, was long and lean, as well, his strong jaw clean shaven, but she could see that the long hair fluttering about his face was dark as sin. He was a man of good birth, no commoner, regardless of his garb. Or, perhaps, he claimed bastardy. She didn't believe it. His bearing alone proclaimed pride and self-confidence, traits no bastard would possess. This man had secrets ... and eyes that would not miss the secrets others might wish to guard. He bore the unmistakable look of a predator.

Chapter Two

Enid cried out quite suddenly. "Jim? What's happened?"

Aslyn glanced quickly at Enid, then transferred her gaze to the oncoming riders once more. It was only then that she realized one of the horses was mounted double.

"Now, don't start yer wailing, love. It's scarce more'n a scratch. Tripped over a bleeding root and caught meself in the leg with me own arrow, fool that I am," Jim reassured her as the riders drew abreast of them.

Enid, apparently, wasn't convinced. Shoving the baby at Aslyn, she rushed over even before the horses had been drawn to a complete standstill, grasping at his leg worriedly, as if she could lift him from the horse.

Aslyn remained as she was, frozen to the spot, her gaze held captive by the huntsman's golden-eyed stare. He nodded slightly, but his hard mouth did not so much as twitch on the verge of a smile as he released her at last from captivity, turning his attention to the soldiers milling around him. "You men--dismount and see if you can get their cart righted."

Without a word, the men dismounted almost in unison. The one who had been riding with Jim on his horse's rump helped Jim down before dismounting himself. The youth among them, who looked to be a squire, gathered the reins of all the horses and led them far enough off the road to secure them, then returned to help his five fellows. After a moment, the huntsman dismounted, as well, and went to help Enid, who was struggling under her husband's weight ... as well she might, for Enid's Jim was a bear of a man.

Shaking herself from her stupor at last, Aslyn followed them, knowing her services would be needed. Jim groaned as he was helped to sit with his back against a tree. At a glance, Aslyn could see that he'd lost a great deal of blood. The leg of his breeches was soaked with it.

Her heart thudded dully in her chest. She had to fight her reluctance to approach him. She should not have been so squeamish about blood, all things considered, but the fact was her own experiences had made her more repelled by the sight, not less so.

"Who be ye?" he said in a growling voice that matched his size as she knelt beside him.

Aslyn met his suspicious gaze with a cool look of her own. She was accustomed to it, but she hated the suspicions always cast in her direction.

"This is Aslyn, love. She's a healer. She came to help when she heard me crying about Bess." She turned a beseeching gaze upon Aslyn. "You can help him, can't you?"

"Phsaw! I've no need of a healer, an' especially not one so young as she. Find something to wrap me up, love ... and bring me a bit of the good stuff, just to warm me bones."

"You will bleed to death if the wound isn't closed."

Enid looked as if she might faint at Aslyn's words. Her hand flew to her mouth to stifle a gasp. The man glared at her. "If ye think frightening the wits out of me woman is the way to convince me to let ye have a go at me, yer dead wrong."

"Don't be more of a fool than you need be," the huntsman said coldly. "Allow the woman to attend your wound."

To Aslyn's amazement, Jim looked cowed. They were much of a height, but Jim was easily twice the bulk of the huntsman. She would not have thought he could be so easily intimidated by a man of the huntsman's stature. Or, perhaps it was not that at all. Perhaps it was the ingrained subservience of the lowborn toward those of higher birth and Jim sensed that in the huntsman even as Aslyn had?

Beyond that, there was something about the huntsman that unnerved her. Undoubtedly it was not merely her imagination, for Jim sensed it too.

Without another word, she stood to hand the baby to Enid and knelt beside the woman's fallen husband. Taking her knife from her pack, she slit the leg of his breeches from knee to hip so that she could get a better look at the wound.

"Here now! These are me good breeches!" Jim objected.

Aslyn allowed her gaze to meet his. "And your good wife can sew them up for your again."

"But they'll be patched," he muttered.

"They would be patched anyway, you great lummox! You've torn them already," Enid snapped. "Stop being so difficult!"

He yelped as Aslyn probed the wound. Aslyn gave him a look. "I'll be as gentle as I can, but it needs to be cleaned. If you've anything trapped inside the wound it could putrefy."

He studied her uneasily for several moments and finally nodded.

Aslyn pinched his leg, forcing the wound to gape. Blood welled to the surface. Jim groaned, gripped the ground on either side of him, but gritted his teeth.

Aslyn frowned in concentration as she peered into the gash. It was always difficult to tell whether foreign matter had been forced into a wound or not because of the blood. Torn tissue looked very little different than bloodied cloth, but Aslyn thought she saw a fragment of cloth from his breeches. Releasing him, she took her pouch of medicines from her belt and laid it out, selecting a long needle. Jim eyed the sharp needle with obvious misgivings. In the next moment, however, he had squeezed his eyes shut and uttered another growl of pain as Aslyn dug around in the wound, removing a fairly large piece of fabric and a number of splinters from the arrow. Finally satisfied, she laid the needle aside and began scooping up snow. Jim let out a yelp the moment she placed the packed ice on his leg.

"What're you doin' now, woman? Tryin' to freeze me ballocks off?" he demanded irritably.

"You'll have no need for them if you're dead," Aslyn said coolly, continuing until she'd packed ice all around his leg. "This will slow the bleeding."

She rose when she was done, took her needle, moved to the tin of boiling water and dropped it in. Removing the tin from the fire, she moved back to the tree where Jim sat and set the tin on the ground next to him.

"What'd you do that for?" Jim asked suspiciously.

"To clean the needle."

"Ye didn't clean it before you poked me with it."

"I always clean it. It's not been touched since the last time I used it ... and cleaned it."

After a few minutes, she began removing the snow. The wound was still bleeding sluggishly, but she was satisfied that no large vein could have been ruptured, else it would have continued to bleed profusely. She reached into the tin and grasped the needle.

When she turned to thread it, she saw that both Enid and Jim were gaping at her, their faces pictures of fright. "Are you a witch, then?" Enid asked breathlessly.

"No."

"Then how'd ye do that?" Jim demanded. "Your fingers aren't burned. I can see that."

"The snow," Aslyn said with determined patience. "My skin was too cold from handling the snow for the water to burn. Try it yourself, if you doubt me."

He didn't looked convinced, or as if he had any desire to test her words. In any case, he forgot all about the incident when he saw that she was threading the needle. "Here now. I'll not be needing that! Look, it's stopped bleeding. All I need is a rag tied about it."

"If it's not closed. It will continue to bleed and it will be too easy for something to enter the wound. It'll be best if it's closed."

Aslyn's nerves were on edge by the time she'd sewn the flesh together. It was an unpleasant task at the best of times, and Jim made no bones about trying to be manful about the thing, yelping each time the needle was plunged into his skin, growling, groaning with pain as the thread was pulled taut. Aslyn was forced to conclude that he hadn't been brave about his wound so much as he was fearful of having it treated. Men were such infants about their hurts.

When she'd finished, she took a clean strip of cloth, sprinkled herbs on it to ward off putrefaction, and bound it snugly around his wound. It was only when she turned to retrieve the tin that she discovered the huntsman stood nearby, watching her every movement. She wondered if he'd been observing her the whole time she attended Jim.

What had he expected? That she would prove herself totally incompetent? Or that she would deliberately harm the man?

With an effort, she pretended she hadn't noticed his rapt attention and took the tin, moving back to the fire.

To her consternation, he followed her. He knelt on the opposite side of the fire as she scooped up fresh snow and set it to boil so that she could clean her needle again. "I am called Kale," he said, lifting his gaze from her hands to her face and studying her with a piercing, unnerving stare that Aslyn could feel even without looking at him.

She allowed her gaze to flicker to his face when he spoke. Up close, she saw that her observations as he'd arrived had not done him justice. She'd had the perception that he was well favored, but assumed, as is quite often the case, that distance had lent him more comeliness than he actually possessed. At a distance, one could not observe the little flaws that could make a world of difference in whether or not one actually was pleasing to the eye.

She saw now that, although his face was harshly angular, he was exceptionally well favored. In the days before, she would have been filled with maidenly confusion and pleasure if she had drawn the attention of such a man.

The interest she drew now made her heart flutter uncomfortably, but she rather thought it was more fear than excitement.

His eyes were golden. She'd never seen eyes that color ... on a human. Perhaps it was the eyes, so near in shade to any number of predators, that lent him the look of one?

"I am Aslyn."

"You are a stranger here?"

She'd had no choice but to admit she was a stranger to Enid, knowing it was too risky to do otherwise when the woman was obviously a local. She was far more reluctant to admit it to the king's man. A huntsman did not commonly lead a band of soldiers. She didn't like to think what the purpose of this group might be. And yet, she had no option, not now, not when Enid and Jim had already indicated they had no knowledge of her.

"I am a pilgrim."

"Traveling from where? To where?"

She debated briefly, but knew it would be better to offer a lie freely, than to pretend outrage at his intrusion into her private affairs. "From Mersea ... eventually to return once I have fulfilled my pilgrimage."

A gleam entered his eyes, briefly and then disappeared so abruptly Aslyn wondered if she had imagined that spark of keen interest at the mention of her origins. One dark brow arched. The other descended. "You are young to begin a pilgrimage, alone."

"Perhaps I am older than I appear?"

His gaze wandered over her face, making Aslyn wish she had pulled the hood of her cloak closer. She sensed the shadows it offered yielded little protection from that piercing stare. "You are not a day above eighteen. Your husband did not object to being left to care for your babes while you went on pilgrimage?"

Despite all she could do, Aslyn's eyes widened in surprise that he'd pinpointed her age so precisely. The hardships she'd endured should have put more age upon her face than that. "I am not wed. There are no babes."

"Why?"

Again, he surprised her. "Why?" she echoed. "I am supposed to know why I was not chosen as bride?"

His eyes narrowed. It wasn't just that he doubted her word. She sensed he didn't like the answer, though she was at a loss to know why. "A beautiful woman has more suitors than she has need of. Try again. The truth this time."

Aslyn blushed. She wasn't certain whether it was because of the compliment, or because he'd so easily seen through the lie. "I did not realize this was an interrogation," she said stiffly, evasively.

An expression, almost of amusement, crossed his features. "You were never in any doubt of it."

That was certainly to the point. Any doubts Aslyn might have nursed that his curiosity was out of a personal interest were neatly disposed of. Aslyn felt her blush deepen. "My betrothed ... died," she responded tightly.

He frowned. A look, almost of anger, flickered in his eyes. Obviously, he did not care for her answer. "And it is for this reason you went on pilgrimage?"

Flustered, Aslyn burned her finger when she dropped the needle into the water, which had begun to boil at last. Instinctively, she shoved the injured finger in her mouth. When she looked at Kale once more, she saw that his gaze had been drawn by the action to her mouth. The look in his eyes sent something warm and liquid flowing through her, wreaking further havoc within her.

She snatched her throbbing finger from her mouth and shoved it into the snow. "Mostly, yes," she said, responding at last to his question.

His gaze, she saw with a good deal of discomfort, had not left her lips. Slowly, as if it was an effort to pull himself away, his gaze moved up her face and locked with her own.

"So ... you crossed the channel to make pilgrimage through a foreign land ... instead of your own."

Aslyn looked down at her finger, examining it, though she knew the burn was as nothing. "No. I traveled within my own country, and *then* crossed the channel."

Amusement lit his features, gleaming in his eyes. "One must wonder what you could have done that would make you feel the need for such an extensive pilgrimage."

Aslyn didn't know how to respond to that. Thankfully, she was not required to. The squire approached them to report that they'd managed to right the cart and repair it enough for travel.

The huntsman rose abruptly. "We should be on our way then and see if we can pick up the trail."

Chapter Three

The cart was full almost to overflowing with family and household goods by the time the soldiers had helped Jim and his wife onto it. Enid turned to smile at Aslyn. "Find yourself a spot on the back."

Aslyn looked at the cart doubtfully. "Thank you, but I believe I'll walk beside the cart."

Aslyn was acutely conscious of the party of men behind them, watching their departure. She was not aware of Kale, however, until he swept her off her feet. Stunned, she stared up at him, her mouth slightly agape as he strode toward the creeping cart and deposited her on a mound of linens in the back.

Without a word, he turned, strode back to his horse and mounted. Pulling the horses about, the group departed in the same direction from whence they'd come. Aslyn watched until they became black specks and finally disappeared over a rise.

The 'town' of Krackensled, Aslyn saw as the cart slowly rumbled up the main thoroughfare, was little more than a large village, though it boasted a maze of crisscrossing roads lined with cottages and a few shops, and as poverty stricken as the majority of the bergs she had seen in her travels. She had learned to expect it. She had not learned to accept it.

Her nurse had often tried to impress upon her that life was not fair, that one should not expect it to be. Fairness was a concept of civilized man that directly opposed the laws of nature. Nature randomly selected individuals and gifted them with beauty, or superior strength or intelligence ... or not. Those with superior strength and/or cleverness, had long since established dominance for their line in the days when true civilization was born. Everyone else was left to scramble for survival.

The rich inherited wealth. The poor inherited more babies, to make them more poor still, except, perhaps, in joy or love. But, however joyful the occasion of a new addition to the family, Aslyn found it difficult to believe the joy could outlast the toil required to rear them or the heartache of burying them, as was so often the case with the poor.

That was not to say, of course, that the poor were passed over when nature bestowed beauty, superior strength or intelligence. She'd seen enough to dispel the prejudices of wealth and privilege she'd been born to. It was merely that those who were fortunate enough to receive those attributes in poverty found them more a curse than a gift. Her own poverty since she'd fled her home had taught her that lesson.

Without the protection of wealth and position, a beautiful girl only became prey for the privileged. The strong were reduced to the status of beast of burden and the intelligent were left to rot in ignorance.

Life was, most assuredly, not fair.

Despite the size of the town, the streets were almost deserted. Aslyn wondered if this was due to the season's inclement weather, the rumors Enid had told her of, or merely typical of the town, which, in truth, did not seem large enough to attract a great deal of commerce. The few people they passed on the road stopped, watching the slow progress of the cart.

Aslyn had learned to gauge the desirability of remaining in a town by the expressions she encountered on the way in. Towns seemed to have a life essence of their own. Some gave one the feeling of welcome. As often as not, they gave one the feeling that one's departure would be more welcome.

Krackensled seemed to fall somewhere between the two. The expressions of those they passed were neither sullen, nor friendly. They were mildly curious or reserved.

Aslyn interpreted that to mean that it would be safe enough to stay for a short time and that, if she had arrived alone, it would not have been.

Jim pulled the cart to a stop beside a rickety shack near the very edge of town. It looked as if it had been abandoned for some time. With an effort, she struggled down from her perch and looked around as Jim and Enid did the same. "The healer, Gershin, lived here. I thought, if you were satisfied with it, I could talk to the landlord for you and see if he would agree to the same terms he'd had with Gershin."

It looked dismal, but beggars could not be chosers. "Do you know the terms?"

Enid shrugged. "Most likely service for his family and a tithe of what you earn in service to others."

Aslyn nodded. She'd expected as much. "That sounds reasonable enough. Are you certain you don't mind the task? I could speak to him myself."

Enid shook her head. "Likely as not, he'd try to gouge you. We owe you as it is and I expect you'll need to look in on Jim again. If you'd be willing to accept it as part of what we owe...?"

Aslyn smiled, relieved by the offer. In her past experience, landlords had been inclined to consider they might as well barter for 'special' favors while they were about it, as soon as they discovered she was unwed and traveling without a companion. "Certainly."

As Enid turned her steps toward the heart of town, Jim jogged the ox into motion, turned the cart down a narrow alley and disappeared beyond a structure almost as ramshackle as the one that had belonged to Gershin. Aslyn caught a glimpse of him and the cart once more as he reached a road that ran parallel to the one where she stood and turned back toward the heart of town. She supposed they'd settled it between them that Jim would take their belongings to begin unloading while Enid made arrangements.

Aslyn turned to survey her new domain. It looked worse than any of the other cottages that lined the dirt packed road, but only by a little. Sighing, she made her way to the door. It was not locked, but the wood had swollen with moisture and was no doubt sealed with ice, as well. She'd battered bruises on her shoulder before she managed to pry the door open sufficiently to squeeze inside. Without any light source, the interior should have looked much like the cave she'd sheltered in the night before, for the house had been constructed of sod and thatch and boasted not a single window. Unfortunately, there were more than a few unplanned 'lights,' allowing sufficient illumination for her to make out the contents.

Without surprise, she saw that it consisted of only one room. A few rickety pieces of furniture littered the space. In the far back was a cot ... no doubt crawling with vermin. Aslyn debated briefly with herself, but decided she was confident that Enid would prevail in her negotiations with the landlord. That being the case, she saw no reason to wait upon word when she could be working at making the place a bit more comfortable.

Moving back to the door, she peered at the hinges and discovered the leather was rotted on the upper hinge. It had begun to separate, allowing the door to sag. Lifting up on the door, she opened it wide to let in more light and, hopefully, allow some of the musty odors trapped inside to escape.

She was reluctant even to touch the mattress, but she most certainly had no intention of using it until it had been thoroughly aired. Grasping one end, she lifted it from the rope frame. Expecting it to be heavy with moisture and probably rotting straw, Aslyn discovered that the mattress, no doubt filled with down, was surprisingly light. Having braced herself for more weight than she'd encountered, Aslyn staggered back a couple of steps as the down filled bedding flew toward her, tripped over something lying on the dirt packed floor, and landed on her rump so hard it jarred the pins from her hair so that they tumbled around her shoulders.

A snicker greeted her mishap.

She turned to glare at the intruder and her heart skipped several beats. A man stood in the open portal, blocking much of the light. She needed none, however. His armor was enough to tell her two things: he was a stranger; and he was a knight, which meant he was a potential threat. She got up with as much dignity as she could muster. "May I help you?" she asked coolly.

"I was told I might find the healer here. Might you be her daughter? Or have I the wrong cottage?"

A patient ... already? Aslyn grasped her hair and quickly coiled it at the base of her skull once more, jabbing pins into it to hold it in place. Smoothing her skirts, she stepped forward. "I am the healer."

He stepped inside, dwarfing the tiny cottage. "I hadn't expected...."

Aslyn ground her teeth but cut him off before he could voice doubts regarding her skill due to her tender years. "Neither had I expected anyone to arrive so soon. I am not even settled in, having arrived in Krackensled less than an hour ago. Is your need urgent? If not, perhaps you could return at a later time, when I've had a chance to settle in?"

"Alas, dear lady, I am afraid it cannot wait. If it were for myself I would gladly wait upon your convenience. My man, I fear, cannot."

Aslyn's shoulders slumped. She glanced around the tiny cottage, but it did not magically appear clean, and, save for the dirt floor, there was no place for his man to lie so that she could attend him. On the other hand, if she attended him outside, like as not, he would be lying upon the snow. "You can bring him in here. I'll need some light. I've not a candle to my name, nor lantern, nor even torch."

He nodded and stepped outside again. In a few moments, the door was blocked once more, this time by three shadows, two men carrying a third. It took some maneuvering to negotiate the narrow doorway, but finally they laid the injured man upon the floor and departed. The knight entered as they left, carrying a torch. After looking around the room and discovering there were no brackets to receive it, he shrugged and held it so that it fell upon his man's chalk white features.

Aslyn knelt beside the injured man. He was unconscious, and bloody from head to foot. It was impossible to even tell where the blood was coming from. "What happened?"

The knight shrugged. "We found him thus at first light. He'd been left on watch."

"This morn?" Aslyn demanded, aghast. "And he has not been attended ... at all?"

Again, the knight shrugged. "There were none among us with knowledge of healing. We brought him here because it was the closest town."

The man was dead. At a guess, he had been for some time. "There was none among you who knew how to plug a hole?" Aslyn asked tightly.

To her chagrin, the knight grinned suggestively. "Indeed, every man of us will avow to a good deal of skill in ... uh ... plugging holes, but it makes the task easier when it's surrounded by a thatch of hair."

Aslyn blushed fierily, but only a little of it was due to his frankly sexual remark. Primarily, she was furious, both at his cavalier attitude toward 'his man' and because not one among them had taken the time to bind the man's wounds. He might well have died anyway, but he had not even had the chance to live. She got to her feet. "I've no skill in resurrecting the dead. I'm afraid I can do nothing for him."

He looked down at the man dispassionately. "A pity."

She stared at the knight. It was a pity as far as she was concerned that the poor man had had the misfortune to be left to the knight's tender mercies. The knight was an attractive man, dark as the devil, but still somewhat above the ordinary in looks, and obviously of high birth. Perhaps that accounted for his callous disregard for the life of a low born soldier, but she found she could not credit that as being entirely the case. Plainly, he had no care for his fellow man, whatever their rank. He exuded a sense of superiority in every look, word and gesture that made it impossible to appreciate his good looks.

She shivered and looked away as the knight transferred his gaze from the dead man to her, unwilling to encourage the man's obviously overwhelming conceit by allowing him to interpret her gaze as an interest in him.

Stepping to the door, he summoned the men who'd brought the man in and told them to 'remove the carcass and find a place to plant it before it began to offend all and sundry by its stench.'

Aslyn's lips curled in distaste at the crass comment. She turned away, dismissing him as she returned to the task of setting the cottage to rights. The knight followed her, placed a heavy hand upon her shoulder. She glanced down at it, up at his face, and then moved away, turning to face him.

He held out a couple of coins. "For your trouble."

Aslyn stared at the coins, but she did not reach to take them. "I did nothing," she said dismissively. "More's the pity."

He dropped the coins on the rickety table. "For your inconvenience then." He looked around the cottage assessingly. "I am Algar of Remey. My men and I are camped nearby on the King's business. If you have need of our service, you need only send word ... Lady...?"

Aslyn's heart thudded dully with alarm. "I've no claim to the title of lady. I am Aslyn ... of Mersea."

His black brows rose. "And your husband? Is he about?"

Aslyn felt the blood leave her face. Any hope she'd nursed that he was only mildly curious vanished. His intentions became frighteningly obvious and he had blocked the only avenue of escape. "Not at the moment."

He laughed, moved toward her. Aslyn backed away, but he followed her step for step until she was pressed back against the sod wall with nowhere else to go. "I was told you were unwed. Why, I wonder, would you lie to me?" he murmured huskily.

"Because your attentions are unwelcome?" Aslyn responded coldly.

"Are they?" he asked with a mixture of amusement and disbelief.

"They are," Aslyn said tightly, wedging her hands between them and trying to push him away.

He lifted a mailed hand, running it lightly along the pulse pounding with fear in her throat. “This little flutter gives your lie away.”

It was on the tip of her tongue to inform him that it was most certainly not desire that sped her heartbeat, but another voice intruded at that moment.

“Fear and revulsion do not equal desire, Algar.”

The knight stiffened at the cold voice, the smile freezing on his face. Slowly, he turned toward the man standing in the doorway of the cottage. He stepped away from Aslyn, his body taut as he faced the man he obviously perceived as a threat. “Kale. What brings you here?”

Aslyn didn’t know whether she was more stunned or relieved at the huntsman’s timely arrival. Relief seemed uppermost. Still, she wondered at it. The knight had not been a part of the huntsman’s party when she’d seen him earlier on the road to town. Perhaps they were part of a larger group, however, for neither seemed very surprised to see the other.

“The King’s business. And you?”

“The same.”

A cold smile curled Kale’s lips. “The King set you upon the business of assaulting his subjects?”

Algar’s face turned a deep hue, but he forced a smile, lifted his brows as if he’d no notion of what Kale was suggesting. “I’ve caused the lovely Aslyn no harm, have I my dear?” he asked, his gaze flickering momentarily to Aslyn. He didn’t wait for Aslyn’s response, which was just as well. “I’ve discovered a flower amongst the weeds and thought only to pluck it ... if she, too, were so inclined, of course.”

“She did not appear overly enthusiastic to me.”

Agar laughed, obviously genuinely amused. “Who can know the mind of a woman when they do not even know their own mind? We had barely ... begun to warm to the subject. I can be very ... persuasive.”

To Aslyn’s relief, Enid peered timidly around the huntsman’s shoulder at that moment. “Aslyn?”

The men turned to look at her.

Obviously alarmed, she took a step back. “Beg pardon, my lords.” She looked at Aslyn questioningly. “Should I come back later?”

“They were just leaving,” Aslyn said, striving to keep the hopeful note from her voice and failing.

Algar chuckled again. “We have been dismissed. Perhaps you were wrong and the lady misliked your interference?”

The huntsman’s gaze locked with her own. However appreciative she was, though, Aslyn had no intention of antagonizing Lord Algar by favoring Kale, nor allowing him to know how thoroughly he had shaken her.

Lord Algar grasped Aslyn’s hand and lifted it to his lips, breathing deeply, as if savoring the scent of her skin, before he brushed the back of her hand with his lips in a light salute. “I will bid you good eve ... for now.”

Aslyn snatched her hand back, clutching the folds of her gown, resisting the urge to rub the feel of his lips from her hand. She watched as Lord Algar strode from the cottage, her chest tight with anxiety over his parting remark.

Kale, after studying her a long moment, turned and departed, as well.

Aslyn’s shoulders slumped. Her knees felt suddenly weak, but there was no place nearby to sit.

“Is something amiss?”

Aslyn shook her head. She had not thought she would be so glad to see the woman again so soon. As kind as she was, Enid was a bit of a chatterbox and Aslyn, who had spent more time alone over the past three years than with company, found the almost ceaseless chatter unnerving ... not nearly as nerve-wracking, however, as Lord Algar. “Not now.”

Enid moved into the room, glancing about the cottage speculatively. “The landlord was happy to accept the terms--not much chance to lease a cottage now. I feel I should have bargained harder, however. The cottage looks worse inside than out, if possible.”

Relieved to have something else to turn her mind to, Aslyn shrugged. “A thorough cleaning and a little patching should make it comfortable enough to suit my needs.” In truth, she didn’t care what the cottage looked like. It was more comfortable than she often had, and, in any case, she had no intention of lingering long in the town, particularly not with soldiers camped nearby.

Enid frowned. “Jim’ll not be up to it any time soon. I’ll ask about. I’m sure I can find someone who would willingly trade repairs for your services.”

“That would be welcome, but don’t worry about it if you cannot. It should be tight enough to hold me for a bit unless it rains. I can mix some daub and fill the crevices in the walls. The thatch might present a problem," she added, frowning as she looked up at the thin patches on the roof where light filtered through here and there.

"You've no wood for a fire, either. You're like to freeze in this doughty place without a good fire to warm you. Jim and I've settled in the cottage that was my mum's before she died, God rest her soul. It's just across the way there, on the next road over. I'll have Jim bring a bit of wood over and get you a fire going to chase the damp away."

The scrape of boots at the door step drew their attention. Aslyn glanced around quickly, more than a little fearful the dark knight had returned. To her surprise, the huntsman stood in the doorway, his arms laden with freshly chopped wood. She hoped that didn't mean that the king's men were camped nearby, but knew even as the thought formed in her mind that it was a forlorn one. He had not been gone long enough to have gone far. It took little imagination to envision all the king's men settled upon her doorstep for the duration of the winter.

Mayhap she'd been a little too hasty in deciding to stay, even for a short time.

Enid's brows rose almost to her hair line as he favored Aslyn with a curt nod, moved to the hearth and set about building a fire.

Aslyn blushed fierily at the curious look Enid sent her. She supposed his actions were out of kindness, but it disconcerted her mightily that he moved about the place with the familiarity of one who belonged. She could not encourage it. She did not want, and certainly could not afford, to become too closely acquainted with anyone ... not Enid, and most assuredly not the huntsman, whose piercing gaze seemed to miss nothing. "I'm most appreciative, but...."

Again the scrape of feet brought Aslyn's attention to the door. She broke off abruptly when she saw a young soldier stood in the opening, holding a pair of candle sticks. "With Lord Algar's compliments." Moving to the table, he set them down, then turned, bowed and departed, all before Aslyn could jog her surprised mind for a polite refusal.

"Wait!" Aslyn called to the soldier's retreating back. He neither slowed nor turned, much to Aslyn's indignation. "I can't take these...."

Enid snickered.

Aslyn glared at her. Kale, she saw when she glanced in his direction, was frowning at the smoldering fire on the hearth.

"I see you're in a fair way to getting settled in so I'll just leave the basket I brought you and be on my way."

Aslyn grasped Enid's arm, giving her a pleading look. "Stay ... a moment." She cast about in her mind. "How is your husband fairing?"

Enid relented, hiding a smile as she gave in to Aslyn's silent plea. "Well enough, I suppose. Limping about, of course, and muttering under his breath, but I checked his bandage. There's been little bleeding since you patched him up this morn."

"Ladies."

Enid and Aslyn both turned startled eyes upon him.

"Good eve."

Aslyn studied him uncomfortably. In truth, she was exceedingly grateful for the fire, however much she would have preferred to build it herself and thus be free of obligation. She had not done so, though, and could not bring herself to be so rude as to allow him to go without expressing her appreciation for his efforts. "Thank you. If you have need of ... of ... uh...." She broke off. Neither 'care' nor 'attention' seemed the sort of thing to utter, particularly not when they could so easily be turned against her.

Kale's lips curled faintly. "If I have need of?" he prodded, his dark brows rising questioningly.

"I'm sure she'd offer you a fine stew for your trouble if she had a hare to toss into the pot," Enid supplied helpfully. "I've brought her what I can spare at the moment, but the roots alone...."

He frowned, glanced around the austere cottage, nodded and left.

Aslyn elbowed the woman in the ribs. "For shame! That was blatant...."

Enid shrugged. "You'd rather go to bed hungry? The roots will not make much of a soup."

Obviously, there was no point in belaboring the fact that Enid had not only discomfited her by soliciting on her behalf, she had encouraged a closer association with the man, which Aslyn was desperate to discourage. Instead, she focused upon Enid's determined efforts to repay her for her help. It was winter. Food was scarce. The basket of food she'd brought could well create hardship for her own family. "It's too much! As much as I appreciate your generosity, Enid, you've repaid me twice over already. You must take your basket with you."

"What? In giving you a spot of tea and a ride into town? We'd have done the same for anyone we passed with no expectation of payment for it. You cannot count that. I figured Jim could patch the roof as soon as he was able, but that'll not be for a while. Anyway, you've not had time to settle in and it's only neighborly to bring a bit of food to tide you over for the night."

"That's too much for so little," Aslyn said firmly.

Enid's brows rose. "My Jim means a sight more to me than a handful of potatoes and carrots, I can tell you!"

Aslyn reddened, mortified to have her words interpreted in such a way. "I didn't mean it that way."

"I never thought you did, but I do." With that she set the basket down and marched toward the door. She turned when she reached it. "I'd stay and help, but I need to get my own family settled in and supper on if we're to eat tonight."

Aslyn nodded and thanked her. She was relieved to have the cottage to herself once more. She'd all but forgotten how nerve-wracking it could be to be surrounded by 'normal' folk, knowing that she must always mind what she said and how she behaved, knowing the danger inherent in allowing herself to let down her guard.

Add to that the pitfall of being a young, unattached female amidst randy soldiers and it was small wonder her nerves were frayed to tatters.

Dismissing her anxieties, she looked around, her hands on her hips. Finally, she returned to the bedding she'd left on the floor and dragged it outside. Gershin had had a line to hang her wash, but the rope had long since rotted. Aslyn tossed the bedding over the T that had held one end, beat it thoroughly to remove as much dust and insects as possible, and left it to air while she cleaned the cottage.

Uneasiness filled her as she made her way back inside, however. She had not been far off the mark when she'd imagined the king's men camped on her door step. They had set up tents no more than a quarter of a mile from the outskirts of town--from her cottage, at the edge of the forest.

Chapter Four

The object she'd tripped over when she'd been removing the bedding, Aslyn discovered, was old Gershin's cook pot. From the look of it, Gershin, like most people, had not been prepared when death took her. She'd left the remains of whatever last meal she'd cooked in the pot to slowly decay. It had long since dried and blackened to an indistinguishable crust. Taking it outside, Aslyn found a stick and scraped the inside of the pot until she'd cleaned it the best she could.

She'd seen a community well as they made their way through town. She had not seen one in the tiny yard that surrounded Gershin's cottage. Sighing, she headed for the well. When she'd washed the pot, she filled it and headed back to the cottage. Thankfully, it was not a very large pot, for her shoulder felt as if it was slipping from the socket only with the weight of the water she was carrying.

There was a stack of wood by her door when she returned. She stared at it for several moments and finally dismissed it, struggled inside with the pot, set it on the hook and swung it over the fire. A brush broom, covered in cobwebs, stood in the corner near the door. Much of the rush had rotted and crumbled, but Aslyn took it and used it to rake down cobwebs around the tiny cottage, brush the dust from the bed frame, the table and chair, and the mantel piece over the hearth. When she was done, she raked the debris littering the dirt floor outside. Examining the broom when she'd finished, she saw it had reached the end of its usefulness, broke the handle over her knee and tossed the pieces into the fire.

The water had begun to boil. Taking her knife from her pack, she selected two potatoes and two carrots and headed back toward the well. When she returned, she discovered that the door was shut. She stared at it uneasily for several moments, and finally moved toward it. Grasping the handle, she put her shoulder against it and shoved.

The door swung open without resistance and Aslyn staggered inside, almost dropping the vegetables she'd just spent the past twenty minutes peeling and cleaning. Irritated, she left the door open, glanced around the cottage to make certain no one waited in the shadows and moved to the cook pot.

Her heart skipped a beat when she saw there was something floating in the boiling water. She stared at it, fighting a wave of nausea, and finally speared it with her knife. It was a rabbit, cleaned and neatly quartered.

Feeling more than a little disconcerted that she'd imagined it might be something unpleasant, she dropped the meat back in the pot and turned to look at the door. Finally, she moved to the table, placed the vegetables there and returned to examine the door. The hinges, she saw, had been repaired.

Uneasiness swept through her as she closed the door. Kale? Or Lord Algar? Or had both of them been busily attending to her comfort? And why? What did they expect in return?

It took no great intelligence to figure out Lord Algar's motives--if, in fact, it had been he who'd seen to it that she had wood for fire, a stout door to close--food. He would not have done it himself, of course. He would have sent one of his men, but was such thoughtfulness in his nature?

A very little thought assured her that she had not misjudged the man, however short their acquaintance. He was not kind, not thoughtful, not considerate. She suspected that he was cunning and manipulative, though, and the deeds could as easily have been performed from those motives as out of kindness.

Although she was more inclined to think Kale responsible for the offerings, the truth was, she could not envision Kale as being kind, thoughtful and considerate either. There was a chilling reserve about him, a sense of absolute self-control that made her distinctly uneasy. It had flitted through her mind, more than once, that he suspected ... something about her. She might be imagining it, of course, but Kale's motives were far more difficult to pinpoint and the doubts suggested Kale was far more dangerous.

She was careful not to look in the direction of the soldiers' camp when she went out to check the mattress. It still smelled a bit too soured for her taste, but she could see no crawling insects. It was not so musty as it had been and, in any case, she did not want to turn it and leave it to air longer. If she did so, she would have to make yet another trip outside and it occurred to her that Lord Algar, at least, was more than likely to interpret her repeated trips to and fro as some sort of encouragement.

At any rate, it was nearing dusk. She would not have been able to leave it much longer anyway.

Dragging the mattress from the post, she hauled it inside.

The rabbit, she saw when she tested it with her knife, was tender. Scooping the vegetables from the table, she dropped them in the pot and went to check her pouch for some herbs suitable for seasoning.

To her surprise and at least partial relief, neither Kale nor Lord Algar showed up on her doorstep to join her for dinner, although she waited until it was full dark before she dismissed the possibility. She ate her stew in solitary contemplation, banked the fire and crawled into bed, wondering uneasily what would come of her chance meeting with two very dangerous men.

* * * *

On the third day after she arrived in Krackensled, Aslyn, who'd been out since first light foraging, both for her cook pot and for medicinal plants and fungi, returned to find a woman sitting on her doorstep. She was cradling something to her chest that had been bundled from end to end.

Weary from trudging through the snow, anxious because she had spotted soldiers more than once as she foraged--which gave her the distinct feeling that she was being watched--and disheartened that she'd returned almost as empty-handed as she'd been when she left, Aslyn had to force a polite smile of interest. "May I help you?"

The woman turned at the sound of her voice and looked up at her, studying her face searchingly. "Enid told me ye were a healer. I come to see if ye'd look at me boy."

"You should have gone in. It can't be good for the child to sit outside in the cold. How long have you been waiting?"

"Not long a'tall."

It was obviously a lie. Either that or the woman was sick herself, for she was shaking all over. Aslyn pushed the door open and held out her arms for the child. After a moment, the woman gave the child up reluctantly and followed her inside. Aslyn frowned when she felt the weight of the child, for it seemed curiously light for its size. "I apologize, but I've little to offer you in the way of comfort. Take the chair, if you like, and sit by the fire while I have a look at the child. But take care, it's a bit shaky. It's like to break and dump you in the floor if you're not careful."

The woman, who looked to be in her mid-thirties, studied her a moment and nodded, but made no move to do either. Instead, she followed Aslyn to the bed, watching her every move as Aslyn removed the woolen blankets to unearth the child. The little boy's eyes were huge in a face shrunken either by prolonged illness, or hunger, or perhaps both. It was impossible to determine his age. She smiled at him as she studied his glassy eyes and then made him open his mouth so that she could see his throat. "What are you called, little man?"

Something flickered in the boy's eyes. He glanced at his mother. "John," he supplied finally.

She looked at his ears. "That's a good, strong name. How old are you?"

"Seven winters."

Aslyn tried her best to hide her shock, but she'd seen toddlers near as big as the boy. "How many brothers and sisters do you have?"

"I don't mean to be rude, but I ain't too keen on you pumpin' my boy."

Aslyn glanced at the woman, subduing her anger with an effort. "If I'm to help him, I must know certain things."

"Gershin never asked so many questions."

"Then Gershin either knew the answers already, since she lived here, or she was a witch. I, myself, am not. And I'm not good at guessing, either," Aslyn responded tartly. "In any case, John seemed uneasy. I was trying to make him feel more comfortable."

She more than half expected the woman to grow angry. To her surprise, the suspiciousness vanished from her face. "Oh. I've six, not countin' Johnny."

Aslyn nodded. "Are any of the others sick?"

"Johnny's the baby. He's always been sickly. The others seem well enough."

"What about you? And his father?"

"I've got a bit of a cold, I think."

Aslyn smiled at John and ruffled his hair. "John, too."

"You think?"

"His throat is a little pinker than normal, his ears, too, but I don't think it's anything serious." She turned to John. "Why don't you wait here while I have a little chat with your mother?"

The woman glanced at her uneasily but followed Aslyn across the room. Aslyn pushed the pot of stew over the fire before she returned her attention to the woman. She considered for several moments and finally sighed. "I know of no gentle way to say this, so I hope you'll pardon me for being blunt. I've seen John's problem more times than I can count. He's starving, plain and simple. He isn't getting enough food to grow, or sustain strength, otherwise the cold would not have affected him so badly."

The woman turned red as a beet, glanced quickly at the child sitting on the bed and then down at the floor. "We do our best."

"I'm not accusing you or condemning you. I'm only trying to tell you that ... you'll not raise that boy if something isn't done. If he's too weak to fight off a cold, he'll have no chance at all if he gets something more serious."

The woman looked like she was going to cry for several moments, but fought it back. "Is there anything, you think, that I could do?"

Glancing at the stew pot, Aslyn saw that it was boiling. Taking one of the wooden bowls she'd found in the cottage, she filled it and took it to the table, then summoned John and bade him eat it. "This will help your feelings a bit, I think."

She waited only long enough to see that he dug in with enthusiasm and then returned to the fire where the boy's mother waited. "You said he's the youngest, the weakest. Perhaps he's simply having trouble fending for himself?"

The woman looked taken aback. "I dole out the food meself."

"Then make sure you give him a bit more, especially meat."

She nodded, but looked a little doubtful. "There's not much meat to be had now, with it winter and all. And the soldiers are camped out here now. They're bound to hunt the woods around here out if they stay the winter."

A frisson of uneasiness went through Aslyn. "They'll not be here long, surely?"

The woman shrugged. "From what I've heard, they've no plans to move any time soon. They're tracking wolves, and the last several attacks were near here."

The blood rushed from Aslyn's face so rapidly that a wave of nausea followed it.

The woman gripped her arms. "Ye best sit down if yer thinkin' about faintin'."

Aslyn stared at her uncomprehendingly for several moments. "No. I just felt a little dizzy for a moment. I should probably eat."

The woman's eyes narrowed. "It had nothing to do with what I just told you?"

Aslyn forced a half-hearted chuckle. "Whatever made you think that? No. I'll admit it's a scary thought ... the possibility of the wolves being near here. But, it's just that I didn't take the time to eat before I left this morning. I expect it was the smell of the food more than anything else."

The woman didn't look convinced. "Not that I'd blame ye, mind ye. The wolves aside, I'm more than a bit uneasy about having soldiers camped on our doorstep meself. There's almost always trouble when the soldiers have too much time on their hands."

"Too true. But mayhap they'll kill off the wolves fairly quickly and be on their way."

The woman glanced over at her son and lowered her voice. "There's somethin' right queer about these wolves, from what I hear tell of it. Ye'd think they was starvin' or they wouldn't be preyin' on folks, but they're real cautious for all that, and wily. The soldiers've been trackin' 'em for months now, an' still ain't managed to catch up with them. Now, don't that sound more'n a little strange to you?"

Aslyn felt her uneasiness return. "How so?"

The woman shrugged. "Don't it seem to you that they'd not be at all cautious if they was hungry enough to be huntin' us?"

"Maybe they've just been lucky--so far. Or the soldiers unlucky."

"Maybe. But folks'r sayin' it's like they *know* the king's sent men to track them down. They ain't sprung none of the traps set for them. An' once it's daylight, they just up and vanish."

Aslyn shivered. "Perhaps their leader is a wily old fellow?"

"And maybe he ain't no wolf a'tall."

Chapter Five

Aslyn had no desire to be drawn any deeper into this particular conversation. Instead of prompting the woman to elaborate, therefore, she changed the subject abruptly.

"I *am* starving. Could I interest you in sharing my stew?"

The woman looked a little taken aback, but shook her head. "I'd best be gettin' back. If you're agreeable, I'll have me man bring you one of our geese for your trouble."

Aslyn held up her hand. "No food," she said firmly.

The woman's lips tightened. "We don't take no charity."

That settled that. Aslyn had been on the point of explaining that she was a penitent and usually took nothing at all, but she could see the woman would take that badly. "Certainly not! I do need a bit of patch work done on the roof, though. Or he could bring some wood for the fire."

The woman glanced up, then nodded.

John, having drained the bowl, had fallen asleep with his head propped on his hands. The woman shook him awake and carefully bundled him up.

"Keep him inside at least a few days--preferably a week. I'm sure you've chores inside the house he could help you with?"

The woman nodded. "Me man won't like it, but I'll handle him."

"And feed him all the soup he can hold. Use fowl, if you can, to make the broth. That'll be better than red meat. Bring him back to see me if he begins to have trouble breathing or seems to be coughing more than you'd expect."

Again the woman nodded, gathered the child up and departed.

Aslyn stood in the doorway watching as the woman scurried down the street. Seven years old and the woman could carry him about as if he was no more than a toddler. With any luck he'd make it through the cold, but she had her doubts the child would see many more winters.

The thought brought the urge to cry. She thrust it away angrily and closed the door. Pity would not help the child, and she had nothing else to give him ... nothing to give any of the hundreds of Johnnys she'd seen in her travels. If she'd been the wealthiest person in the world, she could not save them all, nor even a fraction of them. One person could not. She'd done the best--the *only* thing she could for him.

In any case, she had problems enough of her own. Instead of eating, she paced the cottage, round and round, but she could not outrun her anxieties and finally forced herself to sit and eat. She wanted, desperately, to leave Krackensled, but, from what she could see, that was no longer an option--if it had ever been. The soldiers would be patrolling the area. She would almost certainly be stopped and questioned if she tried to leave, and, unfortunately, the lies she'd told to cover herself precluded any that would allow her passage.

She deeply regretted, now, that she had told them she was on pilgrimage. If only she'd thought of some other tale, something that would have left relatives somewhere that she could claim to be going to visit, or who needed her!

It was pointless to kick herself over it now. She would know better another time ... if there was another time.

But, if what she suspected was true....

She pushed the thought from her mind. Perhaps, she thought hopefully, they would grow tired of waiting long before the moon became full again and move on.

Or perhaps imaginations were running wild because there had been such an unusual number of attacks and it truly *was* nothing more than a roving pack of wolves? If that were the case, then the soldiers were bound to trap and kill the wolves before long.

Surely it could have nothing to do with her ... malady. Surely it could not!

But, in the end, did it matter? She was trapped here. If she stayed, the soldiers might well be hunting her when next the moon was full.

* * * *

It was nearing dusk almost a week after her arrival in Krackensled when Aslyn left the cottage with her cook pot, intent upon cleaning it and filling it at the well. The perpetual rabbit stew had given out at long last. Aslyn could not confess to being sorry to see the last of it. Toward the end it had born little resemblance to that first pot of rabbit stew, for Aslyn had tossed whatever she caught, or gathered, or was 'paid' into it each day--another rabbit a farmer had brought, a few mushrooms, a handful of withered greens--but she found she no longer had much fondness for rabbit stew.

The thunder of hooves brought her out of her abstraction. She looked up to see a group of soldiers approaching from the opposite end of town and checked for a fraction of a second before it occurred to her that whirling around and returning to the house would be the best way to attract attention to herself. She continued on her way after that brief hesitation, her head down, as if she was carefully watching where she set her feet, but she stole a quick glance or two in their direction.

She didn't know whether to be relieved or sorry when they halted at the well and began dipping water for their horses.

She slowed her steps, wondering if they might finish up and leave before she reached them, casting quick, surreptitious glances to the right and left in search of an alternative. Another quick glance told her she'd already passed the only crossing between her and the men. She would not be able to pretend she'd had another destination in mind. Finally, in desperation, she turned and walked up to a cottage. She rapped on the oak panel door, hoping the cottage was occupied and that someone would open the door.

To her relief, she heard the shuffle of footsteps inside.

"Who's there?" a gravelly voice called from within.

Aslyn bit her lip. It hadn't occurred to her that the occupant might not open the door. If she had to yell through it, she might just as well forget about any possibility of escaping the soldiers' notice. She leaned close to the door. "I'm looking for Jim and Enid McCraney. Do you know them?"

The latch clicked and the door opened inward a sliver. "What's yer business with them?"

Aslyn stared at the old woman, taken aback. "I wanted to check to see how Jim was fairing since his accident."

The old woman looked her up and down. "Enid'd not take kindly to yer interest in 'er man," she said bluntly and slammed the door.

Aslyn was left staring at the vibrating panel while color climbed into her cheeks, chasing the cold away. "Thank you," she mumbled. "Would you mind very much if I cut across your yard to the next road over?"

"Me dog'll take a chunk outta yer arse if he gits a whiff of ye."

It took Aslyn a couple of moments to recover from that forthright statement. Finally, deciding, just in case anyone could overhear her end of the conversation, that she should at least pretend she'd had a pleasant conversation with the old termagant,

Aslyn forced a smile. "Thank you very much. I'll be sure to tell them."

She had not heard the horses leave. There was nothing for it, she was going to have to turn back toward home and pretend she'd only gone up the street to see the hateful old woman who'd slammed the door in her face and threatened her with her dog.

As she turned to walk back to the road, however, she discovered Kale was propped against a tree at the edge of the road, not two yards from her. She jumped in surprise, nearly dropping her pot.

A slow smile curled his lips. "I take it she didn't have any to spare."

Aslyn blinked at him. "I beg your pardon?"

He nodded toward the pot she held clutched in her hands.

Aslyn looked down at the pot, stared at it for several long, long moments trying to think of what she might say that wouldn't sound like a lie. Finally, she decided she might as well go along with his assumption since she could think of nothing else. "No. I thought it worth a try," she said, trying to command her complexion to cease fluctuating in pulsing red and white. She would almost have preferred to tell him the truth than to have to claim to have been begging.

He stood away from the tree and walked toward her, his eyes gleaming in a way Aslyn didn't quite like. Taking the pot from her limp hands, he tucked one of her hands in the crook of his arm and guided her toward the road. "It was just as well, I expect."

Aslyn, still too stunned to think very clearly, merely nodded. It occurred to her quite suddenly to wonder where he was taking her and she glanced quickly around. She didn't know whether to be relieved, chagrined or unnerved when she saw he was leading her toward the well.

"I've not tried it myself, but I've been told it tends to be stringy."

"What?" Aslyn asked blankly.

"Dog."

"Dog?"

"I did hear the old woman mention her dog, didn't I?"

Aslyn glanced quickly at his face and then away, feeling blood flood her cheeks in a crimson tide. "You heard...," she said faintly. She realized quite suddenly that he was teasing her and, despite the fact that she had absolutely no desire to have Kale, of all men, flirting with her, she began to see the humor of the situation. She bit back a chuckle, threw him a tentative smile, but it froze on her face as she saw Lord Algar bearing down upon them.

She made an abortive attempt to snatch her hand from Kale's arm, but he caught it, holding her hand firmly in place.

"Lady Aslyn!" Lord Algar said warmly, though his smile was slightly forced, and the look in his eyes as he glanced between her and Kale was anything but warm. "As charming and as beautiful as ever, I see."

It took an effort to refrain from glancing down self-consciously at the horrid gown she was wearing. It was obvious from his speech and manners that he was accustomed to courtly flirtations. Perhaps he thought her ignorant enough to find his flamboyant compliments flattering, but, in point of fact, they had the opposite effect. It was as if he were taunting her and thought her too stupid to realize it. "Mistress Aslyn," she corrected him stiffly.

He fell into step beside her, taking her free hand and tucking it into the crook of his arm. Aslyn gaped at him, tried unsuccessfully to pull away. She glanced at Kale, but he was staring at the road ahead of them, his expression stony.

"Out for an evening stroll, are we?"

"In point of fact, no," Kale said succinctly.

"No?"

Amusement gleamed in Kale's eyes briefly as he looked down at her. It vanished when he transferred his gaze to Algar. "Mistress Aslyn was leery of approaching the well with so many soldiers milling about."

Aslyn glanced at him sharply, flushing when she realized she had not fooled him even for a moment. How embarrassing to think she'd gone through such an elaborate charade, and all for nothing!

Lord Algar's brows rose. "Ever the gallant, eh, Kale? Rescuing damsels in distress."

Kale slid a glance in his direction. "You may count upon it, Algar."

Seeing that they were so intent upon challenge and counter challenge that she might just as well not exist save for being the 'bone' the two were snarling over, Aslyn snatched her hands free, turned and seized her pot from Kale's other hand. "Thank you. Both of you. If you'll excuse me now...."

She didn't wait for a response from either man, or look at them again. For all that, she was acutely conscious of the fact that they took up positions on either side of her, leaning against the stone walls of the well, both men at great pains to appear oblivious to each other, each not so subtly continuing to issue challenge to the other. It grated on her nerves, but she did her best to focus upon scrubbing the cook pot. When she'd finished, she filled it once more.

Any thoughts she'd nurtured that she might slip away unhindered vanished immediately, however. Kale, who'd taken it upon himself to haul the buckets of water up as needed, filled the pot, wrested it from her grasp and held out his arm. While Aslyn was busy ignoring the hint, Lord Algar possessed himself of a hand and tucked into his arm. Surprised, Aslyn turned to glare at him, trying to pull her hand free, whereupon Kale took her free hand, tucked in his arm and gave her a tug.

Giving up the fight, Aslyn allowed them to escort her back to her cottage. She made no attempt at conversation, however, despite Lord Algar's many attempts to prod her into intercourse. Kale remained silent. She wasn't certain whether it was because that was typical of him, or if he was wise enough not to attempt the impossible. In any case, she felt like a prisoner--*was* a prisoner, however courtly their behavior appeared.

Did they fancy that they were courting her? she wondered a little wildly, but she decided she simply could not credit that. The rivalry between them was far older than their acquaintance and, she thought, far more complicated than a simple contest between two randy males for a chosen female.

She was certainly not flattered by the attention, whatever the case. She was more inclined to view it as a comedy of errors, wherein Kale had perceived Lord Algar's interest as being more than it actually was and had set himself up as rival purely for its antagonistic value.

The girl she had been before would probably have been too pleased and too flattered to look beyond the surface. The woman she was had not had that luxury in many a year now. She could not afford only to take things at face value. She felt certain her secret was still that, a secret, because she had not lingered long enough in any one place to allow suspicions to grow, but she could not be sure enough to stake her life on it. Nor could she risk that she would be unintentionally tripped. Either way, her life was forfeit.

She felt a sudden, deep yearning for the life she had once had, a painful wish to be merely a girl, caught up in flattering courtship by two attractive, eligible males. Or even simply to be too blind and shallow to perceive the layers of deception, lust and intrigue that lay in wait for the unwary.

Alas, innocence was not to be had for the wishing. She could not enjoy the attention. She could not preen and find pleasure in it. She could not even enjoy a secret amusement at the situation she had found herself in.

In truth, she was far more embarrassed than amused by the picture they must represent and relieved beyond measure when they came to her cottage once more, until it occurred to her to wonder if they would part company at the door or if she would have to conceive an idea to foist them off.

With an edge of desperation, she pulled free as they reached her door, grasped the handle determinedly and turned, barring entrance, a false smile pasted on her lips. "I must thank you ... both ... for your assistance. I wish I could invite you in for something to war--a cup of tea to warm you, but I have someone coming in a very little bit with a sick child."

To her relief, the men exchanged a look and bowed. Kale stepped forward and set her cook pot on the stoop. Even as he did so, Lord Algar seized her hand and bent over it to give it a salute.

"Until this eve, then, Mistress Aslyn," Kale said, a wicked gleam in his eyes, then nodded and departed before she could say anything at all.

She was left with her jaw at half cock, staring after him in consternation over Lord Algar's dark head. The comment brought Lord Algar's head up with a jerk. As he whipped around to glare after the huntsman's departing back, Aslyn recovered sufficiently to grab her pot and duck inside the door. When Lord Algar turned to look at her suspiciously, she pasted a bright smile on her lips. "Thank you again," she said and hastily slammed and bolted the door.

She braced her back against the door, partly from the weakness of relief, partly from an uneasiness that Lord Algar would not take her dismissal lightly. Her heart was thundering in her ears, making it difficult to listen for sounds of Lord Algar's departure. Finally, however, he left without another word.

Aslyn stared down at the pot hanging on the hook above the fire. She had nothing to put in it. She'd intended to go foraging for something to make a soup once she'd returned with the pot. She didn't dare do so now, however, afraid she'd run up on Kale or Lord Algar again, or worse, both of them.

She turned and looked sadly at the crusty loaf of bread that had been brought to her earlier. It would have gone well with soup. Alone it lost much of its appeal.

Dismissing it, she began to pace the small room, trying to think how she might depart Krackensled without being accosted by either of her 'suitors' or the men with them. It seemed an impossibility. The soldiers roamed the land at night, searching for the elusive wolves. During the day she would be far too easily noticed by villagers and soldiers alike.

Twice, she'd gone foraging and both times she had repeatedly spotted soldiers lurking nearby. She did not believe for a moment that it was purely coincidence, despite the fact that they'd given the pretense of having other matters on their minds.

She was obliged to admit, after much pacing, that it would be worse, given the current situation, to try, than to wait for a better time. If she tried and was caught, then she would be under suspicion and watched even more closely. If she waited, the situation might turn in her favor. There had been no reports of attack in nearly a week. Surely the soldiers would soon leave if nothing happened to keep them in the area?

In the afternoon, a rap came upon her door. She was reluctant to answer it, but she could not simply hide away, as much as she would have liked to. Still, she was cautious, calling through the door before she opened it.

Enid favored her with a curious look when Aslyn opened the door. "You were expecting someone?"

Aslyn smiled weakly. "It pays to be cautious."

Enid hid a smile. "Especially when you're being courted by two such powerful men."

Aslyn turned away as she felt color creep into her face. "They are hardly courting. The rivalry between Kale and Lord Algar is almost certainly older than our short acquaintance. It's difficult to be flattered when they seem more interested in besting each other than claiming the ... uh ... prize."

Enid nodded skeptically.

Irritated, Aslyn asked if she had need of anything.

Enid grinned, not insulted in the least. "Nay. Jim's outside taking care of those repairs, as promised. I thought mayhap you'd like a bit of company."

Aslyn was not currently inclined toward company. In truth she would not have welcomed it at any time, but she found she could not be rude in the face of Enid's determination to promote a friendship. She refused, however, to be drawn into any sort of discussion regarding her 'suitors.' Instead, she played with the baby and listened absently to Enid's recital of all the clever things the baby had done most recently.

Baby Bess seemed none the worse for her accident the previous week. The knot on her head had all but disappeared, leaving a yellowed patch of bruising. Jim was healing well, as well and, with the exception of the continued attacks by wolves, all was right with Enid's world.

Aslyn felt her heart drop to her toes when Enid asked if she'd heard of the latest attack. "There's been another attack?" she asked a little breathlessly.

Enid nodded, her eyes wide. "Just last eve. I'm surprised you've not heard, considering."

Aslyn was almost afraid to ask. "Considering?"

"Will the Red--the farmer that was here to see you about the boils just yester morn. He was on his way home, and nearly there when he was set upon."

"He was ... was he ... killed?"

Enid shook her head. "By God's mercy! Frightened nearly witless, but he was fortunate enough to come off without a scratch. He had chanced to kill a stag along the way and had it upon his shoulders. Doubtless, it was that that attracted them. In any case, when they leapt upon him, they dragged the carcass from his shoulders and he was able to flee while they fought over it."

"The poor man," Aslyn murmured. She did sympathize with his fright, but her own plight was beginning to look more and more desperate and she had difficulty focusing upon anything but unraveling the problem. With an effort, she dismissed her anxieties and directed the subject back to Baby Bess, knowing Enid could not resist following. She wished she could as easily put it from her own mind. It unnerved her to think the man had been set upon so quickly upon the heels of his visit to her. She dearly hoped that Enid had not spread the tale in the same way she'd told it to her, else the villagers would be wary of coming to her door, or worse, become hostile in the certainty that the problems they were having were her doing.

All in all, she was not sorry to see the McCraney family take their leave. As she opened the door for them, however, she discovered she was sorrier still that they had already said their good-byes, for Kale stood upon her stoop.

Chapter Six

Enid threw her a twinkling glance, nodded at Kale and departed, leaving Aslyn staring uncomfortably at her visitor.

"I'd invite...."

"Thank you," Kale said. He handed her a wheel of cheese and strode inside with something wrapped loosely in a piece of thin leather.

Aghast, Aslyn watched speechlessly as he moved to the hearth with the air of one who belongs. He was carrying, she saw, a haunch of meat, already skewered and ready, apparently, for the fire. He arranged it on the spit before he straightened and turned to face her, his expression unreadable.

He had invited himself to dine with her and had brought the main course. Or, did he think she would be the main course, Aslyn wondered uneasily.

After a moment, she pushed the door closed. By tomorrow, she would almost certainly be receiving the looks reserved for women of easy virtue, but it was far too cold to leave the door ajar for the sake of decorum. In any case, she doubted her reputation would survive much longer whatever she did. Kale and Lord Algar had blatantly marched her down the street between them. No doubt the community had been titillated over that and were even now snickering about the healer and her two lovers.

The townsfolk's low opinion of her would not wound her, nor need she concern herself about it as any young, unwed, woman would need to to find acceptance. It might well lead to a precipitate departure for her, however, if for no other reason than that she would be avoided out of censure and have no way of earning her keep.

That might have its advantages. Not that she liked the idea of being run out of town, but it would certainly solve her dilemma over how she might leave without arousing suspicion.

On the other hand, it would also leave her more vulnerable to Kale and Lord Algar, whatever their plans for her.

After studying him uneasily for several moments, Aslyn moved away from the door. "I see you've brought...?" She broke off, uncertain of what the bloody chunk of meat was.

"A haunch of venison."

She nodded and continued to the washstand, pouring water into the basin so that he could wash up. He crossed the room to stand behind her. She glanced up at him over her shoulder, caught by his gaze for several heartbeats before she shook herself and moved away with the realization that he was merely waiting for her to move so that he could wash up.

She watched him as he washed his hands, mesmerized by the movements of his hands and the play of muscles on his forearms, exposed when he'd rolled his sleeves to the elbows. His hands were strong, his fingers long and tapering. Dark hair sprinkled the backs of them as well his forearms. She was still watching as he turned at last, drying his hands on the cloth she'd left beside the bowl for him. He studied her a long moment and finally turned to the bowl once more. Lifting it, he carried it outside to empty the contents.

More than a little dazed by the turn of events--for despite Kale's earlier threat/promise, she truly had not expected him to show up--Aslyn surveyed her cottage when he'd gone outside. She was fortunate to have the little that she did since she had 'inherited' what Gershin had left. However, Gershin had lived alone and had not enjoyed a great deal of prosperity. The cottage contained one small table, one rickety chair and a narrow bed.

Aslyn ignored the bed. There was no sense in stimulating the man's imagination by inviting him to sit on it. There was far more dirt floor in the room that anything else ... and, to be sure, little enough of that considering the size of the cottage. She would never before have even considered such a thing for a moment, but a very little thought told that, unless she was willing to use the bed as a seat--which she most certainly wasn't--she really had no choice but to entertain her guest on the floor.

Irritation surged through her briefly, that she'd been put in the awkward position of entertaining a guest when she hadn't the means for it. She dismissed it with the reflection that Kale had come for a reason. For her safety as well as her peace of mind, she needed to know what that reason was.

If his intention truly was to court her, then she would simply have to find a way to fob him off until she had the chance to move on. If, as she suspected, it was something more, then forewarned was forearmed.

Pulling the old quilt from the bed, she spread it near the hearth, placing the cheese, her knife, the cracked earthen mugs and plates that seemed the least damaged and a bottle of wine near the center. Lastly, she found a dish to hold one of the candles Algar had sent to her, lit it, and set it next to the bottle of wine. She was just finishing the last when Kale returned, knocked briefly and entered carrying a load of wood before she could respond.

His dark brows rose as he surveyed the 'picnic' cloth before the hearth. Until that very moment, Aslyn had not considered the 'table' she'd set might be construed as seductively intimate. She was appalled when she realized that that was exactly what it looked like ... a blanket before the fire, candles--wine.

She glared at him, lest he conceive the notion that that was her intention. "I apologize, but I'm afraid I have little to offer visitors. Rather than suggest we take turns at the table, I thought we might share the blanket." She could have bitten her tongue off the moment the words were out of her mouth. It took no imagination at all to twist those words into a far more intimate invitation than she'd intended. One look at Kale's face was enough to assure her that he'd not missed the, seeming, double entendre.

A faint smile curled his lips. "I should be delighted to share the blanket with you," he responded and continued to the hearth, dropping the pile of wood he carried beside the hearth, then carefully placing a few branches on the fire.

Aslyn blushed. At least a part of it was irritation. If he had openly acknowledged the inadvertently suggestive nature of her comment, she could have set him back on his heels. As it was, he had merely turned it back upon her so that she could not even take exception to his response.

But she knew very well that he had not missed the connotations.

It was even more irritating that he had only to give her that piercing look of his and she began to feel exceedingly warm all over and as breathless as a giddy young maiden. She was more than a little inclined to think it was his fault that she could not open her mouth without uttering something witless.

He left again when he'd turned the spit over the fire. This time when he returned, he was carrying a lute and it was Aslyn's brows that rose. "Do you play?" she asked in surprise.

A slow, infinitely appealing smile curled his lips. It did something drastically disturbing to her heart. "I've a modest skill with it. Mostly I carry it to charm the ladies at court and convince them that I'm a man of breeding and sensitivity."

Caught off guard, Aslyn chuckled. "I had not pegged you for a rogue."

His dark brows rose at the comment. He took her hand, assisting her to take a seat on the edge of the blanket. "Do not let this boyish countenance disarm you. I'm considered one of the blackest rogues unhung."

Aslyn eyed him skeptically as he settled himself opposite her with his back to the wall and began to tune the instrument. There was nothing the least boyish about his face. It was all man--harsh, angular, dangerously appealing. Nor could she imagine him as a seducer of innocents--he seemed far too controlled for that, far too honorable a man--though she had no difficulty at all imagining any number of young 'innocents' casting lures in his direction, hopeful of *being* seduced.

If her own life had not changed ... but there was no point in allowing her thoughts to take that direction. Her life had changed. It would never be the same. And if it had not, then she would have been wed long since and very likely have a babe at her breast by now.

In any case, she was very doubtful that his intentions toward her were of a seductive nature ... however treacherously her body interpreted every word, look and gesture he bestowed upon her. Possibly, he viewed that as a potential bonus to his efforts, but it was not the ultimate goal. Of that she was fairly certain. His behavior toward her had been that of a gentleman from the very first. Unlike Lord Algar, he had made no attempt to take advantage of her situation.

"A breaker of hearts, perhaps," she responded finally, teasingly. "But I cannot see you as a seducer of innocents."

The comment was rewarded by one of his rare grins. "I never said it was true, only that it was rumored ... and, in any case, I don't recall that I suggested it had to do with the seduction of innocents at all."

Aslyn's jaw went slack. "But ... uh...."

He chuckled at the look on her face. Instead of commenting, however, he began to pluck a tune and sang a ballad. Regardless of his claims, his skill was far more than merely modest. He played well, and he sang even better, his voice deep and rich, reaching down into her soul, curling a tight fist around her heart that made her yearn for all those things she'd missed in her life ... husband, hearth, and children ... the passion of a man she could love who loved her in return. She was so enthralled she forgot her guard, clapping enthusiastically when he'd finished, smiling at him warmly. "That was beautiful!"

He bowed his head slightly. After a moment's thought, he played another tune. The ballad he sang, however, was completely unfamiliar to her. It was hauntingly sad, and spoke of a people hunted, misunderstood, despised.

When he'd finished, he set the lute aside and moved to check the meat.

"What is this ballad? I've never heard it before."

He shrugged, intent upon his task. "It's from a legend as old as mankind ... as old as Uthreana, the Earth Mother."

"This is about a people that lived long ago?"

He turned to look at her, his expression unreadable. "Many believe they still live among us."

Aslyn frowned, thinking back to what she remembered of childhood lessons, but she could not recall ever having heard a tale anything like it. "I don't think I've ever heard about them."

He returned his attention to the meat, cutting into it experimentally to check it for doneness. "It's the legend of the werefolk--the beast people--or, as they prefer to call themselves, the brethren, who appear as 'normal' as you and I much of the time, but who are virtually immortal, and change themselves into beasts and roam the night. According to legend, there are those born into the clan, and those fortunate enough to be ... chosen as mates."

A dizzying rush of fright washed through Aslyn as she studied his back, realizing this was no idle conversation. He knew, or he suspected. In either event, her situation was far more dire than she'd supposed. The realization threw her mind into such turmoil that it took a supreme effort of will to force herself to consider how one not guilty, as she was, would react to the story. Should she dismiss it? Or would it be best to express some interest in the subject? Would it be dangerous to show any interest at all?

In truth, despite her fear, the tale held more promise of her possible salvation than anything she'd learned in all her years of travel. If there was any truth at all to it, and surely there must be, she wanted--needed to know whatever he might know about it.

She decided it wouldn't be safe to appear too intrigued and forced a scoffing chuckle that sounded hollow even to her own ears. "Werewolves? But these are just stories simple folk frighten themselves with. In any case, I wouldn't think being 'chosen' a very desirable thing. Who would willingly give up their humanity to become some savage beast?"

Coming onto her knees, she focused her attention on cutting slices of cheese and bread as she sensed him turning toward her once more since she had no confidence that he would not read everything in her face--her fears and her hope.

"Do you prefer your meat red? Or brown?"

Aslyn glanced up at him and then looked at the half cooked slice of meat he had skewered on his knife. A wave of nausea washed through her. "Brown," she said with an effort, wondering if he thought he was testing her by offering the meat virtually raw.

He dropped the chunk of meat onto the nearest plate and returned his attention to his task. "A pity. It's far more succulent when not overcooked."

Aslyn stared at the piece of meat and repressed a shudder.

"But I was referring to werefolk--not specifically werewolves," he continued the previous discussion.

Aslyn met his gaze. This time, however, she truly was confused and had no need to pretend. "Werefolk?"

"They are not limited to taking the form of wolves."

Intriguing as that was, Aslyn realized it was far too dangerous to pursue any further. His piercing stare unnerved her to such an extent that she was certain she would give herself away somehow, if she hadn't already. To her relief, he dropped it and focused upon the meal once he'd placed a slice of meat on her plate.

Uncorking the wine bottle, he poured a measure into each of the earthen mugs she'd set out. "You seem ... surprisingly well educated," he commented, just as Aslyn had begun to relax and enjoy the meal.

She almost choked on the bite of bread she'd just taken and had to take a gulp of the wine before she was able to speak. "I had the good fortune to be reared by a lady of good breeding but no fortune."

He cocked an inquisitive brow. "I thought your father was a sea captain?"

Aslyn did choke that time. When she'd recovered from her coughing fit, she glanced up at him through watery eyes. "Yes. He was. But, naturally, I did not sail with him. I was referring to the woman who kept house for us."

He nodded. Before he could think of another question, Aslyn asked, "And what of you?"

"A younger son of an impoverished gentleman--no prospects," he responded coolly.

Aslyn colored, felt irritation surface. It took an effort to curb the urge to slap him. She had not been fishing for information of that type, or for that reason, and he damned well knew it. “Which is of no interest to me as I’ve no interest in attaching a husband,” she said tartly. She’d been sorely tempted to say ‘you’ rather than ‘a,’ but decided he was not so thick skinned as to need anything more pointed.

His eyes gleamed. “No?”

“I plan to enter the nunnery when I finish my pilgrimage and return to Mersea,” she said tightly. Let him stew on that!

He frowned. “You must have loved him very much.”

The comment threw her for a curve, particularly since she could tell from his expression that the thought displeased him far more than he liked, or than he was willing to allow her to see. Unfortunately, she wasn’t altogether certain what it was that she’d told him before that had provoked the comment. She stared at him, trying to remember exactly what she’d told him about herself. It was the pitfall of deceit. One must lie to suit the occasion, which meant if one stayed in one place too long, one could begin to hang oneself with lies.

She must have mentioned her betrothal, she finally decided, either to him or to someone he’d questioned. She had never been inclined to elaborate, however--she was at least wise enough to realize her limitations and she couldn’t help but wonder what her exact words had been to lead him to this conclusion. Regardless, there could be only one answer. She’d already told him she would enter a convent. She had to have *some* excuse for choosing to do so. She looked down at her food to keep from giving herself away by her expression. “Yes,” she lied.

He refilled her cup. “You are far too young ... and far too beautiful to hide yourself from the world in a convent. Your destiny lies elsewhere.”

Aslyn wasn’t about to allow herself to be sucked in by his flattery. With his probing questions and comments, he’d made it clear enough that his only interest in her was in discovering if she had anything to do with the attacks. How could he imagine her as some sort of hideous beast capable of such ferocity and yet so simple as to fall for the grains of flattery he sprinkled out between his probing questions? Or, perhaps, believing her to be of the werefolk, he thought her mind could only be simple?

She smiled dismissively and turned her attention to her meal, trying to show enthusiasm she did not feel. In truth, she’d lost her appetite long since, which was a shame considering he'd provided the best meal she'd seen in many months.

"You surprise me."

"How so?"

"In virtually every way, in truth. More specifically, I'd expected either a coy prompt for more flattery, or a denunciation ... or a polite 'thank you.'"

Aslyn didn't look at him. She was doing her best to curb her temper. "Was I rude?"

"Surprisingly."

She glanced up at him then. "Perhaps I didn't consider it a compliment?"

"You thought, perhaps, that it was mere flirtation?"

She did not care, at all, for the feeling that she was being toyed with, as a cat might play with a mouse. Anger made her incautious. "I did not make the mistake of thinking it a 'mere' anything. I am curious, however, to know why you pretend an interest in me that you obviously do not feel."

He was silent for so long that she thought he would not answer at all. "You could not be more wrong."

Aslyn threw him an uncomfortable glance. She didn't doubt that she was meant to believe he was expressing an interest in her when in truth his interest was merely in tripping her up. He was a true hunter, and one far more dangerous than any she had ever encountered before. She would do well, and live longer, if she could bring herself to ignore her attraction to him and guard herself.

Chapter Seven

Since she could think of no response to his comment, Aslyn focused her attention upon pretending to finish her meal. When she reached the point where she thought she might choke if she tried to force down another bite, she wiped her hands then took the remaining cheese and carefully wrapped it. Collecting their plates, she rose and took them outside to scrape them, leaving the soiled dishes outside to be cleaned in the morning. When she returned, she discovered that Kale was once more strumming upon his lute. The meat was still hot, but she wrapped it carefully, tied it with string and put it outside the door, covering it with her overturned cook pot to keep stray animals from dragging it off.

She explained to Kale that she'd left it in the snow to cool so that it would be easier to carry when he left, hoping he'd take the hint and depart. In truth she was exhausted from the turmoil of his visit, for she'd run the gamut of emotions since he'd arrived. More disturbing and unsettling still was the fact that, despite everything, beneath it all had lain a simmering desire she could never completely ignore. Every look, every gesture, his slightest touch had burned her with awareness of herself as a woman and him as a desirable male.

She could not recall a time when she had ever been more agitated. She needed to be away from him to recover her equilibrium and think.

He cocked an eyebrow at her. "I brought it, and the cheese, for you."

Aslyn did not want to take it. It was one thing for him to provide their meal, quite another for him to be supplying her with food. However, she did not feel up to the challenge of a debate with him over the matter at the moment. She merely thanked him therefore, stood uncertainly for a moment, and, when she saw he had no intention of departing, sat on the edge of the blanket again.

She fidgeted for some moments, realizing the obligation of manners and wishing she could ignore it. Finally, reluctantly, she invited him back to dine with her once more on the food he'd provided.

The look he bent upon her was far too perceptive for her comfort, but he did not comment upon her lack of good manners in making it far too obvious she had only asked out of politeness. "Thank you, but we are leaving in the morn and may not return for some time."

"Oh?" Aslyn asked, trying to keep the hopeful note from her voice.

Apparently, she didn't succeed, for he sent her a narrow eyed glance. "We've heard word that there was an attack near Beaver Falls. There's little chance we can track the pack now, but we leave at dawn to try."

Aslyn nodded, folded her hands in her lap and thought hard of something she might say that would send him on his way without making her appear more rude than she already had, or worse, suspicious.

She noticed after a moment that Kale was holding the lute out to her, waiting for her to take it. Unbidden, longing welled up inside her. She had loved to play when she was younger, but it had been years since she'd touched an instrument. She doubted very much that she could even remember the tunes she had once played, or the words to the songs. Moreover, commoners rarely owned such things. It would certainly look suspicious if she possessed a skill she should not have. She shook her head. "I don't know how to play."

He eyed her skeptically for several moments, then indicated again that she should take it. "It's not difficult to learn. I'll show you."

Reluctantly, Aslyn took the instrument and held it awkwardly, hoping he'd interpret that as inexperience. He rose, moved behind her and knelt so that his splayed knees were on either side of her. Reaching around her, he placed her fingers on the strings, explaining the chords to her. Aslyn stiffened, more disturbed than she liked by his nearness, but allowed him to guide her fingers since she seemed to have no choice in the matter.

Her back burned where he brushed against her. His male scent engulfed her with his essence, sending a heady wave of longing through her that demolished rational thought. Her heart thundered erratically, making her breath rush quickly in and out of her lungs as if she were trapped beneath a heavy weight that made her fight for air. The harder she tried to struggle against it, the more ensnared she became until she was hardly conscious of his hands over hers except for the currents that seemed to spread from his fingertips into her hands, rush along her arms and strum some wanton chord inside of her.

At last her hands fell idle and she gave up all pretense of learning the strings, mesmerized by the movement of his thumb as he rubbed it back and forth across the back of her right hand. He captured her hand in his finally and lifted it for his inspection. Almost against her will, her gaze followed the movement until she was looking up into his golden gaze. "You have been bitten."

The comment sent a shaft of fear through her, dampening the heat surging through her, though even fear did not dispel it completely. She moistened her dried lips. "I ... It was a hound when I was a small child," she lied, knowing it was no such thing, though she could not recall how or when she'd gotten the scar.

He touched the tiny, white scars with his lips, brushing them back and forth against her flesh in a way that sent a fresh surge of heat through her. As she watched, he turned her hand palm upwards and placed a kiss on the sensitive flesh there. When their gazes met over her hand, she knew he meant to kiss her.

Her mouth went dry at the thought. Her heart lurched painfully. She hovered breathlessly in anticipation, fighting the urge to give in to her body's urges.

With an effort, she withdrew her hand and looked down at the instrument in her lap, knowing if she allowed him to kiss her she was lost. After a moment, Kale rose. "I should go."

There was a note in his voice that told her he would have far preferred to stay. She knew in that moment that she desperately wanted him to ... and that he was far more dangerous than she had perceived.

She closed her eyes against the desire, trying to close her mind to the little voice that urged her to take what joy she could of life. She was cursed. She knew in her heart that she would never find the cure, never be a wife and mother. It mattered little that it went against everything she had been brought up to believe in to even consider taking a lover. What she'd become against her will went against everything she'd been brought up to believe in, and it had deprived her of any chance of love and marriage.

In the end, it was fear that made her reject the offer she wanted so badly to accept ... not the fear of condemnation by her peers--she had already been condemned to damnation by her malady--but rather the fear of loss. Far better never to have loved, she thought, than to have loved and lost.

She knew if she gave herself to him she would be giving all of herself, not just her body and her passion, but her heart and her soul.

Without a word, she offered up his lute.

He studied her for a long moment but did not take it. "I'll be back for it," he said finally and strode toward the door.

She found she was too weak to rise at once when the door had closed behind him. Finally, however, she rose and bolted the door.

After banking the fire and dousing the candle, Aslyn shook the blanket and made her way to her bed, but she found little rest. She ached for his touch with a yearning that filled her mind with heated dreams.

It took an effort to drag herself from her bed the following morning. Still bleary eyed, she made her way to the necessary behind the cottage, noting as she did so that the camp had been struck. A mixture of relief and sadness filled her. She should be glad the soldiers had gone. It meant her secret was safe. It meant she had the chance to leave without the danger of being caught fleeing the area.

It meant she would probably never cross paths with Kale again.

The urge to weep at the thought was strong. She quelled it with an effort, turning her thoughts to the necessity of leaving while she had the chance. Somehow, however, she could not seem to find the energy to gather her few belongings and set out. She'd slept so little the night before that her head ached, making coherent thought nearly impossible. She was tempted to simply crawl back into her bed and try to sleep for a few hours. She was certainly in no condition to travel as she was. She would need to move fast and put many miles behind her if she was to attempt it at all or she would run the risk of still being too close to Krackensled when ... if ... the soldiers returned.

A sickness had crept into the village, she soon discovered, when first one and then another of the townsfolk appeared upon her doorstep with a child bearing spots. A different sort of dread seized her when she realized what it was--small pox. She did what she could, but in truth there was very little she could do except to warn them to keep the sick as far from the well as possible. Her supply of medicinal herbs was low and even if that had not been the case, there were none she knew of that would cure the illness. The strong would survive. The weak would die.

She was so weary when she finally crawled into her bed that night that she could hardly keep her eyes open, and still her dreams were plagued by Kale's touch. When she woke the following day feeling worse, if possible, than the day before, she began to wonder if he had somehow placed a spell upon her. Her obsession with Kale seemed unnatural. He had done no more than kiss her hand.

But he had not merely kissed her hand. He had enfolded her in his embrace. Remembering the feel of his arms around her, the brush of his chest against her back, the woodsy scent that clung to his flesh, was enough to send a rush of heat throughout her body.

If she were truthful with herself, she had been lost long before he had touched her.

As much as she would have liked to discount her feelings as the result of some sort of black magic, she knew very well that it wasn't. With no more than a careless caress, Kale had aroused a sensual awareness in her that she began to doubt that she would ever be able to put to rest. She might flee from him, but she could not flee the memory of her body's response to his nearness.

She lost count of the days, for she found little rest at night, and none at all during the day. Finally, however, the traffic to her door began to slow as the small pox ran it's course with surprising speed. The death toll was relatively small in numbers. She'd seen whole villages wiped out by the disease, but, doubtless because it was far too cold for anyone to be out unless absolutely necessary, more families were untouched than those that were hit. The villagers were convinced that it was her doing and lavished gifts of appreciation on her, much to her embarrassment. It did no good, however, to claim she'd done nothing to earn their gratitude.

Weariness finally took its toll and Aslyn slept dreamlessly throughout the night and most of the following day. It was nearing dusk when she finally roused herself enough to rise. Disoriented, it took some moments to realize that she'd slept throughout a night and entire day and that it was not morning approaching, but evening when she opened her door at last.

Shaking off the haziness of sleep, she made her way around the cottage to the necessary, trying to recall when she'd eaten last. If the clamor of her stomach was anything to go by, it had been days.

As she was returning to collect her cook pot, however, she heard the snap of a twig close by and it drove all thoughts of hunger from her mind. She froze, instantly alert, and turned slowly toward the sound. A snow fox stood less than two yards from her, watching her with a steady, golden eyed gaze.

He was by far the largest fox she had ever seen, nearly as big as a small wolf. In fact, for several moments she thought it was a wolf, but as she stared at him in fright, she began to notice the subtle differences.

Her fear subsided somewhat, but she could not help but be uneasy about discovering a fox virtually at her door step. After a moment, when he made no move to leave, she took a cautious step back. To her dismay, the fox took a step toward her.

Aslyn stopped, studying him. He did not appear to be mad, but perhaps hunger had driven him this close to town? If that were the case, then he was easily as dangerous as a wolf, for he was as big and his teeth sharp enough to rend her flesh.

She took another step back. She was on the point of whirling to run when the fox leapt at her. Uttering a shriek of fright, she jumped back, tripped and went down even as the fox struck her chest. Disoriented by the fall, it took several moments for Aslyn to realize that the fox was standing over her, on top of her, his forepaws planted firmly on her breasts.

She stared up at him, holding her breath, fearful that any moment he would go for her throat and rip her to shreds. Instead, after several long, agonizing moments of fright, the fox stepped off of her. Watching him warily, Aslyn lay still for several moments, hoping that he would be satisfied with having felled her and flee into the woods once more. Instead, he sat, still watching her.

She frowned, wondering at his curious behavior. It was almost as if he was tame. Slowly, she sat up. When the fox made no attempt to pounce upon her again, she began struggling to her feet. As she placed her palm against the ground to push herself up, however, the fox darted forward, nipping her hand with his sharp teeth. She wasn't even aware of the branch she'd clutched when she'd fallen until the fox darted at her, but the moment he did, she swung, catching him on the shoulder. What he might have done had she not struck him, she was never to know, but the branch was sufficient to dissuade his attack. He broke off with a yelp and loped off, disappearing against the background of the snow long before he could have reached the trees.

Aslyn stared after him, trying to spot him against the mounds of snow, but she caught no more than a glimpse of him before he vanished completely. The throb in her hand finally caught her attention and she lifted it to examine it. Despite the blood, she discovered it was little more than a scratch. Undoubtedly, he had only caught it with the edge of his teeth. If he'd had time to bite, he would have inflicted a good deal more damage.

A sense of uneasiness filled her, and she glanced back in the direction that the fox had disappeared, wondering if it had been mad after all. As bizarre as its behavior, however, she knew it could not have been mad. If it had been, nothing short of killing it would have stopped its attack.

Finally, she was forced by her stomach's demands to dismiss it. Reaching down, she grasped a handful of snow and rubbed it across the back of her hand until the bleeding slowed. Returning to the cottage, she cleaned the wound thoroughly, then soaked it in a dish of steeped herbs and salt to promote healing and prevent the wound from putrefying. When she was satisfied, she collected her cook pot and walked down to the well to fill it.

She had just filled the pot and turned to start back when a woman's screams rent the air. The sound tore through Aslyn like the slash of a knife. She dropped the pot from suddenly nerveless fingers. Her head whipped around from side to side as she searched for the source of the horrible sounds. Around her, she saw the villagers pouring from their cottages as they, too, were drawn by the cries. Almost as one, they began to move, slowly, but quickly gaining speed. Many grasped broomsticks, axes ... anything they came across as they rushed toward the shattering cries.

As one, they halted abruptly as they reached the next street and saw a man and woman on their knees in the middle of the muddy road. The man was covered in blood. The woman was holding a wad of bloodied rags, rocking back and forth. With an effort, Aslyn forced her feet forward, moving almost like a sleepwalker until she was near enough to recognize the woman.

It was Ana Halard, little John's mother .

A terrible dread seized Aslyn as she stared at the distraught woman, studied the torn rags the woman was clutching. Even as one of the nearer bystanders gagged, turned and threw up, she knew what it was.

The man kneeling before Ana looked up at Aslyn, tears streaming down his cheeks and Aslyn finally recognized him as John's father. "I tried to fight 'em off. I did. But it was no use. No use a'tall. Them vicious bastards 'ad already torn 'im to shreds."

Aslyn felt the strength leave her knees. She sank onto her knees beside them. "John?"

Ana Halard turned to look at her. "I told 'im not to take me baby to the woods. I told 'im. He said I was pamperin' 'im. Said he'd never be a man if I kept 'im tied to me apron strings."

Aslyn touched the woman's shoulder. "Hush. Don't say these things."

"It's true!"

Aslyn turned to Halard. It was impossible to tell, however, if the blood spattering his face and covering his chest and arms was his or the child's. "Are you hurt?"

He ignored the question, climbed awkwardly to his feet. Swaying slightly, he looked down at his wife, blubbering now like a hurt child himself. "I only did what I thought was right."

"You got 'im killed!" she screamed at him. "He was too small to be out gathering wood. You should've taken one of the older boys."

"Stop it!" Aslyn cried angrily, but she knew that both the boy's parents were too hurt and shocked to really know what they were saying. She glanced around at the villagers. "Someone help Mr. Halard to my cottage so I can see to his wounds."

The crowd around her simply stared at her blankly, too shocked and horrified themselves for anything to filter through to them.

"I don't need no tending. I'm for finding those damned wolves and killing them, ever last one of them! Who's with me? Who'll help me hunt them down and slaughter them? Before they pick us off one by one!"

A low rumble began amongst the villagers. Like the growl of an animal, it built into an enraged howl. They surged forward, following Halard as he lurched toward the woods he'd so lately exited. Stunned, Aslyn watched them race into the woods, most of them completely unarmed, those few who were armed carrying little more than sticks. A very little thought told her, however, that they were mad with fear and fury and nothing short of a hail of cannon fire would halt them. They could not be reasoned with and might well turn upon her if she tried to stop them.

In any case, Ana needed her. She turned her attention to the boy's mother. She was still clutching John's torn and battered remains to her, rocking him back and forth. She touched the grieving woman on the shoulder. "Mrs. Halard, please, let me help you. Give him to me. I'll take care of him."

It wasn't until the woman turned to look at her that she realized there were tears streaming down her own cheeks.

"There ain't nothin' nobody can do fer me baby anymore."

Aslyn swallowed against the lump in her throat. "We have to ... prepare him."

The woman began to wail aloud. "No! No, no, no! He's scared of the dark. My baby's scared of the dark. You can't put 'im in a dark hole."

Aslyn glanced around helplessly. To her surprise she discovered a half a dozen women standing around the two of them, their faces filled with pity and horror. As if they read her mind, they surged forward, grasping the woman and pulling her to her feet and then half carried her to her cottage. Aslyn remained where she was, watching them, slowly becoming aware of her own wrenching sobs.

She could not force the image of the battered child from her mind. Image after horrible image clicked before her mind's eye, each one banished by one more horrible than the last.

He had been a weak, sickly child. She had known in her heart that he would never grow up, but she had thought he would die in his bed, not in terror and pain. She couldn't bear the thought of the torment he'd suffered before he'd found peace. What must his mother be going through? Small wonder the woman was out of her mind with grief, to lose a child under such terrible circumstances.

It made it worse that he had been doing so well when last she'd seen him, his face smiling up at her, glowing with growing good health. Had it been only the day before that Ana had brought him to show her how much better he was doing?

It dawned on her then and a coldness crept through her that had nothing to do with the icy ground.

John had been to see her only the day before.... The last victim of the wolves had been Will the Red, and she'd seen him the very morning of the day he was attacked.

Chapter Eight

Was it only a coincidence that the last two victims of wolf attacks had been with her only hours before their attack? It seemed too absurd to believe, and yet the attacks that had begun months ago had always been close by, wherever she was. She had assumed that she was responsible for at least some of the attacks, but had also known she could not possibly have been responsible for the majority of them. She had also assumed the attacks were widespread, not concentrated to her vicinity. But, what if she was wrong in that line of thinking? What if she was somehow drawing the wolves?

She had been told that the soldiers had decided to camp in the area because the last several attacks had been nearby. They were tracking the pack, had been tracking the pack for months ... and they had been led virtually to her door.

Shaking her head, she mopped the tears from her cheeks and slowly got to her feet and looked around. She was alone.

It had grown dark. She lifted her head to stare up at the sky. The moon had risen, but it was no more than a pale sliver in the sky. Tomorrow, or perhaps the day after, it would not appear at all and the dark of the moon would lie upon the land. For how many days, she wondered? Did it matter? Soon the full moon would rise and her time would be upon her.

It seemed impossible that she could have lingered so long, impossible that she could have so completely lost track of passing time.

A sudden urgency filled her to leave Krackensled, at once--that very night.

She was running by the time she reached her cottage.

Flinging the door open, she did no more than push it toward closed, only vaguely aware that she had not shut the door completely, nor bolted it, as was her habit. It nagged at her, but she dismissed it. It could take no more than a few minutes to gather her things and she would be on her way anyway.

In truth, she had brought very little with her. Deciding to take the ragged quilt, she rolled it and bound the ends with string, then spread a cloth on the bare mattress and retrieved her spare shift and gown from the pegs on the wall, bundling them quickly and placing them in the middle of the cloth. Her healing herbs were always kept in their own pouch and she merely grabbed it up and set it beside the bundle. Looking quickly around, she saw that she had gathered all she had brought with her, but her stomach was rumbling once more, reminding her she'd not eaten. Taking her knife, she cut a large wedge of cheese, meat and a chunk of bread to bundle in her pack and then cut some thin slices to stack together so that she could eat it as she walked.

She had just slung the blanket over her shoulder when she heard a sound behind her. It froze the blood in her veins.

"Going somewhere?"

Slowly, she turned and stared at the man filling the doorway.

She did not recognize him. It was the first time she'd seen him without his armor. Instead, he was dressed in leather, as Kale usually dressed, a dark cloak slung about his shoulders.

But it was not the way he was dressed that made him unrecognizable. It was the wildness in his gleaming, golden eyes, in his wind swept hair ... the blood smeared on his jerkin and breeches.

Aslyn's heart slammed into her chest so hard all the strength went out of her body and it was only by force of will that she kept from wilting into a puddle of terror on the floor. "What are you doing here, Algar?" she whispered through parched lips.

Instead of answering at once, he lifted his head, sniffing the air. His eyes were gleaming with malice, and lust, when he looked at her once more. A savage grin curled his lips. "How could I resist the scent of a female in heat?"

Aslyn felt her jaw go slack as the words sank slowly into her fear numbed mind. Insulting as the comment would have been under other circumstances, she was no longer human ... but she-beast. Why had it not occurred to her before? Even when she had speculated the possibility that the pack was trailing her, that she was leading them, it had not dawned on her to wonder why they might be drawn to her.

It made so much sense now of things that had seemed to make no sense at all before.

Small wonder Kale had needed only to brush against her, to leave his scent on her skin and her mind had clouded with the need to mate with him.

"Good God!"

His grin widened. "I doubt there would be many who would be willing to agree He has anything to do with us."

Sluggishly, her mind worked its way around the comment. "You knew!"

He chuckled, stepped inside and pushed the door closed behind him. "The moment I saw you again."

"How? How could you possibly know--again? What do you mean, again?"

He cocked his head to one side, studying her. "I'm hurt. You don't remember?"

She stared at him, cast her mind back, but no matter how hard she jogged her memory, she was certain she had never met him before she had come to Krackensled.

"You bore the mark. It distressed me no end that I had not been the one to give it to you, but I knew you were meant to be mine. Unfortunately, your father had seen fit to bestow you upon another. I had to ... dispose of my rival. But when I looked around again, you'd vanished."

Aslyn swallowed against the lump of sickness welling in her throat. "It was you? You ... butchered Wilhem?"

He stared at her a long moment and began to laugh. "You thought you'd done it?"

Fury surged through her, suddenly, violently, pushing all other considerations to the back of her mind. "You killed John! You monster!"

He shrugged. "When the beast is upon me...."

Aslyn shook her head, too angry to think straight, but one fact stood out. "No. It doesn't make any sense. The moon isn't full."

A thin smile curled his lips. "It makes no sense to you, my dear, because you were not born into the clan. You were marked, long ago, chosen as mate by one of the brethren. But his loss is my gain," he added with a chuckle, beginning to advance slowly toward her.

"You summon the beast. It doesn't control you."

"Exactly."

"Then you *are* a monster! You chose to slaughter that poor, innocent child!"

Again he shrugged. "The hunger must be appeased when it comes upon me. I only chose the one handiest to feed upon."

Aslyn backed away. "You marked me! You stole my humanity, made me into a monster like you!" she exclaimed, lifting her hand.

His eyes narrowed, all traces of humor vanishing as he stared at her hand. "What happened to your hand?"

"As if you didn't know!"

Rage filled his eyes. He leapt at her, grasping her hand and lifting it to sniff it. He growled, low in his throat. "You are mine! I meant to have you when you came into your first season, but you escaped. I've searched for you for three long years. I'm of no mind to allow you to escape me again!"

Aslyn snatched her hand from his grip and leapt away from him. "Nay! I'll not allow you to touch me, you monster! I'd die, rather!"

He lunged for her. She screamed as his arms closed around her. Dropping down, she managed to slip from his grasp, but he caught hold of her hair before she could get away. Pain shot through her scalp as he jerked her upright and flung her toward the bed. She skidded across it and slammed into the wall so hard it shook from the impact, clods of dried mud raining down around her.

He reached for her again, dragging her toward him so that her gown rode up around her waist. Aslyn kicked him, rocking him back momentarily. Knocking her legs out of his way, he tried to grasp her flailing arms. She slapped at him, curled her fingers and clawed his arms, but the leather made her efforts ineffectual. He lunged at her, forcing the breath from her as he landed on top of her. The bed creaked, groaned and finally gave way under their combined weight.

Aslyn was still struggling to drag air into her lungs when Algar flew from her. She blinked, rubbed the dirt from her eyes so that she could see.

Kale was standing over Algar, breathing heavily.

Relief and joy flooded her, but both vanished almost immediately as it dawned on her that Kale was no match for Algar. As strong as he was, Algar probably outweighed him by twenty pounds or more. Moreover, Algar was not human. He had the strength of the beast.

She screamed as Algar bounded from the floor and crashed into Kale. Forced back by the other man's superior weight, Kale slammed into the table, shattering it into splinters of wood. Before Algar could leap upon him, he rolled away, coming to his feet once more in the half crouch of a knife fighter's stance, a wicked blade gripped tightly in one hand.

Algar drew his blade as well, circling Kale, blocking the only way in or out of the cottage.

Aslyn scrambled crab-like across the floor, seized a piece of the table leg and hurled it in Algar's direction. His eyes widened in surprise as it struck him on the shin. Distracted, Kale's head whipped around. Algar roared and charged. Aslyn grabbed up another board and hurled it. His eyes widening in surprise, Kale jumped aside. The block of wood missed him by mere inches and smacked into Algar's forehead. He stumbled. Before he could recover, or Aslyn launch another missile, Kale launched himself at Algar, swinging his blade so fast it was a mere blur of motion, slicing three long cuts across the leather jerkin Algar wore.

Algar leapt back, landing on one of the pieces of wood Aslyn had thrown at him. It rolled, pitching him backward through the doorway.

Kale rushed at him, launching himself at the fallen man, but Algar recovered quickly. Jerking his feet up, he connected with Kale's belly as he descended. Lifting the huntsman, Algar used Kale's own momentum to pitch him head first into the cottage yard.

Aslyn could no longer see Kale, had no idea of whether he was too hurt to recover quickly enough. As Algar scrambled to his feet, she caught sight of her own knife. Snatching it up, gripping it tightly in her fist, she rushed Algar even as he turned to attack Kale once more. She wasn't even aware of screaming until Algar swung back toward her, but she was far quicker than he. She embedded her dagger in his shoulder up to the hilt before he could swing at her to fend her off. He roared as she sank the blade home, swinging at her with his balled fist and catching her across the jaw.

Pain exploded inside her head, sending bright, white lights through the darkness that settled over her like a cloak even as she flew backwards and struck the wall. Stunned by the blow, it took her several moments to fight the darkness off, to roll onto her knees. Even the certainty that he would follow the blow by an attack was not enough to will strength into her limbs. Finally, however, she managed to stagger to her feet and look around.

Dimly, outside, she heard the sounds of a struggle. Crawling across the floor, she found a leg of the table and, after several aborted attempts, managed to get to her feet. Weaving like a drunk, she focused on the door and made her way across the cottage, slumping against the door frame as she reached it, surveying the area outside. Algar, she saw to her immense relief, had vanished. Kale was struggling to get to his feet.

He looked up at her, studied her for a long moment. A smile tugged at his lips. "I hope you don't mean to use that on me."

Aslyn blinked, looked down at the table leg in her hand. "He's gone?"

The smile vanished. A grim look took its place as he turned and stared off into the darkness that shrouded the land. "Yes. Unfortunately."

Aslyn's knees buckled, and she sat abruptly.

Kale was on his feet in an instant, striding toward her. Without a word, he scooped her into his arms and carried her inside, kicking the door closed with his foot. After surveying the damage inside the cottage, he moved to the hearth. Kneeling, he sat her so that her back was against the wall nearest the fireplace. "Don't move."

Striding across the room, he lifted the mattress from the broken bed frame and returned. Setting it in front of the hearth, he scooped her up once more and settled her carefully on top of it. "Where are you hurt, sweeting?"

Stunned as she was by all that had happened, the endearment warmed her, perhaps more so because he didn't seem even to realize that he'd said it. "I'm not hurt," she said shakily. She was shivering, her teeth trying to clatter together despite her efforts to control the jerking in her jaws. Dimly, she was aware of a dozen or more areas on her body that throbbed dully with pain, but she knew they were bruises only, nothing serious enough to claim as wounds.

"Don't try to be brave. Tell me."

Aslyn shook her head, fighting a sudden urge to burst into tears. "I'm not at all brave. He frightened me half out of my wits. But, I'm not hurt. Truly. It's nothing more than bruises."

He ignored her disclaimer, searching her for any sign of cuts or broken bones. Finally, he sat back on his heels, studying her bruised face, and renewed fury leapt into his eyes. "I will kill him by inches when I find him."

Aslyn grabbed his hand when he made an abortive movement, as if he would rise. "Don't! Please don't go. Not tonight. He might come back. Besides, you're hurt. I need to see to your wounds."

He shook his head. "It is nothing. Scratches that will heal quickly enough."

"At least let me see so that I might be easy in my mind."

He studied her a long moment and finally shrugged. "When I return. I need to see to my horse first. I won't be gone long."

Anger surged through her as she watched him leave. He was bleeding. The wounds might not be severe, but she would have far preferred to check them before he went to see after his horse.

Of course, it would be cruel to leave the poor, dumb beast outside indefinitely, but surely his own needs should come first?

Or did he mean to go after Lord Algar, despite the fact that he'd told her he would not?

Anxiety quashed the anger. She bit her lip, tempted to rush after him, but in the end she merely rose and bolted the door. Turning, she surveyed the shambles of the cottage. It contained very little now that was not broken.

It hurt to walk, to bend, to lift ... even bending her head created a fiercer pounding inside her skull, but the shattered remnants of the furniture and crockery represented any number of 'traps' for the unwary. Slowly, moving like an old woman, she collected the broken pieces of wood that were the remains of bedstead, table and chair, and piled them beside the hearth to burn. Her own meager belongings were scattered about the room. She made a pile of the broken crockery near the door and collected her belongings, tying them in a bundle and leaving them near one wall, out of the way. She'd just collected the last fragments of crockery that she could see and started toward the door when someone tried the door, then rapped on it sharply.

"Who is it?" Aslyn called out in a breathless squeak.

"Who are you expecting?" came the dry reply.

Dropping the crockery on the pile beside the door, Aslyn unbolted it and pulled the door open. Kale strode inside, surveyed the room and turned to her as she bolted the door behind him.

"You are a stubborn woman."

She smiled tiredly and, on impulse, threw her arms around him, hugging him tightly. "I thought you would not come back," she said in a voice muffled against his chest.

His arms came around her briefly, but then he pulled away, guided her back to the mattress on the floor and made her sit. She was about to protest when he joined her. She reached for the ties of her shirt. "Here. Let me see to your hurts."

His brows rose, but he didn't argue as she loosened the ties and pulled his tunic over his head. To her surprise, but with a great deal of relief, she saw he had not underestimated his injuries. There were a number of scrapes, along his ribs, and on his arms, but none deep enough to require attention. Already, they had closed and ceased to bleed. He had a number of bruises, as well, on his chest and back, and a long, dark mark on his shoulder that made her wonder if she'd struck him with the table leg when she'd thrown it.

She relaxed. Realizing she was still shaking, she pulled her cloak more snugly about her and shifted closer to the fire. "You are no more hurt than I, thankfully."

He frowned, looked around the cottage. After a moment, he rose and took the rolled quilt from the pile near the wall, pulled the ties from it and returned, shaking it out and wrapping it around her shoulders. "Which I owe to skill, and you to pure luck," he responded coolly. "It was foolish of you to endanger yourself needlessly."

Aslyn frowned at him, but discovered she simply didn't have the energy to argue with him. Giving in to her aches and pains, she lay down on the mattress, trying to ignore the throbbing in her cheek. "I should've allowed you to fight him alone, I suppose, but I was not entirely confident that you could beat him and thought it best to add my poor efforts to yours, lest I be left to fend him off again, alone."

He chuckled.

She opened her eyes, a little surprised that he had taken the insult to his manhood so calmly. He shifted until he was laying beside her. "Next time, make certain I am not in the line of fire before you begin throwing the furniture."

Aslyn stiffened slightly as he pulled her into his arms and settled her against his chest, but as his warmth seeped into her, she relaxed once more. "I missed you," she mumbled.

"More accurately, I ducked," he murmured in a voice laced with amusement.

She shrugged. "I still missed you."

"True."

She sniffed, finding she had to fight the urge to burst into tears. "I lost my dagger."

He shook. When she opened one eye a crack to look at him, she saw that he was trying to suppress a chuckle. "He took it with him, I'm afraid. As much as I appreciate your efforts to defend me, that was most ignoble of you to stab him in the back."

Again, Aslyn shrugged. "Is it my fault he didn't turn around?"

"He had his back to you to begin with."

Aslyn lost interest in the subject. "How came you here?"

"Upon a horse."

She shook him, weakly. "Do not jest."

"It's truth."

"I know you came upon a horse! How came you here, now?"

"Ah. We had been tracking the wolf pack for nigh a week when it occurred to me that they appeared to be moving in a broad circle. I left the men to follow them and returned to Krackensled in case they were doubling back as I suspected."

Aslyn shuddered, felt tears well in her eyes. "They did. They killed a child. Poor little John Halard. His father had taken him into the woods to help him gather firewood."

Kale's arms tightened around her. "I'm sorry, sweeting."

The words seemed to rupture a dam of grief inside her. Aslyn wept until finally, completely exhausted, she drifted off to sleep.

She swam upwards toward awareness sometime later to the sensation of warmth generated by Kale's hand as he stroked her back soothingly. The effect upon her, however, was anything but soothing. Her breasts, pressed tightly against his chest ached with need, as did her woman's place between her thighs. She moved restlessly against him, uncertain of exactly what it was that she needed to quell the ache, but certain that Kale could assuage the need.

He stilled her movements. "Sleep, Aslyn."

She was too hot and achy to sleep. She nuzzled her face against his bare chest, pressed her lips there. He jerked at the touch of her mouth as if branded. Reaching down, he cupped her chin and urged her to look up at him. "Don't tempt me. I'm a man, Aslyn. I've only so much resistance. You're hurt. Rest."

Aslyn sighed, feeling a sense of defeat wash over her. Finally, she snuggled against him and drifted away once more.

Kale was gone when she awoke.

Chapter Nine

Aslyn woke to a sense of well-being, although she wasn't certain what had evoked the sensation. When she stretched, however, an involuntary groan of agony tore from her, bringing her wide awake. She sat up slowly, painfully, and looked around as memory flooded back.

The sense of well-being, she finally realized, had come from curling next to Kale during the night. It had given her the sense of being protected and cared for ... something she'd lost so long ago she had ceased even to realize how much she missed it.

That sense vanished the moment she realized she was alone.

Rising with an effort, she made her way to the door and around the side of the house to the necessary, not really surprised when she saw no sign of Kale, but vastly disappointed.

When she returned, she stoked the fire and pushed the cook pot, filled with snow, over it to warm while she searched the cottage for food. She hadn't eaten in so long, she felt dizzy and weak, although she supposed a part of the dizziness and weakness was from the battle the night before. The cheese and meat she'd sliced for her journey had fallen on the floor when Kale had crushed the table, and thereafter been stomped into the dirt. Opening her bundle, she took the pieces she'd carefully wrapped and looked around for her knife before she recalled that she'd lost it in the scuffle. Finally, she had to settle for gnawing bites from the edges of the food. When she'd eaten her fill, she carefully wrapped the food again, bundled it into her pack and removed her spare gown and shift.

The water, when she tested it, was tepid on the surface, and the next thing to scalding nearer the bottom. Stirring it with a stick, she lifted the pot from the fireplace, sat on the mattress and bathed. Not surprisingly, she was filthy from the scuffle. She blushed when she thought about offering herself to Kale when she must have looked completely unappealing--battered, bruised and filthy, her hair a tangled mat.

She was glad he'd left while she was still sleeping. At least he'd spared her the humiliation of waking up and facing him after that little episode.

He'd also been kind enough to tell her he didn't want to hurt her when she was already hurt. She remembered that. It was one of the things that had made her feel so protected and secure. Fortunately, she'd been too groggy with sleep, and suffused with animal lust to figure out that what he'd really meant was that he couldn't bring himself to give her a roll when she'd already been wallowing in mud. "I will die of embarrassment if I ever have to see the man again," she muttered to herself.

And that wasn't even the worst of it. When she caught a glimpse of her reflection in the water she gasped in horror. One whole side of her face--the side where Algar had clobbered her--the side that still throbbed almost as badly as it had the night before--was horribly bruised and swollen.

She looked like a monster.

The thought made her cringe inside.

She was a monster.

Damn Algar to hell!

She covered her face with her hands. All these years she had wandered, searching for a cure that didn't exist! And Algar, damn him, had taken her life away from her, killed her betrothed--made her unfit for any decent man.

The image of John's battered little body popped into her mind and she shuddered. Shying away from it, she got up abruptly.

Kale, she knew, had gone after Algar. His men had not yet returned. Now was the time to leave if ever there was one. She simply could not face Kale again, not after what had almost happened between them the night before--not when she knew now without a shadow of doubt what she was.

Nothing good could come of staying.

Moving purposefully now, ignoring the multitude of aches and pains, she gathered her belongings and left the cottage. It was still early, the streets deserted.

She frowned, wondering why no one else was about, but then remembered that most of the villagers had gone out to search for the wolf pack. God alone knew how many had returned, or in what condition, but she could not allow that to concern her. She had her own survival to consider.

She glanced around. New snow had fallen during the night, making it difficult to discern the tracks from the night before, but it appeared that Algar had headed north. She was tempted to head south, but thought that might be too predictable. Kale had told her the soldiers had tracked the wolf pack in a wide circle that seemed to be heading back toward Krackensled ... which meant going west was out, since there was too much danger of running into the soldiers.

She decided to head east, but just in case Kale got it into his head to follow her, she turned south when she left the cottage, following the main road until she found a cross road that was almost as well traveled.

It took her almost an hour to reach the forest east of town. To her relief, she encountered no one, but she was still a mass of nerves before she reached the tree line. There she waged another, brief, inner debate. She could make better progress if she followed the road. The snow was almost as high, and worse, it had been churned up by the passing of several carts, but there were no deep drifts to worry about, no possibility of stepping inadvertently into a trough.

If anyone came to look for her, however, she would be all too easy to spot and have no hope of escape. She left the road and entered the forest, struggling through soft snow that came almost to her knees. She was sweating with effort and breathless even before she had traveled far enough that she could no longer see the village. She glanced up at the weak sun, trying to gauge the amount of time that had passed and saw that the sun was already high in the trees.

Cursing, she forced herself to move faster, refusing to stop to rest, but only slowing when she was so winded she could hardly catch her breath. She began scanning the forest ahead of her, choosing a landmark that looked to be a quarter of a mile, or a half a mile away, and then counting her miles as she reached them. By the time the sun was overhead she thought she had gone at least five miles, but it was a rather dismal projection. A man on a horse could travel that distance, even in the snow, in less than a quarter of the time it had taken her.

She stopped, briefly, to eat a few bites of cheese, bread and meat, washing them down with the remains of the bottle of wine she and Kale had shared the night before. There was hardly enough to make it worth the effort of having carried the bottle, but it helped to chase the chill from her bones.

When she'd finished, she dug a hole in the snow, buried the bottle and carefully smoothed the snow over it again. She glanced back over the trail she'd left behind her when she'd finished, realizing that she might as well have saved her strength. She'd left a trail behind her that a blind man could follow. Kale was a huntsman. Were he so inclined, he would have no difficulty whatsoever in tracking her down.

Tired as she was, she looked around until she found a fallen branch and began to work her way backwards, smoothing over her footsteps as she went. It took her twice as long to manage half the distance she had traveled earlier. Her back began to feel as if it was going to crack and break in two, but she persevered until she thought she had traveled at least two miles, then changed directions and began to move in a south easterly direction.

By late afternoon Aslyn felt she had put sufficient distance between herself and Krackensled to consider stopping for the night. In truth, she was afraid she had little choice in the matter. It was the time of the dark of the moon. If she had been traveling by road, the stars might have shed enough light that she could have kept going, but she had elected to take to the forest. Granted, many of the trees were bare, but it was an old forest and the trees were huge, growing closely together with branches intertwining overhead.

She would have to build a fire. It was far too cold even to consider doing without one, regardless of the dangers inherent in doing so. While she trudged through the snow, she'd had no difficulty staying warm, but once she stopped she would begin to freeze without one ... unless she was fortunate enough to discover an unoccupied burrow or den she could squeeze into.

Hopefulness surged through her when she came upon a steep slope above a frozen stream. Like any natural stream, it meandered, but it ran in a general north/south direction. Cautiously, she made her way down to the surface of the stream and began to follow the bank south, studying the banks for any sign of a cave or even a crevice deep enough to offer some shelter. She was so intent upon her search that it was some moments before the rhythmic sound she heard fully registered as being one not of her own making.

Horse hooves.

Aslyn froze, turned her head to determine the direction and discovered that there was a rider baring down on her. Despite the dimness of approaching dusk, despite the distance, she knew the moment she spotted him that it was Kale ... and he had spotted her.

Her heart lurched in her chest. For several moments, she couldn't seem to force her panicked mind to react. Finally, however, the rhythmic pounding formed in her brain as the word 'run, run, run.' Looking wildly around, she realized the only possibility she had of escaping was to climb the bank. As steep and as slippery as it was, she felt certain the horse would not be able to climb it and, if Kale had to find another place to climb the bank she would have time to hide.

The moment the idea formed in her mind, she tossed her burdens aside and climbed for all she was worth. When she finally managed to reach the top, she paused long enough to catch her breath and to spare a glance to see if Kale had spotted her escape.

To her horror, she saw that Kale, instead of following the stream until he reached the point where she'd climbed up, had urged the horse off the stream the moment she left it ... and the horse was climbing the bank like a mountain goat. Spurred by the certainty of instant capture, Aslyn took off through the trees at her best speed.

It took Kale all of five minutes to run her down. She felt the heat from the horse a split second before Kale leaned from its back and snatched her off her feet, plunking her across his lap.

She kicked her feet, trying to wiggle off, whereupon Kale dealt her half frozen rump a ringing spank.

Aghast, she went perfectly still for about two seconds before it fully sank into her mind that he'd had the unmitigated gall to spank her. She struggled to lift her head and gave him her best 'I'll kill you' look.

Unfortunately, the evil look he was giving her frightened her considerably more than hers, apparently, did him.

"Going somewhere?" he asked in a cold, tight voice.

He grasped her then, lifting her until she was sitting before him on the saddle, instead of lying face down over it. She scowled at him. "I am."

They glared at each other for a full minute in a silent battle of wills. "Indeed you are, but not where you think," Kale said finally.

He turned the horse then without another word and kicked it into motion.

Aslyn gasped as the horse lurched forward, grasping frantically for something to hold on to. She needn't have worried. Kale held her tightly against his chest with one arm.

"Put me down this instant!" she demanded when she'd recovered sufficiently from her fear of falling to manage it.

"No."

Aslyn turned to look at him in disbelief. "Why?"

He took his gaze from the path long enough to focus a cold, narrow eyed glare upon her. "Because Algar wants you. You cannot run fast enough, or far enough, to escape him."

Rather than frightening her as she supposed had been his intention, his words wounded her to the quick. She looked away, determined not to allow him to see the hurt in her eyes.

It was not, after all, as if she could have failed to know that Algar wanted her, or that Algar would certainly try to track her down. Although Kale could not have known that Algar had admitted to her that he'd been searching for her ever since she'd fled her home, he must surely know she was not so stupid as to think Algar would suddenly decide to stop pursuing her, only because she had shown herself unwilling.

It hurt, though, to realize Kale's only interest in, or concern for her was in using her to trap Algar.

She didn't trust herself to speak for some time afterward, fearful that she would find a warble in her voice, or worse, burst into tears. By the time Krackensled had come into sight, she had recovered sufficiently from her hurt to be angry once more but also to realize that, as compelling as her reasons for leaving were, she could not voice them, and even she was obliged to admit that any lie she might come up with could only sound weak and foolish.

He had no right to hold her against her will. The king had not sent him to harass innocent travelers, but to track down and slaughter the wolves wreaking so much havoc on the populace. However, she was in no position, unfortunately, to demand release, or, more accurately, to enforce her demands.

They left his horse at the livery near the center of town and walked the remainder of the distance to the cottage. Any hope Aslyn had that he might simply escort her there and leave were dashed immediately.

He opened the door, ushered her in and immediately closed and bolted the door behind them. In truth, Aslyn was barely even aware of his actions. She thought for several moments that he'd brought her to the wrong cottage.

The packed dirt floor had been covered, virtually every square inch of it, with carpets. Two high backed, overstuffed chairs had been set before the hearth. A small table between them held a silver candelabra with a half a dozen burning tapers. In the place where the rickety table had sat, stood a handsome, gleaming oak table and two matching oak chairs. A screen behind the table partially blocked her view of the bed, but she saw the narrow bed that had been destroyed in the scuffle had been replaced by a wider one with an elaborately carved foot board.

She turned to look at Kale questioningly and saw that he had discarded his tunic. He advanced upon her, a purposeful look in his eyes. Startled, Aslyn took a step back, lifting her hands to hold him off. He ignored the weak defense. Scooping her into his arms and carrying her to the bed, he dropped her in the middle of it. Aslyn bounded upright as he sat on the edge and proceeded to remove his boots.

"What are you doing?" she asked, more than a little stunned.

He stood up and began removing his breeches. "Something I should have done long ago."

Aslyn's eyes widened as he pushed the breeches from his hips, her gaze focusing of its own accord on the swollen male member jutting from the thatch of hair low on his belly. Heat suffused her as she stared at it. Her heart commenced a frantic tattoo against her chest wall, making her breath short and fast.

She moistened her dry lips. "But...."

Grasping the neck of her gown, he ripped the ancient, threadbare fabric from neck to waist as if it were no more than paper. Aslyn gasped in shock, staring down at her exposed shift, worn to the point that it was virtually transparent. As he reached for her last defense, she scurried away. The rending sound of tearing cloth told her, however, even if the sudden, chill kiss of air had not, that she had not successfully eluded him. Clutching the tatters of her clothing, Aslyn scrambled to the far back of the bed, glancing wildly around for an avenue of escape. The bed was wedged into a corner, however, leaving two sides blocked by walls, a third by Kale.

She leapt for the foot of the bed at the same moment that Kale leapt toward her. He caught her around the waist, dragging her back.

She placed her palms against his chest. "What are you doing? Why?"

He grasped her arms, forcing them to the bed on either side of her head. "Claiming what is mine ... what has always been mine."

A strange mixture of anger and desire rushed through her at his words, at the look in his eyes. "You're no better than Kale," she said coldly.

Something flickered in his eyes. For several moments, she thought he would release her and withdraw, instead, after that brief hesitation, he lowered himself until his bare chest was resting against her breasts, until his mouth hovered mere inches from her own.

Aslyn stared up at him, her gaze focusing upon his hard mouth, and something warm and liquid flowed through her, washing the anger away, leaving only the desire. She had wondered from the first moment she'd seen him what it would feel like to be desired by him, kissed, caressed. She lifted her lips to him in mute appeal.

He swallowed, his gaze flickering to hers momentarily before he closed the gap between them and pressed his mouth to hers. Fire flooded her at the first touch of his lips. She opened her mouth to him, conquering even as she surrendered.

A shudder ran through him as he thrust his tongue into her mouth, tasting her essence, exploring, touching off currents of liquid fire that flooded her belly with molten flame, raced through her veins, bringing her whole body into sizzling life. She wrapped her arms around him, unaware, and uncaring of when he'd ceased to hold her captive.

She ran her hands along his back, exploring every inch of him that she could reach, even as he explored her body with his hands.

His body was as she had imagined, taut muscles everywhere she touched, his skin smooth and as soft was her own along his back, faintly abrasive on his chest and arms where hair grew. She moved restlessly beneath him, enjoying the texture of his skin as it brushed hers, feeling her nipples harden into stiff, throbbing peaks.

He broke the kiss, moving down to cover one hard peak with his mouth. Aslyn gasped, groaned, cupped his head to her. Threading her fingers through his hair, she tugged, offering her other breast to him when he finally, reluctantly, released the nipple he had teased until she was writhing in mindless ecstasy, groaning as if she was dying.

As heavenly as the suction of his mouth on her breast was, it was not nearly enough. She wanted ... needed more.

She began to struggle against him and when he lifted slightly away, she kissed him as he had kissed her, exploring his body with her mouth. He groaned, allowing her exploration, holding himself in check with an effort that made him tremble beneath her touch.

The tremors running through him were echoed by her own body, a sense of urgency building within both of them until they reached a point where neither could wait longer to join their bodies. Aslyn spread her legs for him, reaching for his throbbing male member to guide it inside her even as he moved to wedge his hips between her trembling thighs. Looping an arm beneath one thigh, he lifted it as he pushed fully inside of her in one swift thrust. Expecting the pain of having her maiden head breached, Aslyn gasped, tensed against a pain that was insignificant beside the pleasure of feeling his flesh become one with hers. She nipped his shoulder, then sucked it to soothe, curling her other leg around him and arching her back to urge him on.

He needed no more. He was shaking with the effort to hold himself in check and at that began to thrust inside her in long, powerful strokes that fed the hunger in her belly for the caress of his man's flesh. She countered each stroke, tilting her hips to urge him deeper, meeting each thrust with a grind of her hips that drove them both to the edge within moments.

He went still suddenly, squeezing his eyes shut, every muscle straining against giving into his body's demand for release. She cried out in frustration, thrusting her hips against him until he uttered a long, low growl and began to move again, hard and fast. He bit down on her shoulder as his climax seized him, his body jerking against hers with his release. The nip of his teeth sent her over the edge of pleasure. It culminated in an explosion of ecstasy that ripped through her entire body, leaving lassitude in its wake.

She went limp beneath him, barely conscious.

Chapter Ten

Minutes passed while they fought for breath. Finally, he gathered himself and rolled off of her and onto his back beside her. Aslyn found herself drifting in a hazy state of blissful repletion. After a while, she realized, dimly, that she had not put up much of a fight to fend him off. She had offered little in the way of maidenly objection. She had certainly not behaved as a maiden when he had touched her.

She found she didn't care.

She should have. What he thought of her was important to her. She had never given herself to any man before and she feared her behavior might make him think otherwise, but in the end, she realized that nothing beyond the moment really mattered. There was no future--not for her--not for them.

It still bothered her. They might have little time together, but she wanted it to be good between them. She wanted warm memories to take with her.

She should be furious with him for his presumption that she would simply yield herself to him only because he had claimed her. If she could rouse a healthy dose of outrage, she would be considerably more convincing as a maiden who'd been robbed of her virtue.

She could not seem to rouse any sense of outrage, however. She could not, in fact, dismiss the urge growing inside of her to join with him again to see if it was as wonderful as the first time.

She rolled onto her side, studied him for a long moment, and then reached over and plucked gently on one of his chest hairs. One corner of his lips twitched, threatening a smile. She tugged a little harder.

"Ouch!" he exclaimed dutifully, and then spoiled it by chuckling. "What was that for?"

Aslyn thought about it a moment, but she was in no mood to start a fight by pretending outrage she didn't feel. "Just checking," she murmured and lay back down again.

"For what?"

"Life."

Laughter rumbled from his chest. He lifted his head, flicked his flaccid member and collapsed again. "For the moment, there is none."

A gurgle of laughter escaped Aslyn before she could stop it. "So much for ravishing me."

Kale rolled onto his side, propping his head on his bent arm and staring down at her, his expression a cross between amusement and worry. "I did not pleasure you?"

Aslyn tried to look despondent but failed. "You know very well that you did."

He grimaced. "Actually, I was not altogether certain. I lost control." He flopped back on the bed, staring at the ceiling. "I do seem to recall hearing something between a yodel and a cat screech."

Aslyn punched him playfully and rolled over on top of him, smiling down at him. "You can do it again, if you like."

His lips twitched. "With your permission?"

The sense of playfulness vanished as she studied his face and realized that the passion she felt for him was only a part of what she felt. Her heart--her soul--was as deeply, irrevocably his as her body--as she had known it would be. She wasn't certain which had come first, or if it even mattered. The two could not be separated.

Small wonder it had cut her so deeply to think he cared only that he could use her to trap Algar.

She lowered her gaze, forcing a smile. "With all my heart," she said playfully, swallowing with some difficulty against the lump of misery that had risen from nowhere to lodge itself in her throat.

He caught her chin, forcing her to look up at him and she felt her smile fall a little flat. "Forever?"

She looked away, forced a chuckle. "For tonight at least," she said flippantly, then, when he frowned, she reached down and cupped his male member. "If I can rouse him from slumber."

It hardened at her touch, grew to fill her hand to overflowing.

He rolled onto his side so that she landed on the bed beside him. Cupping her face in his hands, he lowered his head and kissed her with such tenderness she thought she would cry. She found she could not bear his tenderness. It made her feel as if her heart would break.

She pulled away from him, nipped his shoulder and then his earlobe, running her hands over his chest, his arms and then reaching down to cup his erection. His response was almost instantaneous, heated, aggressive. He moved his mouth and hands over her, possessively, as if to claim every inch of her body as his own.

She pushed him onto his back and crawled atop him, spreading her thighs and rubbing her woman's flesh against him. He lifted her hips and thrust upward, impaling her to the hilt. She cried out, ground her hips against him and finally leaned forward, pulling away slightly then pushing back again.

Before she had caught her rhythm, he surged upward, tipping her onto her back and thrusting into her again and again until she felt herself climbing toward the peak of pleasure once more, felt him striving to reach his own culmination.

Abruptly, he pulled away, rolled her onto her stomach and lifted her hips for his thrust. She groaned when he embedded his hard flesh deeply inside her, pushing back against him to feel him more deeply still.

Gripping her hips, he thrust again and again, setting a rhythm that was fast, hard, demanding. She braced herself on her arms, arching her back, squeezing her eyes tightly shut as she felt her body tensing toward the ultimate release. She screamed when it caught her, carrying her over the edge.

He cried out as well, holding her tightly against him as his seed flooded her.

He groaned when he pulled away from her at last and lowered himself shakily to the bed, breathing harshly as he strove to catch his breath.

Aslyn found she had little desire to move and no strength for it. She was more than half asleep when he gathered her to him, pulling one of her legs over his hips and sliding one of his between her thighs. She muttered a half-hearted complaint as he slid one arm beneath her head and wrapped his arms around her, but his arms tightened when she tried to pull away and she subsided, too tired to argue.

He was studying her when she woke near dawn. She blinked the blurriness from her vision, disconcerted. "Did I oversleep?" she asked a little uncertainly.

He shook his head slightly, lifting a hand and brushing a tendril of hair from her cheek, then lifted a stray lock, studying it. "It glows like fire."

It was the bane of her existence, the main reason she rarely went outside without a hood to cover the brilliant beacon her auburn hair became the moment light touched it. "It's most unkind to remark upon it."

He cocked an eyebrow. "It's beautiful. Almost as beautiful as you are."

Aslyn covered her face with her hand. "Hardly. I look like a monster with my face all swollen."

He pulled her hand away. "The swelling and bruising are almost gone."

Aslyn frowned, certain he was only saying that to try to make her feel better. To her surprise, however, she discovered her face felt almost normal ... which was strange. Surely, as badly battered as her face had been, it would have taken far longer to heal? Or, had she simply lost all track of time?

She knew better, however, and finally decided it must have been the cold that had helped the swelling go down so quickly.

Dismissing it, she glanced around the cottage. "Where did all of this come from?"

He frowned, lay back against the mattress, staring at the ceiling. "I brought them. I would have caught up to you far sooner if it had not taken so long to haul it all here. Then, too, I'd thought you had only gone out. It only occurred to me after you'd been gone for hours that you'd ... decided to leave."

Aslyn grimaced, covering her face with the coverlet. A very little thought assured her that there was nothing she could say that would make her actions any less offensive. She could not recall ever feeling quite so horrid. It didn't matter that it had never occurred to her that Kale had left on her account, to shower her with gifts such as those that now adorned her humble cottage.

She could always say she was sorry ... but it was such an insignificant response to something so horrendous as what she'd done and could not convey the depth of her feelings on the matter.

Worse still, nothing had changed. She could not stay, no matter how badly she might want to, and she could not explain to Kale why she could not stay.

"Were you so convinced I could not protect you from Algar that you thought you had to flee?"

Stunned, Aslyn snatched the covers down and stared at him. "No! That had nothing to do with it!"

"Then why?"

Unable to bear the censure in his gaze, Aslyn rolled onto her side, staring at the wall. "I cannot explain."

"Can't? Or won't?"

"Either."

He was silent for several moments. "You left because of me."

Aslyn sighed, wishing she had tried to come up with a convincing lie. "I left because I had to... Because it was time... And ... because I was afraid of wanting something I could not have."

Kale came up on his side once more, facing her, a teasing light in his eyes. "This is an intriguing statement. Care to elaborate?"

Dismayed as she was that she'd said far too much, Aslyn couldn't help but respond with a smile. She reached for him. "Why don't I just show you?"

They had just gotten warmed up when there came a rap on the door. The sound jolted Aslyn back to reality as effectively as an ice bath. Kale was harder to convince. Finally, however, Aslyn managed to slip away and crawled from the bed.

Her gown and shift lay in tatters on the floor beside the bed. She held them up, staring at them in consternation, then turned to give Kale an admonishing glare. He grinned, lifting his brows and wiggling them at her wickedly. Aslyn suppressed a chuckle.

Dropping the useless garments, she went to the door.

"Who's there?"

"Jim Baker. Be this the house of the healer?"

Aslyn cursed under her breath. "It is. I'm not able to see anyone today unless it cannot wait."

"It be bad. I come yesterday, but you was gone."

She bit her lip, but there was nothing for it. Her clothing was in shreds. Worse, she'd dropped her bundle when Kale had given chase and he had not retrieved it so she didn't even have her spare. She couldn't invite him in wearing nothing but a torn shift, or wrapped in a bed sheet. "If you could come back in an hour, I can see you."

"An hour?"

"Yes."

"All right then."

He sounded more bemused than sullen, but Aslyn still felt uncomfortable about having to send the poor man to wait yet another hour.

Shrugging it off, she returned to the alcove and took her shift and gown from the floor, looking around for her bag of healing potions, which contained her needle and threads.

Kale sat up, snatched the fabric from her hands, wadded it in a ball and tossed it across the cottage. It landed in the hearth and immediately caught flame. "No!" Aslyn exclaimed, but before she could dash to the hearth to drag it out and stamp the flames out, Kale snatched her up and flung her to the bed.

Aslyn glared up at him angrily, trying futilely to fight him off while there was still a chance of retrieving the clothing. "Stop it! That's the only thing I have to wear!"

He returned her glare with one of his own. "I'll not have my woman wearing something not fit for a beggar."

"You'll not have your woman wearing anything at all!" Aslyn snapped angrily. "For I have nothing else. The other was lost yesterday."

Kale grasped her arms, holding them to the bed on either side of her head. "I brought clothing for you."

Aslyn went still. "You what?"

"I brought...."

Aslyn cut him off, her face suffused with color. "You were that certain I would give myself to you like some ... some lowborn slut!"

His eyes narrowed. "You believe being my woman makes you a slut?"

Aslyn looked away. "I never agreed to being a kept woman."

"You gave yourself to me willingly."

The comment sent a jolt of discomfort through her. She could deny that she had, but then both of them would know she was lying, so what was the point? Beyond that, he was right. Why cavil now at being a kept woman, or for that matter his certainty that she would agree to it?

Her morality had become so ingrained that she took comfort from the appearance of it even when it was a lie? What possible difference could appearances make to her of all people?

The fight went out of her. She shook her head. "Nay, enthusiastically."

His brows rose in surprise.

She smiled faintly. "We have an hour."

* * * *

The gowns he'd brought were completely inappropriate for her trade. They were beautiful, and made of fine fabrics. Aslyn gazed at them with a mixture of dismay and pleasure when Kale spread them across the bed for her.

"Kale ... they are beautiful, but I cannot wear these to treat the sick."

Kale shrugged. "You are mine, now. You've no need to."

She stared at him a long moment. "I don't help because I need to. I help because I want to. You must understand this about me ... I cannot look upon those in need and do nothing."

He sighed heavily, caressing her cheek with his hand. "I sensed that about you. I don't suppose it weighs with you that I am loath to share your attention with anyone else?"

Aslyn couldn't prevent a smile. "You'd tire of my undivided attention soon enough ... the very moment you decided to dash off upon a hunt and found that I was baggage you'd as soon not lug along."

"You are wrong. I would take you with me to dress the meat," he murmured, a teasing gleam entering his eyes.

Aslyn gave him a look, but chuckled, then turned to study the gowns once more, trying to decide which looked the simplest of them. Kale moved behind her, reached around and unfurled a roll of light wool. Aslyn stared at the gown blankly for several moments, then twisted around to hug him tightly. "You do know me," she said as she looked up at him.

He smiled faintly. "In all ways."

She looked away uncomfortably. "I should dress."

"A pity."

She threw him a doubtful glance, but took the gown and selected a shift to wear under it. As simple as the gown was, it was still far and away better than anything she'd worn in many years. She felt pleased with it and at the same time uncomfortable, fearful of ruining it. Finally, she took a length of linen and tied it about her waist as an apron.

Kale had dressed, as well. She glanced at him, but she didn't feel comfortable about asking him where he might be going. Instead, she asked if she should prepare a noon meal for the two of them.

His face was grim, all business again. "My men should have arrived by now. I need to check on them and see what the delay is."

Aslyn nodded.

He caught her chin. "You will not leave the cottage while I'm gone."

It wasn't a question. It was an order. Resentment flickered through her, but she dismissed it. As urgent as her need to go was, she could not chance being caught by Kale again. The only way she might have a chance was if she allayed his suspicions, allowed him to believe that she would stay. "I won't."

He studied her a long moment and finally nodded. "Keep the door bolted. Don't open it unless it's someone you know."

She nodded. "You think he'll come back?"

"I know he will. It's only a question of when."

"Kale...," she said, halting him as he opened the door. She had been about to tell him that Lord Algar was a werewolf, but quite suddenly it occurred to her that that was not necessarily true. He was a killer. He seemed to believe he had some special powers, but she had not seen anything to indicate that he was anything but a man ... a vicious, possibly crazed, killer ... but still a man, and, regardless of the tales Kale had told her about the werefolk, she wasn't so certain he believed in them, or would believe her if she claimed Algar was one. Then, too, whatever Algar was, or was not, she knew without a doubt that she had become one of the werefolk. She didn't particularly want to set Kale's mind in that direction. She certainly did not want to tell Kale what had led her to believe Lord Algar was a wolf. "Take care," she finished.

He nodded and left. Jim Baker arrived so closely upon the heels of Kale's departure that she had to wonder if he'd waited outside. Embarrassed as she was that he might have witnessed the intimacy between her and Kale, she was far more ashamed when she discovered the man had a terrible gash that should have been tended promptly.

His wife, he said, had done her best to stop the bleeding, and wrapped it tightly, but it had continued to bleed sluggishly. One look as she unwrapped the bandage was enough to make her wonder that he'd been able to walk to her door. It was not a terribly deep gash, nor did it seem any large veins had been ruptured, but it was a long, gaping cut. She cleaned it carefully and stitched it closed. "What happened?"

He looked sheepish. "We went into the forest to track the wolves that had attacked the child. It had grown dark and we didn't take torches so we couldn't see. Something leapt from the brush. Someone yelled that it was the wolves and everyone panicked. I didn't see who hit me."

"But you don't think it was the wolf?"

He shook his head.

"Did anyone get bitten? Or clawed?"

Again, he shook his head. "I don't think so ... except, maybe, Halard, when he fought the wolves off of his boy. I think they were long gone before we even went into the forest."

Aslyn nodded, trying to keep the fear from her expression. "But Halard was bitten?"

Baker scratched his head. "I don't know for certain. He never did say, but he didn't seem to be hurt bad. If he had been, wouldn't he have come to you?"

"I was ... gone most of the day yesterday ... looking for medicinal plants. Not an easy thing to find this time of year."

Baker nodded and rose. "How much?"

"A couple of loaves of bread?"

He nodded. "Just come to the bakery when you want them."

Her shoulders slumped when she'd closed the door behind him.

Halard had almost certainly been infected. How long, she wondered, before he changed?

Chapter Eleven

Aslyn paced the floor when Baker had left, wondering what, if anything could be done. She was strongly tempted to simply go to the Halard cottage and ask after him, but Kale had specifically said she was not to leave the cottage.

Not that she would have, under ordinary circumstances, considered staying only because he had ordered her to do so. The problem was, she *had* to go, and soon. Tonight would be the second of the dark of the moon. She was running out of time and if she failed to convince Kale that he could trust her, then he would not let down his guard enough to allow her to escape before it was too late. If he came back and found her gone....

And what if she did go? What if she saw with her own eyes that Halard bore the marks of the wolf? It might mean nothing at all. She suspected Algar was indeed a werewolf and the leader of the pack. But what if it was only wolves?

Even if her suspicions were right, what possible good could it do anyone for her to know it? She would have to convince the villagers that Halard was a danger. Who would they be more likely to believe? Her ... a stranger among them? Or someone they'd known for years?

She finally decided to go. Kale had not been gone long. He had seemed to think he would not be back in time for the noon meal. It would not take long to walk over to the Halard cottage and it seemed likely that Kale would never even know she'd left the cottage.

Seeing Halard might make no difference at all to anyone but her, but it might at least make her easier in her mind if she saw him and spoke to him about the attack.

Taking her cloak, she bundled it closely around her, pulled the hood on and left the cottage, walking quickly. The Halard's cottage was on the next road over and she took the cross road that Jim McCraney had used the day that she'd arrived.

She faltered when she realized that she would be going into a house of mourning. She wasn't certain she could stomach seeing John dressed for burial, most likely displayed for the mourners who came to pay their condolences.

After several moment's hesitation, she proceeded as she'd begun.

It wasn't difficult to locate the cottage. Neighbors from up and down the street were congregated in tight little knots out front. Many glanced at her as she made her way to the door and uneasiness washed over her.

Had it begun already--the suspicions? Or, was it merely her imagination that their looks were accusing? She had worried after John's attack that they might begin to consider her to blame because the last two victims had been to see her shortly before they were attacked. When people were gripped with fear it took no more than that, and sometimes considerably less, for them to begin to choose a victim of their own to blame for their misfortune.

Now she knew the attacks were her fault. Algar had tracked her here. Perhaps the attacks on John and Will were even more directly her fault than that. Perhaps Algar had singled them out because they bore her scent upon them.

Was it her own sense of guilt that made her feel their stares were accusing?

Shaking the sense of uneasiness, Aslyn tapped on the heavy oak panel door. Ana Halard opened the door. "What are ye doin' here?"

Taken aback, Aslyn stared at her blankly for several moments. "I came to pay my respects and to see if Mr. Halard had injuries that needed attention."

Ana's lips tightened. "He don't need no help from the likes of you."

The uneasiness returned tenfold. Aslyn was tempted to simply turn around and leave. As strong as the cowardly prompt was to turn tale and run, though, she had to know just how deeply the resentment was running against her, and what she'd been condemned for. "I don't understand."

"There weren't no trouble 'round here till ye came. Ye brought it with ye an' I don't want ye 'round my family no more," Ana Halard said through gritted teeth.

Aslyn took a step back. "I'm sorry for your loss," she said stiffly, then turned and retraced her steps with as much dignity as she could muster. The looks she encountered on the way out were even more pointed and angry than before. It took an effort to pretend she didn't notice, and even more effort to hold her pace to a walk when her instincts urged her to run. That would be the worst thing she could do, though. People tended to revert to the simple animals when they were frightened, losing their thin veneer of civilization with amazing speed and, like any other predatory animal, chasing what ran.

She was clammy with fear by the time she reached the cottage once more, further unnerved by the fact that there seemed an uncommon number of people on the road before the cottage, all turning to look at her as she passed.

She was shaking when she at last bolted her door behind her, but she felt little relief, knowing she was now trapped in the cottage. The day passed in nerve-wracking suspense. She could not even see outside without opening the door to peer out, since the cottage possessed not one single window--and peering out could be interpreted as a sense of guilt far too easily. She nerved herself a couple of times to go out to the necessary behind the cottage, partly out of need, partly because she knew it was necessary to appear as if she was going about her daily routine, and partly so that she could see what was going on. Each time she went out she saw knots of villagers up and down the road, talking, often glancing toward her cottage.

Kale returned late in the afternoon, near dusk, his face grim, drawn from weariness and some other emotion Aslyn couldn't decipher. She was not left long to wonder over it, however.

Kale poured himself a tumbler of mead and collapsed in one of the chairs before the hearth, staring into the flames broodingly. Despite her uneasiness over the situation in the village throughout the day, Aslyn was immediately aware that something was very wrong.

She moved to the chair next to him, stood uncertainly for several moments and finally sat on the edge. "Will you eat?"

He glanced at her, studied her a long moment, almost as if he hadn't heard the question, and finally shook his head.

Aslyn frowned. She didn't like to prod him for information when he was obviously laboring under emotions he was having difficulty grappling with, but he was making her more nervous by the moment. "Did you find your men?"

A look of nausea crossed his features. "Yes."

Aslyn's heart lurched in sudden, painful dread. "They returned with you?" she asked hesitantly.

He set the empty glass down on the table between the chairs and scrubbed his hands over his face. "They were dead. All of them."

"Oh my God!" She slid off the chair and knelt before him, slipping her arms around him and laying her head in his lap. "Kale, I'm so sorry!"

He pulled her up onto his lap, folding her into his arms, squeezing her tightly a moment before he relaxed his grip, holding her loosely against his chest. "I should have been with them. If I hadn't decided to try to head the pack off, I would have been."

Aslyn shuddered at the thought. "And you might have been killed with them."

"And I might have been the difference between life and death. If I had been there, they might not have been overwhelmed."

"You can't know that. You can't torture yourself with the thought that you might have made a difference. You took a greater risk by coming back here alone. How could you have known?"

"I should have guessed it was a trap. We've been tracking the pack for weeks now."

Aslyn said nothing for several moments, wondering if she should voice her fears about Algar. But she knew, regardless of what suspicions it might provoke about her, she had to say something. "Do you think ... Is it possible these wolves are ... not just wolves?"

"It's far more than a possibility."

Aslyn pulled away and looked at him. "You think they're all...."

"Werewolves? Yes."

It was worse, then, even that she'd thought. She had considered it very likely that Algar was exactly what he claimed to be, and that he was leading the pack, adding human cunning to animals already cunning in their own right. She had wondered if his men knew, or suspected that he was leading them a merry chase, posing as soldier by day to foil all attempts to capture the pack. It had even occurred to her to wonder if some of his men might also be as he was, werewolves. She hadn't considered that the men he led by day were the same pack he led by night. Small wonder Kale's men had not stood a chance against them. "What will you do now?"

"I have the unpleasant task of telling their families. And then I must gather more men and find them--and put an end to them once and for all."

Chapter Twelve

As little as Aslyn liked the idea that Kale had been appointed to the task, she knew that he was right. The killing must be stopped. Someone had to do it. She just wished it was someone other than Kale who must risk their life.

With some effort, she persuaded Kale to eat. He'd had nothing, she felt sure, since he'd left, nothing even to break his fast before he left. She coaxed him over to the table and sat with him, though her appetite was no better than his.

The urge was strong to tell him about the atmosphere within the village, but she quashed it. He had worries enough. He did not need to be concerned for her when his mind should be focused upon his task.

She only hoped the villagers would not take it into their heads to set fire to the cottage while they slept.

Tomorrow, at first light, Kale would leave to perform the unpleasant task of informing the families of the dead men about their loved ones.

She would leave as soon as he was gone.

For the first time since she had left her home, the idea of leaving brought with it a wealth of grief. She wanted, more than she had ever wanted anything in her life, to stay with Kale. She wished desperately that she might at least have had a few more days with him, but she was nothing if not practical. She had no choice but to go when the opportunity was there.

In any case, whatever her circumstances, even if she were not a werebeast, the villagers had convinced themselves that she was at the root of their problems. If she stayed, Kale would almost certainly stay, and she would be risking his life as well as her own.

There were no choices, except the choice of life over death.

When they had finished their meal, Aslyn drew Kale to the bed, kissing every inch of his skin she revealed as she undressed him. And when he had done the same for her, she made love to him with all her heart.

* * * *

When Kale rose before dawn and dressed, Aslyn pretended to sleep on undisturbed, although she'd wakened to full alertness the moment he stirred. It took more of an effort than she would ever have thought to lie still, to breathe slowly, shallowly as one deeply asleep. Her heart was hammering in her chest with a combination of nerves, fear and grief. More than anything, she wanted to 'wake,' to coax him back into bed so that she could share her body with him once more ... just one more time.

But once more would never be enough to quash the sense of loss that even now seemed as if it would suffocate her. She could not take his essence with her by doing so. It would not lessen her sorrow, and she doubted she could make love to him again without giving away the sense of desperation she felt.

She waited when he had gone, counting the minutes, listening for any sound that might warn her that he'd forgotten something and returned. In a little while she heard the sucking, clopping sound of a shod horse galloping through snow. The sound grew louder as he neared the cottage and then began to fade once more as he gained distance.

Aslyn sat up, pushed the covers away and moved the edge of the bed, dropping her face into her hands. Oh, for the luxury of lying in the bed, clutching his pillow and weeping till she could weep no more!

She shook the urge off and rose. Dressing quickly in the woolen gown Kale had brought her, she rolled the quilt and tied it, then looked around. In truth, there was little she needed to take and the less the better. She had no use for the beautiful gowns Kale had brought, though the temptation was great to take just one.

She dismissed it and moved to gather food into a small bundle, tying it at her waist as she did her bag of medicines. Donning her cloak, she slung the blanket roll over her shoulder and moved to the door of the cottage, easing it open no more than a crack so that she could look out. It was still dark out, though light had begun to filter through the darkness, lifting it sufficiently that she could see almost to the center of town.

The streets appeared deserted.

She slipped outside, closing the door firmly behind her and moved quietly to the edge of the road.

She needed a horse.

She could release it once she'd gained some distance and allow it to find its way home, but she had to cover as much distance as possible as quickly as possible if she was to have any chance of winning free of the place.

It was dangerous even to consider stealing one, and yet even more dangerous to try again to leave without one. She could not take a chance that Kale might decide to come by the cottage to check on her and discover her gone. She had to make certain, this time, that she was far away by the time he discovered her gone, too far for him to find her.

The livery was on the next road over. As loathe as she was to pass by the Halard's cottage after what had transpired there the day before, she had little choice but to do so. Otherwise, she would have to follow the main road to the center of the village, cross over by way of the crossing road and back track--or worse, cut through a cottage yard and risk running into someone out to visit their necessary, or someone's dog.

She crossed the road in front of the cottage, moving briskly, but as quietly as possible. Within moments, she'd reached the next road. After peering down it to make certain no one was about, she made the turn and focused upon the livery nearly halfway down the road, glancing neither right nor left until she neared the Halard's cottage.

She could not resist looking as she neared it, however, and her heart nearly leapt from her chest as she did so.

The door was standing wide.

She stopped abruptly, staring hard at the dark opening. As she did, she saw the door was not open. It had been shattered. The oak panels lay in splinters just inside. She moved closer, certain her eyes must be playing tricks on her.

It was not, as she had more than half hoped, a trick of the uncertain light and shadows. The door had been shattered inward.

The pack had returned for Halard.

Aslyn broke into a run. There was little doubt in her mind that the entire family had been slaughtered, and none that the village would become a raging mob the moment someone discovered the attack. They would be coming for her.

She slowed as she neared the paddock of the livery, knowing she might spook the horses if she rushed them. Only two stood in the paddock behind the livery. Stopping only long enough to still her pounding heart and slow her breathing, Aslyn moved slowly to the paddock, speaking softly, coaxingly. The horses lifted their heads the moment she came within view, snorted, stamped the ground.

It took far more patience to coax the nervous beasts than she felt like allowing them, but she had no choice. Finally, she managed to get hold of one, slipped her blanket roll around its neck and leapt onto its back. There was no time to gather saddle and tack, and she had no desire to run additional risk by going into the stable.

For all that, she was not accustomed to riding bareback, had never tried it before and wondered for several moments if she would even be able to stay on animal's back. In truth, she had not ridden in so many years that she was no longer accustomed to riding at all.

Finally, she managed to guide the horse to the gate and open it. She made no attempt to stop the other horse from slipping out as she rode out. With any luck at all, it would lead anyone who tried to follow her in a different direction entirely. Grasping the blanket roll tightly, she nudged the horse with her knees until she had it pointed in the direction in which she wished to go and gave him his head. In truth, she had no destination in mind. She simply wanted to travel in the opposite direction from which Kale had gone.

She had managed to reach the edge of the village when the first hue and cry went up. She had no idea whether it was due to her theft of the horse, or if someone had discovered the Halard family massacre. She pulled the horse to a stop when she reached the edge of the forest, turning to look back. Smoke was wafting from the far end of town.

They had set her cottage ablaze. Either they thought she was still inside and had not yet discovered the missing horses, or it was out of pure malice.

She nudged the horse once more, allowing him to follow the road until the first rays of the rising sun touched the road before her, banishing all shadows. She urged him off the road then, into the forest, winding her way southward.

She had decided upon a destination. She was going home.

The horse began to tire before they had gone many miles. She allowed him to walk for a while, to rest and then urged him to move a little faster. For all that, the going was slow in the deep snow. She did not stop to rest the horse, or eat, when the weak winter sun rose to its zenith. She was hungry, and tempted by her stomach's clamoring to try to eat while she rode, but a very little thought dissuaded her. It was all she could do to remain on the horse as it was. She had no desire to risk falling off only because she could not wait to eat.

When the sun slipped at last behind the tops of the trees on its downward path, Aslyn dismounted. She was stiff from riding so long and her legs gave out beneath her as she touched the ground.

It had been her intention to point the horse toward Krackensled and give him a sharp encouragement to find his way back. She didn't get the chance. The moment she fell, the horse bolted. She watched his departure in some dudgeon, for she had not had the chance to retrieve her blanket roll from around the horse's neck.

Apparently, the horse thought the bouncing roll was something attacking it, for it careened wildly through the trees, floundering in the snow several times in it's panic to outrun whatever it was that had it by the neck.

"Fool!" Aslyn snapped, sorry now she hadn't gotten the chance to whack it a few times with a tree branch.

There was no hope of retrieving the blanket roll. She could only hope the stupid beast managed to free itself of the thing before it was found. Otherwise they might track it back to her.

She was going to freeze without a blanket.

She sat, pulled the small bundle from her belt that held her food and ate enough to quiet her stomach's protests and then bundled the remains once more and set out. The days were short. She had a couple of hours, perhaps as much as three, to find shelter for the night.

She didn't waste time trying to cover her tracks. She could not spare it, and, in any case, she had decided to go home. She could not afford to change directions several times to throw off pursuit. She had to make her way to the coast and cross the channel as quickly as possible.

Once she crossed into Norandy, she was fairly certain she would be safe from any and all pursuit. Until then she risked death at any turn.

There were many times during the trek that she cursed Algar, and even more times that she cursed the fates. If she had to be a werewolf, why could she not have the same ability as Algar apparently had, to shift at will into a beast more capable of traveling through the snow?

It was a waste of energy. She was as she was. She could not change it, however much she wished she could.

As she fought her way through drifts of snow, tangles of leafless briars, and staggered up rises and slipped down dales, she wondered what sort of reception she might expect when she returned home.

Would her father be glad to see her, alive and apparently well? Or would he send her away? Would he slay her when he discovered what she'd become?

She would have to tell him, whatever the outcome, else she would be a danger to everyone she cared for when the full moon rose and she was taken by her beast. Dismal as the prospect was of being locked in the castle dungeon during those times, it would have to be done. She could not trust herself. She certainly could not expect her father to trust her.

It was almost dusk when she came upon an abandoned cottage. A sense of hope, relief and nervousness assailed her when she first spotted it, but she realized quickly enough that no smoke rose from its crooked chimney and no smoke meant no one would be inside, waiting to attack her.

Still, she approached it cautiously, stopping to listen every few feet, checking the cottage and the area around it. When she finally reached the door and peered inside, she saw that the cottage had evidently been abandoned for quite some time. Much of the thatch had rotted and fallen in, aided by the weight of the snow. The door had also fallen in. The interior of the cottage was bare of anything save snow, dusty cobwebs and rotting poles and thatch.

It would not make much of a shelter, either against the elements, or the wolves if they had tracked her, but it was all there was.

With an effort, she stood the door upright and propped it against the door frame. She stared at the hearth doubtfully for some moments, wondering if the chimney would even pull, wondering if she could build a fire in it without catching the roof on fire, and if she even dared risk it when she knew she was being hunted, but she finally decided she would need to take the chance of building a fire if she was to survive the night.

It was full dark by the time she managed to find enough branches to build a modest fire. By the fire's feeble light, she cleared the debris inside the cottage far enough from the hearth that it would be less likely to catch fire. An almost constant breeze wafted through the tiny building, finding its way through every crack, but it was tiny puffs, not gusts. The dirt floor was free of snow near the hearth, and dry. She curled up as close to the fire as she dared and warmed her hands until the stiffness left her fingers, then opened her pack of food and ate a small portion.

She was very nearly as miserable inside the ramshackle cottage as she had been trudging through the snow, but a full stomach, enough warmth to thaw her somewhat and exhaustion combined to make her eyes drift shut almost the moment she curled up beside the hearth.

She wasn't certain how long she slept, but the howl of wolves woke her.

Chapter Thirteen

The sound was distant, indistinct. At any other time, her exhaustion would have deafened her to so slight a sound, but she'd been subconsciously listening for sounds of pursuit since she had left Krackensled. She was instantly wide awake, looking around uncertainly, wondering what had wakened her.

It came again, a mournful cry taken up by many throats.

Baying.

They had caught her scent.

Aslyn leapt to her feet, looking around her. There was nothing to use for a weapon, of course, beyond the branches she'd dragged in to make a fire.

She had not thought, when she had stopped, beyond the immediate need to find shelter from the weather for the night. The cottage offered little enough of that. It offered no security. She would be no better off inside the cottage than outside if the pack caught up to her. In fact, far worse off, because she would be trapped, with no place to run.

The door was barely standing on its own. There was no way to barricade it, nothing to use to fortify it.

Pulling the door away from the opening, Aslyn moved outside, stood in the clearing surrounding the cottage and listened. When the sound came again, she turned slowly, finally determining that the sounds were coming from the north west, she began to trot southward, hoping to conserve energy while still maintaining enough speed to stay ahead of the pack.

The area was unfamiliar to her. If she'd been a few miles further west of her position, she might have seen landmarks she recognized. She might have remembered something that might help her.

As it was, she could only strain to see through the darkened landscape, searching for some place she might hide and escape their notice, a burrow, or cave large enough to conceal her, but still small enough she might have some hope of barricading the opening to protect herself from attack.

She saw nothing. It seemed she ran for miles, and all the while the sounds behind her became louder as the pack closed in upon her. In desperation, she began to look up at the trees as she approached them. Being treed was the last thing she wanted, but it began to seem it might be her only hope of escaping the wolves.

She was so busy looking up at the trees that she failed to see the chasm of darkness before her. When the earth suddenly dropped from beneath her feet, she hit the ground and began to roll, over and over. Striking a young sapling that almost cracked a rib, she came to a halt at last, but she was too dizzy to rise at once. When she finally managed to stagger to her feet, she discovered that she had rolled down onto a frozen stream.

It was wide, but she had no idea how deep it might be. Near the center a narrow track remained unfrozen. Looking around, she finally found a long branch and made her way carefully to the rushing water, leading with the branch. The ice thinned to the point that it shattered under the branch before she got within a yard of the open water. She slipped when the branch broke through the ice and landed on the ice so hard it cracked under her.

Holding her breath, she stabbed at the open water again and found that it was not nearly as deep as she'd feared it might be. When she tried to get up, she broke through. The freezing water snatched her breath from her lungs. She struggled--to get up, to catch her breath, floundering in the knee deep water until she was soaked to the skin without a dry thread to her name.

Finally, she managed to get her feet under her and, using the branch, levered herself up until she was standing. Finally, she managed to draw in short, panting breaths.

Her boots had filled with water when she'd fallen. With her first step, water gushed up and out of them.

She found she could not cross. Each time she stepped up on the ice, it broke beneath her weight. The baying of the wolves was far more distinguishable than it had been before she tumbled down the ravine into the stream. She wasn't certain of how long she had struggled in the icy slush, but she knew it was far too long.

Turning, she began to make her way downstream, trying to put some distance between her and the wolf pack. When she had rounded a bend and was out of sight, she tried once more to cross, still with no luck.

She could not feel her feet. It felt as if she was walking on stumps, except that pain shot up her legs each time she stepped down and her knees threatened to buckle. She was panting so loudly by now, she had to hold her breath to listen for sounds of pursuit, but she knew they were closing in on her.

Frantically, she searched the edge of the stream for a place to hide, a tree to climb.

The banks were slick with snow and ice. Here and there a small tree, perhaps as big around as her thigh, grew, but she could not climb anything so flimsy and it would do her no good if she could. If her own weight did not bend it double, it would take no more than a push to bring her down, or shake her from the precarious perch. Further up the bank, she saw that there were larger trees, but she doubted she could reach them in time, or climb them if she could, for she saw none with branches low enough she could hope to grab a handhold and pull herself up.

As she rounded yet another bend in the stream, however, her situation went from very bad to catastrophic. A small, mostly frozen, waterfall blocked the mouth of the stream. Aslyn stared at it in dismay, realizing she had trapped herself.

She could hear the wolves behind her, knew they'd reached the stream and were searching for her scent. Any moment, they would discover that she had not crossed and they would be on her. Casting around frantically, she saw that the banks were steeper here even than those she'd already passed.

Trying to be quiet no longer seemed an issue. She began to struggle toward the nearest bank, breaking ice as she went, slipping, falling. She heard them behind her before she ever managed to reach the bank and turned, staring in frozen horror as they rounded the bend in the stream and came into view.

It was like a vision from hell. They were mounted upon horses as men, but it was the eyes of wolves that looked out at her from wolf faces and claws that held the reins. She thought for several moments that it was a trick of shadow, or that, perhaps, they had donned the hides of wolves. As the leader lifted his head and bayed, however, she realized that they had shifted into part man, part wolf.

The sound made the hair at the base of her skull prickle and sent a shaft of panic through her. She screamed as they leapt from the horses. Whirling, she struggled to climb the bank. When she saw she was making no progress, she leapt to her feet and raced mindlessly toward the waterfall. She discovered when she reached it that the half formed intention of climbing it was an impossibility. The water had frozen over in flow, forming a slick curtain of ice from the top to the base, where it had mushroomed into frozen curls. It could not be more than eight to ten feet high, but it might just as well have been fifty. She could find no handhold to climb.

Slowly, she turned to face the men/beasts. They shifted as she watched, becoming men. At a signal from their leader, they spread out across the stream. Lord Algar grinned at her. "I've always enjoyed a good chase. We'll have to do this again sometime, just for the sport of it. But right now, we must be on our way."

Aslyn could only stare at him in horror and revulsion, so frozen with fear and cold from the icy water her jaw was locked in spasms of chills. As she stared at him, however, too panicked to even think of how she might escape him, something large and dark leapt from above her, landing in the stream between her and Algar.

Dark as it was, she knew him instantly, and hope surged through her as his men, following his lead, landed on either side of them, spreading out across the stream as Algar's men had, facing the wolf men.

"Renegades, we have been charged by High Chief, Renoir, to bring you to justice for your crimes against *the people*," Kale said coldly.

Algar's face contorted into a mask of rage. He spat at Kale's feet. "We do not recognize Renoir as our High Chief any longer! We're of no mind to obey his laws."

"*Our* laws," Kale corrected. "It is not your choice to decide which laws you will obey and which you will not. You have endangered the entire clan by your actions. You will be tried by the people for your crimes against them."

Algar roared. "We will face trial by combat ... now!" He dropped to the ice on all fours. Around him, his men did like wise. As Aslyn watched, they shifted, their bodies changing form and contour, splitting the man clothing they wore so that she could see the fur that sprang from their skin.

Kale, too, dropped to all fours. Aslyn stared at him a moment, then, stunned, turned to look at the men with him. They, too, had dropped. As she watched, they shifted to beasts all around her--wolves, bears, cats. When she turned to look at Kale again, a large snow fox stood where he had knelt only moments before. Almost as one, they roared a challenge at the werewolves they faced.

Aslyn staggered back in shock as they launched themselves into battle, roaring, swinging great paws studded with wicked claws, their sharp teeth bared and gleaming in the meager light the stars in the heavens offered.

Two wolves leapt upon the bear nearest her. With a roar, the bear swatted the wolf that leapt at his throat, sending it flying. The wolf's head struck her shoulder in flight, knocking her to her knees in the icy stream. The blow didn't hurt that badly, but it broke through her shocked paralysis enough that she began scrambling toward safety as the battle waged around her, wolves, bears and cats locked in a fight to the death.

A wolf landed, snarling, in front of her. Even as he leapt for her throat, however, his wickedly sharp teeth bared, a white blur collided with him. The fox's jaws locked on the wolf's throat, ripping away a chunk of flesh and fur. Blood spurted from the wound, spraying Aslyn across the face and chest. She screamed, nearly gagging, wiping frantically at the blood.

Whirling away, she struggled in the opposite direction, dodging the beasts that fought all around her, swaying, skidding on the ice as they leapt with bared teeth to rend flesh and shatter bone. A cat crashed to the ice just to her left, rolling with the wolf that was snapping and tearing at it. The two combatants collided with her, knocking her down. She gasped as the icy water splashed over her. Before she could get to her feet, the whirling fighters caught her again.

As she scrambled to crawl away from them a shadow fell over her. When she whirled to see the newest threat, she discovered one of the great bears was standing over her. Reaching down, he scooped her up with one arm, holding her against his furry chest. She fought and clawed at the beast, struggling to break free even as he lumbered across the ice with her.

He dropped her onto a mound of snow as they reached the stream bank and Aslyn whirled to flee, expecting any moment to feel the crushing weight of his jaws, or a blow from one of his great paws. When neither came, she spared a glance backward and discovered the bear had turned away. He stood just below her, as if guarding her from the battle still being waged on the ice below her.

Aslyn hesitated, wondering if it was safe to stay, but as she glanced out over the carnage of the battle, fear and revulsion spawned renewed panic and she turned away, climbing. She had no destination in mind when she reached the top of the bank at last. She only knew she could not stay. She had to get as far away as she could.

She had not even gained the edge of the forest that surrounded the stream when something huge slammed into her back. Blackness clouded her mind and sight as the impact of the blow propelled her forward and her head cracked against something hard and unyielding.

Chapter Fourteen

Aslyn roused slightly as she felt the warmth of hands, turning her over, wrapping something around her. With an effort she lifted her eyelids fractionally. Kale's worried face swam before her vision. Satisfied that she was safe, she closed her eyes again, enjoying the warmth that was slowly seeping into her frozen bones.

Dimly, she heard voices around her; men's voices, talking, groaning in pain; and the soft wicker of horses, and the shuffle of hooves against packed snow. She moaned when she was lifted abruptly, feeling pain shoot through her skull and claw its way through her body.

When she became aware again, she realized that she was on a horse and the warmth against her cheek was Kale's chest. The steady beat of his heart comforted her and she was tempted to simply drift off again, but something nagged at her, something that she needed to tell him. "Can't go back. Burned the cottage," she mumbled with an effort.

His arms tightened around her. "I know. I'm taking you home."

She smiled at the word, realizing there had never been a sweeter one, or one more cherished.

* * * *

Aslyn woke to find herself in a strange bed. As groggy and sluggish as her mind was, she was in no doubt of that. Blinking, she looked around the dim room in confusion, wondering where she was, how she'd come to be there.

She discovered that Kale was propped in the bed beside her, watching her.

She stared at him a long moment. "Where am I?"

"Home."

She frowned, more confused than ever. "The cabin? This doesn't...."

He shook his head. "Our home."

Aslyn sat up abruptly, discovering in the process that she was naked. Grasping the cover, she clutched it over her breasts. Her head swam at the sudden movement and she lifted one hand to press it against the throbbing pain. "How? What happened?"

Gripping her shoulders, he pushed her gently back until she was lying with her head on the pillows behind her. "My men and I captured the renegades and brought them home to stand trial."

Aslyn rubbed her head. "There was a battle...." Her eyes flew open and she stared at Kale. "I didn't imagine it, did I?"

Kale frowned a look of uncertainty crossing his features. "No."

"You're...."

"A werebeast." He lay back, staring up at the ceiling. "I cannot undo what I've done, Aslyn. In truth, I confess I feel no remorse for it, though I am sorrier than I can say that it has been the cause of so much pain and hardship for you."

Aslyn turned her head to stare at him uncomprehendingly. "I don't understand."

Kale rolled onto his side again. Reaching over her, he lifted her hand and brought it to his lips. She remembered then. It was the hand the snow fox.... Kale had bitten her. She tried to snatch her hand back, but he held it. Rubbing the fresh marks with one finger, he then traced the pale, white scars beneath them.

He looked into her eyes. "I was only a youth myself when I saw you the first time. In my eyes, I saw a tiny princess and in that moment decided to claim you for my own. I marked you. It was not Algar, but it was my mark that led him to you."

Aslyn frowned, trying to make sense of what he was saying and drawing a blank. It dawned upon her finally that the dream she'd dreamt for many years had been no dream at all. She had always thought the scars were from some long forgotten mishap as a child. She had never considered that the bite she remembered from her 'dream' had been real and the scar had been the result.

"In truth, it was a child's game I played then. I imagined you growing up to be a princess and myself as the knight who would come to steal you away, but even then I knew when I marked you that you could not escape the fate I'd given you. When you attained womanhood, your beast would take you.

"My father punished me, of course, sent me to Renoir as squire, here in the valley of the clan. I thought that I had outgrown that childish infatuation. Perhaps, I had. But when I saw you on the road to Krackensled, I saw my mark upon your hand and knew your beast had led you to me."

"*You* made me a werebeast?" Aslyn said, trying to grasp the thought. She was a werefox, not a werewolf, not vicious, not one who preyed upon humans. Was it less revolting because she found she was not the same as Algar? Or was it less revolting because of her love for Kale?

"Yes. I gave you the mark of the beast, my mark. The second mark was to warn Algar of my claim upon you ... lest he think the beast who'd claimed you had released his claim. The third sealed your fate, binding you to me."

"Third?"

"The night we made love, we mated for life."

Aslyn thought about that for several moments, searching in vain for indignation. "You did not give me a choice."

"No. I was ... afraid you would choose another."

Aslyn frowned. "This is a very strange way to tell me you love me," she said irritably.

He turned to look at her, studied her a long moment and finally smiled. Reaching for her, he pulled her across his chest. "It is far more than loving. It is a mating of two souls."

Aslyn's brows rose. "Just the same."

"You didn't tell me you loved me," he pointed out.

Aslyn sniffed. "Mayhap I do ... mayhap not. I was not wooed as I fully deserved."

Kale looked deeply into her eyes, then growled, rolling until she was beneath him. "Do not play your games with me, woman! Say it!"

Aslyn chuckled. "I might, but only if I hear the words I want to hear."

"You're a stubborn wench!"

"That is not the three little words I want to hear!"

"I ... love ... you," he growled.

Aslyn thought about it. "That was not very prettily said, growling at me as if I was plucking the hair on your chest!"

Kale cut her off by kissing her. She looked up at him dreamily when he released her at last. "You could always show me how much you adore me," she said a little breathlessly.

His golden eyes gleamed. "With all my heart," he said.

The End

Printed in the United States
66477LVS00004B/232-255

9 781586 087944